"THE BEST SPY STORY THAT HAS COME OUR WAY IN A LONG, LONG TIME."

The New York Times

CAUSE FOR ALARM

"Unsurpassed for slippery intrigue, totalitarian villainy, exciting chases, hairbreadth escapes, and a general air of authenticity. Excellent."

Saturday Review

ERIC AMBLER

"THE GREATEST OF MODERN SUSPENSE WRITERS."

Cleveland Press

Books by Eric Ambler

ERIC AMBLER
CAUSE FOR ALARM

YOUR ASSURANCE OF QUALITY · BANTAM BOOKS · NEW YORK

*This low-priced Bantam Book
has been completely reset in a type face
designed for easy reading, and was printed
from new plates. It contains the complete
text of the original hard-cover edition.*
NOT ONE WORD HAS BEEN OMITTED.

CAUSE FOR ALARM

*A Bantam Book / published by arrangement with
Alfred A. Knopf, Inc.*

PRINTING HISTORY
*Knopf edition published February 1945
2nd printing . . . September 1945
Bantam edition published June 1964*

*Bantam Books are published by Bantam Books, Inc. Its trade-mark,
consisting of the words "Bantam Books" and the portrayal of a bantam, is registered in the United States Patent Office and in other
countries. Marca Registrada. Printed in the United States of America. Bantam Books, Inc., 271 Madison Ave., New York 16, N. Y.*

TO JOYCE

"Such subtle covenants shall be made,
Till peace itself is war in masquerade."

DRYDEN, "Absalom and Achitophel"

DEATH IN MILAN

THE MAN standing in the shadow of the doorway turned up the collar of his overcoat and stamped his numb feet gently on the damp stones.

In the distance he could hear the sound of a train pulling out of the *Stazione Centrale,* and wished he was riding in it, lounging back in a first-class compartment on his way to Palermo. Perhaps after this job was done he would be able to take a holiday in the sun. That was, of course, if They would let him. It never seemed to occur to Them that a man might like to go back to his home occasionally. Milan was no good. Too dry and dusty in the summer; in the winter these damnable fogs rolled in from the plains and ricefields, damp and cold and bringing the smoke from the factories with them. It was getting misty already. In another hour you wouldn't be able to see your hand in front of your face, let alone anything else. That meant that Buonometti and Orlano wouldn't be able to see what they were doing. There would have to be another night of watching and waiting in the cold. He had no patience with it. If this Englishman had to be killed, let him be killed easily, quickly. A dark stretch of pavement, a knife under the ribs, a slight twist of the wrist to let the air inside the wound, and it was done. No fuss, no trouble, practically no noise. Whereas this. . . .

His gaze travelled up the dark façade of the office building across the street to the single lighted window on the fourth floor. He shrugged resignedly and leaned against the wall. One hour or two, what difference did it make? What did They care if he got pneumonia?

Only once during the next twenty-five minutes did he move. The footsteps of a stray pedestrian echoing along this deserted business street caused him to shrink back into the shadow. But of a passing policeman he took no notice, and grinned to himself when the uniformed man seemed deliberately to avoid looking his way. That was one advantage in working for Them. You didn't have to worry about the police. You were safe.

He straightened his back suddenly. The solitary light had gone out. He stretched his cramped muscles, adjusted the brim of his hat and walked quietly away towards the telephone booth at the end of the street. Two minutes later his work for the night was finished.

The door of the office building opened and two men came out. One of them turned to shut the door behind him. The other did not wait. With a muttered *"a rivederci"* he crossed the road and disappeared in the direction of the station. The man who had shut the door turned and stood there watching him out of sight.

He was a stoutish, middle-aged man with rounded shoulders and a way of holding his arms slightly in front of his body, as though he were trying perpetually to squeeze through a very narrow opening. That posture had been his life. He had squeezed his way by, rigid yet without dignity; an ineffectual, apprehensive man who had fed his self-respect on dreams and always satisfied it.

He felt in his jacket pocket, lit a cigarette, rebuttoned his overcoat and started to walk in the opposite direction. At the first corner he hesitated. On his right a little way down the main thoroughfare the words CAFFÉ FARAGLIO in neon tubing glowed through the fog. His hesitation was only momentary. He turned right and crossed to the *caffè*.

He found a table near one of the heating stoves and ordered a *caffé latte* and a *Strega*. The spirit he drank at a gulp. Then he took an envelope from his pocket, dropped his hands below the level of the table top and drew a thick roll of one hundred lire notes from it. He counted them carefully—there were twenty-five—and transferred them to a wallet. Then he drank his coffee, paid the waiter and went.

The fog was thickening. Now it lay in patches so that at one moment he picked his way cautiously along the side of the pavement, while at the next he was able to step out briskly. A crowd pouring out of a cinema jostled him, and he turned down a side street to avoid them.

He was going in the direction of the Monte di Pieta quarter in which he lived. As, at last, he crossed the Corso Venezia to turn down the Via Monte Napoleone he saw a black limousine drawn up by the kerb. But there were other cars about and he took no notice of it. It was not until he was threading his way through the net-work of streets behind the public gardens that he noticed that the car seemed to be following him. He could hear it whining along in low gear just behind him and see the yellow glare of its headlights through the fog. He walked on, telling himself that the driver had probably missed the way. Then it happened.

The fog had lifted for a few yards ahead. He stepped into the road to cut off a corner. A fraction of a second later the car accelerated violently. Jerking round quickly, he saw it swing over towards him. The headlights grew suddenly larger, blinding him. He shouted and tried to jump clear. The next moment the car hit him.

He felt a terrible pain shoot through his legs up to his waist and a second shock as he hit the ground. For a moment he lay still. He was dimly aware that he was lying across the kerb. He tried to raise himself. Then the pain surged up to his chest and there was a thin, high singing noise in his head. He knew that he was losing consciousness and he put up a hand to grasp the wallet in his pocket. It was his last conscious movement.

The car had stopped several yards farther on. A man got out of the seat next to the driver, walked back and, bending down, thumbed back one of the injured man's eyelids. Then he returned to the car.

"*Sta bene?*" said the driver.

"*No.* He is still alive. Go back and make certain."

The driver shifted the gear into reverse, peered through the rear window and the car moved back to the corner.

"Now!" said the man beside him.

The car jerked forward. The wheels bumped twice and came to rest against the kerb. The man in front got out again and again walked back. When he returned to the car he was wiping his fingers on his handkerchief.

"*Sta bene?*" said the driver.

"*Bene.*" He got back into his seat and slammed the door. "As soon as we have reported to headquarters," he said as the car moved slowly across the tram-lines along the main road, "I shall drink half a bottle of cognac. This fog gets on to my chest."

It was twenty minutes before a child ran screaming to its mother that there was a man lying bleeding in the street.

Chapter I

FIRST CAUSES

ONE THING is certain. I would not even have considered the job if I had not been desperate.

Early in January, the Barnton Heath Engineering Company decided to close down the greater part of its works.

It was the day after I had asked Claire to marry me that the first blow fell. I had walked into my office that morning feeling very pleased with life. Not that, strictly speaking, I had any cause to feel pleased. She had promised to "think about it carefully" and let me know. Still, I felt pleased. A girl like Claire would, I assured myself, have made up her mind immediately if she were going to refuse. She was probably terrified that, if she didn't strengthen her position by reducing me to a state of jittering suspense, I might be tempted to play the dominant male and expect her to give up being a very promising surgeon in order to become a second-rate housekeeper. She has a dangerous theory that, when two persons get married, a court of inquiry ought to sit in order to determine from the available evidence which of the two is better fitted to assume responsibility for the housework—the husband or the wife. I had, however, not the slightest intention of asking her to give up her work. Quite apart from the fact that I did not wish her to do so, I knew perfectly well that, if it came to a trial of wills, she would win. She is very beautiful and very intelligent.

Towards lunch-time I was going over a batch of costs with my assistant when I received a message from the head office in London saying that Herrington, the General Manager, would like to see me that afternoon. Summonses from Herrington were rare. Wondering what it was all about and irritated at having to interrupt my work, I caught the two-forty-five at Barnton Station. At half-past three I saw Herrington. At four o'clock I was walking slowly down Queen Victoria Street with a letter in my pocket informing me that "owing to circumstances beyond the control of the Board," my services had to be dispensed with.

Herrington's carefully chosen words of regret still lingered in my ears.

"Damned unfortunate, Marlow, but there it is. The Barnton Heath works just aren't paying. Nothing to do with you, of course. Labour's too expensive so near London. Felstead has warned us that he can't renew his contract at our price, and things are too shaky at the moment for us to risk keeping your show going. Question of cutting our losses. Hard-lines on you, of course. And hard-lines on us, too. Good production engineers don't grow on trees. You won't have any difficulty in getting fixed up. If there's anything I can do, let me know."

So that was that. I had a month in which to find another job. And "things were shaky at the moment." Production engineers might not grow on trees; but then nor did jobs. "Trade recession" they called it in the newspapers. As far as I could see there wasn't a great deal of difference between a trade recession and a good old-fashioned slump. "If there's anything I can do, let me know." Well, yes, there *was* something he could do. He could find me another job. But probably he hadn't meant quite that. Nice chap, Herrington, but a little too charming. Dammit no! That was humbug. He wasn't a nice chap. I'd always loathed him like poison and he'd detested me. He'd probably been quite pleased to get rid of me. He'd never quite forgiven me for making him look a fool over the original Felstead estimates. Still, there it was. No use getting sorry for myself. I knew plenty of people who might put me on to something good. I might even get something better. No need to panic, anyway. Plenty of time. I'd telephone Dowsett in the morning and see if he knew of anything going. There were the men to be thought of, too. They were Hallett's responsibility, of course, and he would do his best for them; but it would be devilish for some of them, all the same. The girls would quickly be absorbed by neighbouring factories. Girl labour was at a premium in the Barnton district. The skilled men would not have much trouble either: those munition people two miles away would jump at them. It was the rest, the unskilled, the clerks and storekeepers with wives and families, who would suffer. I ought to be thanking my stars.

When I got back to the works I went straight to Hallett.

"You've heard the news, of course," I said.

He sniffed. "Yes. Herrington wanted me to break it to you, but I told him to do his own dirty work. He actually had the nerve to suggest to me, too, that we keep quiet about it so far as the works were concerned until three days before we shut down. There's the tail end of the Felstead contract to complete, and I suppose he's afraid of the production figures falling off over the month. I told him to go and boil himself. Quite apart from the fact that a good many of them ought to do some quick saving if they can, the girls in the turret shop are organising a social club. Their foreman tells me they're going to ask me to be President. I shouldn't be able to look myself in a glass if, knowing what I do, I let them go on with it."

I nodded. "You're right. I was thinking of that side of it while I was coming down. You and I are about the only people sitting pretty over this business."

He looked at me curiously. "You think so? I hope you're right, Marlow. Personally, I've got a wife, three kids and a house on mortgage to think about. My idea is that the only people who are sitting pretty, as you put it, are Herrington, his plump-backed Board and the dear shareholders. Did you see the last balance-sheet?"

"No?"

"It was a sight for sore eyes. The Forces of Fat, Marlow, move in strange and mysterious ways. Who are we, the mugs who do the job, to question their wisdom? All the same, I *do* question it. But, then, I'm only a blank-dash Socialist."

I left him composing a round-robin to the foreman. Not till then did I remember that I was meeting Claire at seven o'clock.

I broke the news over the soup.

She was wearing a new hat—a fact upon which I had been careful to comment—but it was not the sort of hat behind which she could hide while she thought of something to say. She looked as though she wished it had been.

"That's bad, Nicky," she said. Her voice was quite steady. She paused and then added: "I hope that you're not going to let it interfere with the wedding."

We were eating in a Chinese place, and I have heard that the Chinese are a very difficult race to astonish; but I seem to remember seeing the cook, a Cantonese with a figure like a water butt, goggling incredulously at us through the service door. By the time I had returned to my side of the table, the entire restaurant was buzzing with comment. There was some giggling. Blushing, we got on with our food.

"And now," said Claire some minutes later, "that that is settled, what are you going to do about keeping me in the style to which I have been unaccustomed?"

A wave of remorse swept over me. "Look here," I urged weakly. "This is all wrong. We shouldn't be talking about marriage at this time. Things are pretty bad at the moment. It may be months before I can get the job I want. That's all right as far as it goes. The bank will stay friendly for a bit. But I wouldn't like to make any statement about my prospects. Not for publication, that is. What would your father say?"

"He'll say exactly what I tell him to say."

"But . . ."

"Listen, Nicky." She wagged her chopsticks at me. "You're thirty-five, five foot ten in your socks and handsome to boot. More important, you're a very clever engineer. Hallett told me so that night we had dinner with him and his wife. Why shouldn't you get a good job? Things may be slow just now, but not for first-rate men. Don't be so silly. Besides, I'm twenty-nine; and a female in my position who isn't married by that time ought to be forced to eat her own scalpel."

She succeeded, almost, in convincing me. At all events, for the rest of that evening we forgot about such things as money. To be more precise, we went to a cinema, sat in the back row and held hands. The film, I remember, was very bad. We enjoyed it enormously and took a taxi to her home. Her father gave me a whisky and soda and asked me what I thought of the foreign situation in general with particular reference to the prospects of the Rome-Berlin axis breaking over the Czech question. I forget what I replied. After a bit he looked at us over his glasses, smirked and trotted off to bed. I went home finally by an all-night tram. I was in excellent spirits. I hummed a tune to myself. She was right, bless her heart. I knew my job. I should be all right. It was the man without qualifications who suffered when trade "receded."

But I was wrong.

It took me about two and a half months to find out just how wrong: two and a half months of raised hopes and disappointments, of fruitless interviews and abortive correspondence. Towards the end of my last week at Barnton, I was offered a job at two-thirds the salary I had been getting and turned it down. Six weeks later I would have given my left arm for the chance; but it was too late. I knew that Hallett had thought me a fool and, when he carefully refrained from saying "I told you so," it didn't improve matters. He himself had accepted an offer at fifty per cent. less than Barnton had paid and seemed relieved. I began to get worried and, I am afraid, irritable.

Claire was amazingly good about it all; but I was in a mood to imagine things, and began to suspect that she was losing confidence in me. Foolish of me, no doubt. She, too, was worried; but not as much by my difficulties as by the effect they were having on me. The plain truth is that I was rapidly losing confidence in myself. Then we had a slight quarrel. In itself it was trivial, but other circumstances were to render it important.

We were sitting, rather gloomily, over tea. It was a Tuesday afternoon, and she had left the hospital for an hour to hear the result of an interview with a Birmingham man who was in London for the day. The result was negative. The man from Birmingham had been very pleasant and had given me introductions to two firms from both of which I had already drawn blanks. She heard the news in silence.

"Well," I added bitterly and very childishly, "when do we get married? Or would you prefer to call it off?"

"Don't be a fool, Nicky." She paused. "Anyway, I don't see why all this should interfere with our plans. Just because things are a bit tiresome at the moment, there's no reason why we shouldn't go ahead." She paused again. "After all," she went on lightly, "I've got a perfectly good job and they talk about giving me more money soon."

"That's very nice, darling," I snapped. "And what am I supposed to do? Sit in the furnished bed-sitting-room and darn your stockings?"

It was rude and unpleasant enough, but it was only the beginning. I said a lot of things I didn't mean; pompous things about a man having a certain substratum of "self-respect" to consider and the ignominy of living on a wife's earnings, none of which bore the slightest relation to what she had meant.

She sat tight-lipped and silent until I had finished. Then she said: "I didn't think you could be such an ass." With that she got up and walked out of the shop.

Of course, we made it up that evening. But there was a reservation about the reconciliation of which we were both conscious. When I left that night, she put on her coat and walked with me a little way.

"You know, Nicky," she said after a while, "you've done a terrible lot of apologising to-night. I feel rather bad about it. I know very well it's all my fault really. If I'd had a grain of imagination I'd have known that you'd got enough to worry about without having a confounded nitwit of a girl talking marriage at you to make it worse."

I stopped dead in my tracks. "What on earth are you getting at, Claire?"

"Go on walking, darling, and I'll tell you." We went on. "You remember that engineering paper you left in the hall the other night?"

"Yes, what about it?"

"I had a look through it, Nicky. You'd marked an advertisement in the Appointments Vacant Section. Do you remember it?"

"Yes, vaguely."

"Well . . . ?"

I spluttered. "Good heavens, Claire, you're not suggesting . . . ?"

"Why not? It fits your qualifications exactly. It might have been designed specially for you." And then, as I began to expostulate once more: "No, listen, Nicky. It would do you good."

I halted again. "Now you listen to *me*, sweet. There are some things which are fantastic and absurd, and this is one of them."

She laughed. "All right, but here"—she produced a piece of paper from her bag and thrust it into a pocket of my overcoat—"I tore it out in case you might want to change your mind. Good night, darling."

When at last I continued my walk to the station, I had completely forgotten about the piece of paper.

A week went by. Those seven days were the most depressing I have ever spent. For the first six of them nothing at all happened. Then, on the morning of the seventh, I received a letter from a famous engineering firm in answer to an application of mine in reply to an advertisement for a works manager in one of their smaller factories. I was to call at their offices at three o'clock that day.

At three o'clock I was there. With me in the reception room were two other men. Both were middle-aged. Both, I guessed, were there on the same business as I was. I was right.

I was the last to be seen by the works director. He greeted me with an air of patient amiability.

"Oh yes"—he glanced at my letter lying on the spotless blotting-pad in front of him—"Mr. Marlow, isn't it? Yes, yes. Now, I asked you to call for a special reason. Quite frankly we consider you a little too young for consideration in connection with the post under discussion at the moment." He primped his moustache wearily. I waited. "However," he went on, "we *could* use a young, unmarried man with your qualifications in connection with an important contract we have just secured. Mind you, I'm not making you a definite offer. If you're interested we'll discuss it further. The—er—salary, naturally, is not very large. You probably know how bad things are at the moment, eh? And, of course, it would mean signing on for four years. Still, I don't suppose that would worry a young man like you. It's a great place, Bolivia, a great . . ."

I interrupted the flow. "Where did you say?"

He looked surprised. "Bolivia. The Chaco war," he went on confidently, "showed them the need for relying upon their own resources in time of war. It is a question of establishing two factories and putting them on an economical production basis. The experience alone. . . ."

But I had risen. I could feel that I had become very red in the face. "Thank you very much," I said curtly. "I am afraid, however, that my time is valuable this afternoon. I must apologise for wasting yours. I feel sure that you will find the man you want quite easily."

He stared at me for a moment, then shrugged. "Naturally. Good afternoon. Pull the door to behind you as you go, will you?"

Outside, I bought an evening paper, crossed to a teashop and ordered a cup of tea. Then I noticed that, seated at the next table was one of the men I had seen in the reception room. On a sudden impulse, I leaned across to him.

"Excuse me, sir. I hope you'll forgive my asking; but, as a matter of interest, do you mind telling me if you have just been offered a post in South America?"

He looked startled. He was a grey-haired man with a heavy, intelligent face and large, capable hands. He examined me suspiciously. Then he grinned.

"So they tried that on you too, did they? Well, I don't mind telling you. He did offer me a job in South America —at three quid a week. Said I was too old for the job advertised. Bolivia and three quid a week! Me! I told him what he could do with it. I don't think he liked it much."

"I suppose, then, that the other man got the real job."

"Real job?" He laughed derisively. "There isn't any real job, my friend. That's just a way of getting good men cheap. I've seen that game before. They cut their price to compete with the United States and the Monroe Doctrine. Then they have to make their precious profit. I might have fallen for it, but luckily I've got a job of sorts, selling small tools." He indicated an attaché-case on the chair beside him. "Cheap Jap stuff."

I offered him a cigarette. We went on talking. Bit by bit I learned something of his career; and, as I listened to the quiet, almost casual account of the work he had done, I knew that here was a man beside whose qualifications and experience mine were second-rate. This man knew his job supremely well. Other things being equal, no management with any sense would have hesitated to choose him in preference to me. And yet, here he was selling small tools, "Cheap Jap stuff." When I asked him how business was, he smiled.

"I wouldn't know about that," he said ruefully; "I'm not much good as a traveller. It's a very difficult thing to be good at. I've no patience, very little tact, and I'm always getting people's backs up by showing them how they ought to run their businesses. Besides, I can't help telling them just how bad my stuff is. I'm trying to improve, but it's tough going." He called for his bill. "It's time I was off. Glad to have met you."

When he had gone I tried to read my evening paper. Herr Hitler had reaffirmed the principle of the Rome-Berlin collaboration. Signor Mussolini had made another speech from the balcony of the Palazzo di Venezia. The chairman of an armaments combine had announced complacently that profits for the previous year had proved extremely satisfactory and had expressed confidence in the future of the company. Another Balkan state had gone Fascist. A Croat living in the Paris suburbs had dismembered his mistress's body with a hatchet. A banker had welcomed improved prospects for foreign lending. There were two pictures on the front page: one of two grinning and embarrassed soldiers riding on a new type of tank, the other of a famous statesman, looking like an apprehensive vulture with a fishing-rod in one hand and a very small fish in the other. On page four was an article entitled: "In thy strength, O Britain . . ." by an ex-naval officer who, I happened to know, was also a director of a naval construction yard.

I put the paper down, finished my tea and felt in my pocket for a match to light a cigarette. My fingers encountered the piece of paper. I drew it out, smoothed it on the table and read the advertisement through again very carefully.

REQUIRED by Midland firm. Thoroughly experienced production engineer to take charge of Continental office. Must speak fluent Italian and have had experience of high-production practice. Language qualification essential. Generous salary and commission to right man. Excellent prospects. Apply, stating age, experience (in detail) and when available, to Box 536x.

I don't know what had possessed me to mark it. Maybe it was the bit about the Italian that had struck me as odd. After my parents had died I had shared a room with an Italian fellow-student who had taught me his language in exchange for mine. It had all been part of a plan to spend our summer vacation walking south from Naples. The plan had never matured. We had quarrelled a week before we had been due to start. But my Italian had remained, nourished by an occasional novel from Hachettes and, lately, vague ideas about a honeymoon in Rome.

I put the paper back in my pocket. It was out of the question, of course. Absurd. Claire, bless her heart, was talking nonsense.

But the fact that I put the paper back in my pocket instead of throwing it away was, I think, significant. Almost without my knowing it, the seed of the idea was swelling in my mind. That evening when I arrived at my flat, the seed bore fruit. There were two letters for me. Both had the word "regret" in the first line.

I had a bath, changed my clothes, sat down by the fire and lit a cigarette. For ten minutes I remained there, thinking. Then I got up. There was, after all, no harm in writing. It would probably come to nothing, anyway. Besides, even if I were offered the job, I could always change my mind.

"By the way," I remarked casually later that evening; "just as a matter of interest, I've written for that Italian job. I wouldn't take it, naturally, but there's no harm in seeing what it's all about."

"I thought you'd be sensible, darling," said Claire.

Chapter II

SPARTACUS

FOUR DAYS later I received a letter from The Spartacus Machine Tool Company Limited of Wolverhampton. It was signed by a Mr. Alfred Pelcher, the Managing Director, and requested me to call upon him at Wolverhampton the following day. "Should," the letter concluded, "our meeting not produce any result to our mutual advantage, we shall be pleased to refund to you the travelling expenses from London."

That sounded fair enough. The following day I walked out of Wolverhampton station and asked to be directed to the Spartacus Works. After a bus ride and a ten-minute walk, I came to them, a dingy, sprawling collection of buildings at the end of a long and very muddy road. The view did nothing to raise my drooping spirits. Neither did my reception.

As I approached, a decrepit looking gate-keeper appeared out of a wooden office and asked my business.

"I want to see Mr. Pelcher."

He sucked his teeth and shook his head firmly. "No travellers seen except on Tuesdays and Thursdays. It's a waste of time to try other days."

"I'm not a traveller. I have an appointment with Mr. Pelcher."

He bridled. "Why didn't you say so? I've got my job to do. I can't be expected to know everything. I'm not," he added unnecessarily, "a ruddy crystal gazer. Here"—he grasped my arm—"over there and up the stairs." He indicated a flight of steel stairs set against the side of a black brick building on the opposite side of the yard and retired, muttering, to his office.

I thanked him, clanked up the stairs and pushed open a door marked "SALES OFFICE AND ENQUIRIES. *Please walk in.*" Beyond it was a small frosted glass window, labelled "KNOCK." I knocked. The window slid open with a crash and a fat, pale youth with the beginnings of a moustache peered through at me.

"I want to see Mr. Pelcher."

"Reps., Tuesdays and Thursdays," said the youth severely. "There's a notice at the gate. I don't know what some of you chaps are coming to. It's a waste of your time and mine. You can't see him now."

"I have an appointment."

He shrugged. "Oh well! Name?"

"Marlow."

"O.K."

The window slammed again and I heard him asking over a telephone for Mrs. Moshowitz. Then: "Is that Mrs. Mo? This is your little Ernest speaking from the Sales office." There was a pause. "Now, now! Naughty, naughty," he went on playfully. He lapsed suddenly into the lingua franca of the gangster film. "Say, listen, sister. There's a sucker here named Marlow. He claims he has an appointment with the Big Boy. Shall I let him have it in the stomach or will the Big Boy give him the works himself?" Another pause. "All right, *all* right, keep your stays on." He slammed down the telephone, reappeared at the door and announced that he would himself take me across to Mr. Alfred's office.

We descended the stairway, turned to the right along an alleyway littered with rusty scrap and climbed up another flight of stairs to a door with a Wet Paint notice hanging on the handle. My escort kicked the door open with his heel and informed the elderly and harassed-looking Jewess who glared at him indignantly across a sea of blue-prints that I was the man for Mr. Alfred.

This I was beginning to doubt. What I had so far seen of

the Spartacus Machine Tool Company had impressed me so little that I was within an ace of leaving then and there, without seeing its Managing Director or troubling about my travelling expenses. I was a fool, I told myself, to have wasted a day on such a wild goose chase. But it was too late to think about that now. I was being shown into Mr. Alfred's room.

It was large and very untidy. Stack upon stack of dusty files and tattered blue-prints formed a sort of dado round the green distempered wall, the upper part of which was decorated with many framed catalogue illustrations of machines and two yellowing gold-medal award certificates from Continental trade exhibitions. A coal fire smoked below a mantelpiece groaning under a pile of technical reference books, an *Almanach de Gotha*, a bronze Krishna mounted on a teak plinth and a partly concealed copy of *Etiquette for Men*. In one corner was a bag of golf-clubs. In the centre of the room, behind an enormous table strewn with labelled machine parts, correspondence trays, wooden golf tees, engineering trade papers and boxes of various sorts of paper clips, sat Mr. Alfred Pelcher himself.

He was a small, bald, cheerful man of about fifty with rimless, bi-focal spectacles and a soft, soothing manner which suggested that he had judged you to be in a very bad temper and was determined to coax you out of it. His dress—clearly the product of a compromise between the demands of a morning in the office and an afternoon's golf—consisted of a black lounge suit jacket, a brown cardigan and a pair of grey flannel trousers. He had a habit of wrenching desperately at his collar as if it were choking him.

When I entered the room he was fiddling busily with the curser of a two-foot slide-rule and transferring the results of his calculations to the margin of a copy of *The Times Trade and Engineering Supplement*. Without looking at me he waved the slide-rule in the air to indicate that he was nearly finished. A moment or two later he dropped the slide-rule, sprang to his feet and shook me warmly by the hand.

"How very good of you to come all this way to see us." He pressed me into a chair. "Do sit down. Now let me see, it's Mr. Marlow, isn't it? Splendid." He waved a deprecatory hand at his marginal calculations. "Just a little problem in mechanics, Mr. Marlow. I've been trying to work out approximately how many foot-pounds of energy an eighteen handicap man saves on an average round by having a caddy to carry his clubs for him. It's a tremendous figure." He chuckled. "Do you play golf, Mr. Marlow?"

"Unfortunately, no."

"A great game. The greatest of all games." He beamed at

me. "Well, well now. To business, eh? We wrote to you, didn't we? Yes, of course." He relapsed into his chair again and stared at me through the lower half of his spectacles for fully thirty seconds. Then he leaned forward across the table. "*Se non è in grado,*" he said deliberately, "*di accettare questa mia proposta, me lo dica francamente. Non me l'avrò a male.*"

I was a little taken aback, but I replied suitably: "*Prima prendere una decisione vorrei sapere sua proposta, Signore.*"

His eyebrows went up. He snapped his fingers delightedly. He lifted the slide-rule, banged it down on the table and sat back again.

"Mr. Marlow," he said solemnly, "you are the first person to answer our advertisement who has read it carefully. I have seen six gentlemen before you. Three of them could speak tourist French and insisted that most Italians would understand it. One had been in Ceylon and had a smattering of Tamil. He declared, by the way, that if you shouted loud enough in English anyone would know what you were driving at. Of the other two, one spoke fluent German, while the last had been on a cruise and spent a day in Naples. You are the first to see us who can speak Italian." He paused. Then a sudden expression of alarm clouded his features. He looked like a child who is about to be hurt. "You *are* an engineer, aren't you, Mr. Marlow?" He plucked anxiously at his collar. "You are not, by any chance, an electrician or a chemist or a wireless expert?"

I summarised my qualifications briefly and was about to refer him for greater detail to the letter I had written when I saw that my letter was on the table in front of him and that he was nodding happily over it while I talked. Mr. Pelcher was evidently not quite so ingenious as he appeared.

When I had finished, he slid the letter discreetly under his blotter and emitted a loud sigh of relief. "Then *that's* all right. I feel that we understand one another, Mr. Marlow. Now tell me"—he looked like a small boy asking a riddle—"have you had any sales experience?"

"None at all."

He looked crestfallen. "I was afraid not. However, we can't have everything. A good engineer who can speak Italian with reasonable accuracy is something you don't find every day. Excuse me one moment." He lifted the telephone. "Hallo, Jenny, my dear, please ask Mr. Fitch if he would mind stepping over to my office for a moment." He put the telephone down and turned to me again. "Mr. Fitch is our export manager. A very nice fellow, with two bonny children, a boy and a girl. His wife, poor soul, is dead. I think you will like him."

"I wonder," I said, "if you would mind giving me some idea of what the post involves, Mr. Pelcher?"

He clasped his forehead. "Good heavens, of course. I thought I'd told you. You see, Mr. Marlow"—he clutched at his collar—"we are not a very big concern. We specialise in one particular class of machine. You probably know that." I didn't, but I nodded. "We have," he continued, "a slogan. 'There is a Spartacus machine for every high-production boring job.' It is, within limits, a comprehensive description of our activities. Actually, however, we have been concentrating more and more during the past year or so on high-speed automatic machines for shell production. About a third of our shop space is at present given over to that work. It was started more or less as a side-line. I had some ideas on the subject of that type of machine. We worked them out. They were successful. We secured world patent rights on the design of the Spartacus Type S2 automatic. Incidentally, the word Spartacus was my idea originally. It's good, don't you think —Spartacus the slave—neat. However, to return to the S2. We hold world patent rights, and I must say they've proved very valuable to us. We have licensed some of our American friends to manufacture; but we retained the European market for ourselves. I think we were wise. The Germans have produced a machine to compete with the S2, but it's no better than ours, and we have had a good start. Business with the Continent has been really brisk. The Italians, in particular, took to the S2 immediately. The ordnance department of the Italian Admiralty were very interested. Firms installing our machines were able to reduce their costs quite phenomenally. We have, of course, been approached by British concerns, but frankly we have been kept so busy with export business that we haven't bothered so far to cultivate the home market. The Italians have been so very helpful, too, in arranging the financial details. As a rule, you know, it's quite difficult to get money out of Italy in these days. In our special case they pay with drafts on New York. You see, they need the machines. Very friendly of them. About a year ago we decided that it would pay us to open an Italian office. I couldn't spare the time to keep on running over there all the time. Milan is, as you may know, the centre of things from our point of view. We got hold of a very good man for the job. You may have heard of his sad death. Ferning was the name."

"I can't say that I know of him."

"No? It was mentioned in the trade papers. But perhaps

a man of your age doesn't read the obituary notices." He chuckled and pulled so violently at his collar that I thought the stud would snap. He became serious again. "Poor Ferning! A nervous, sensitive sort of fellow I always thought. But then you can't always judge by appearances. He made an amazingly good thing of the Milan office. With an order we got from Turkey, we've sold practically the whole of our present output of S2 automatics for the next two years. It's a nice machine. Naturally, that is only on our present production basis. We're putting up a new shop, and as soon as that is going we shall be in a position to accept all the orders we can get. Bad luck about Ferning. The poor chap was run over a few weeks back. A very sad affair. As far as we can gather it was foggy and he was walking home when it happened. Killed outright, fortunately. The driver of the car, whoever it was, didn't stop. Probably didn't even know he'd hit anybody in the fog. They're sometimes pretty thick in Milan, you know. Unmarried, thank goodness, but he leaves a sister who was dependent on him. Very hard lines."

"Yes, very."

"Ferning's assistant, Bellinetti, is carrying on at the moment. But we are not regarding that arrangement as permanent. A good assistant, no doubt, but not yet ready for responsibility. Besides, he's not a trained engineer. That's what we need, Mr. Marlow. A trained man, a man who can go into the works and show the customer how to get the best out of our machines. With the Germans so active at the moment, we've got to keep well in with the people who matter, and"— he winked broadly—"and co-operate with the Italian officials. However, Mr. Fitch will tell you more about that." He lifted the telephone again. "Hullo. Is Mr. Fitch coming over, Jenny? On his way? Good." He clawed at his collar and turned to me again. "Naturally, Mr. Marlow, if we were to come to terms we should want you to spend a week or so here in the works before you left. But there again, that's something we can discuss later. Of course, you may not like the look of *us*"—he chuckled as if at the idea of such a fantastic possibility—"but I must say I feel that we might profitably discuss the matter in more detail first."

I laughed politely, and was about to intimate that more detail, and in particular more detail in connection with the financial aspects of the job, was precisely what I *should* like, when there was a knock at the door.

"Ah!" said Mr. Pelcher, "here's Fitch."

Mr. Fitch was a very tall man with a long, thin head and a way of holding himself that made him look as though he were standing under a low, leaking roof on a wet day. He surveyed us from the door with the mournful air of an elderly borzoi being teased by a pair of fox terrier puppies.

"This, Fitch," said Mr. Pelcher briskly, "is Mr. Marlow. He is a trained engineer and he can speak Italian."

Mr. Fitch shambled forward and we shook hands.

"I was just telling Mr. Marlow," pursued Mr. Pelcher, "some of the circumstances of our Italian connection."

Mr. Fitch nodded and cleared his throat. "The bottom's out of the export market," he asserted gloomily.

Mr. Pelcher laughed and twitched at his collar. "Mr. Fitch has been saying that for ten years now, Mr. Marlow. You mustn't take his pessimism too seriously. Nothing less than doubling our turnover every year would satisfy him."

Mr. Fitch looked at me doubtfully. "Do you know Italy very well, Mr. Marlow?"

"Not as well as I should like to," I replied evasively.

"Play golf?"

"I'm afraid not."

"Fitch," said Mr. Pelcher fondly, "is a scratch golfer. Hits a terrific ball and as accurate as the devil. However"—he dragged his thoughts back to earth with a visible effort—"to business! Perhaps you'd like to have a look round the works, Mr. Marlow? Fitch, do you mind showing Mr. Marlow round? When you've done, come back here and we'll have another chat."

Whatever the shortcomings of the Spartacus offices, they were nowhere visible in the works. The Works Manager, to whom I took an instant liking, was obviously competent and the standard of work being turned out was extraordinarily high. "Pelcher," said Mr. Fitch, as we crossed from one shop to another, "likes everything just so. He's a fine engineer. If he had his way and we hadn't got a Board of ex-Generals and Members of Parliament with a titled nitwit thrown in, this place would be twice the size. He's a damned smart business man too. But did you ever see anything like his office? He's a lousy golfer as well. The last time I played with him he took a slide-rule out to deal with problems of drift and wind resistance. Not that it made any difference to his game. On the first tee he spent two solid minutes with the slide-rule and then pulled his drive somewhere round the back of his neck."

As if to make up for this burst of confidence, Mr. Fitch maintained an unhappy silence for the rest of the tour; but it was with slightly more zest that I ascended for the second time the stairs to Mr. Pelcher's office.

Back in London that evening, I gave Claire a résumé of the day's findings. "I think," I concluded, "that they'll probably offer me the job. Of course, I shan't take it. The money they've got in mind is ridiculous. The lira may be in our favour, but that's nothing to do with what the job is worth in pounds sterling. And Italy, too! The whole thing is out of the question."

"Of course, darling," said Claire.

We said no more about it.

Two letters arrived for me next morning. One was from Mr. Pelcher, formally offering me the post of manager of the Spartacus Milan office. The other was from Hallett. His new job did not start for another fortnight. He thought I would probably be fixed up by now. Could I possibly lend him five pounds?

I went for a short walk, smoked a couple of cigarettes, sat down and replied to both letters.

Three weeks later I caught the Folkestone boat-train.

To my intense relief there was nobody at the station to see me off. I had said good-bye to Claire the previous night. She was, she had said with somewhat emotional practicality, too busy at the hospital to spare time to come to the station. Later on she had wept and explained, unnecessarily, that it wasn't that she couldn't spare the time, but that she didn't want to make a fool of herself and me on the platform. "After all," we kept on assuring one another, "it's only for a few months, a temporary job until things get better here." By the time it was time for me to go back to the hotel into which I had moved, we had managed to evolve an atmosphere of bright camaraderie that spared both our feelings and our pocket handkerchiefs.

"Good-bye, Nicky, darling," she had called after me as I had left, "don't get into trouble."

And I had laughed at the idea and called back that I wouldn't.

I actually laughed.

Chapter III

THE PAINTED GENERAL

IT IS on my second evening in Milan that General Vagas comes on the scene.

Looking back now, the whole story seems to begin with that meeting. What had happened to me apart from that seems of no significance. Yet if it is easy to be wise after an event it is easier still to let that wisdom colour an account of the event itself, to the confusion and irritation of the reader. It is as if he were listening to a joke being told in an unfamiliar foreign tongue. I must tell the story in a straightforward manner. General Vagas must, so to speak, take his place in the queue.

At eight o'clock that evening I sat down in my room at the Hotel Parigi to write to Claire. She has kept the letter and as it describes in a more or less condensed form what had happened to me since my arrival and the impressions I had formed of the Milan staff of the Spartacus Machine Tool Company, I have incorporated it. It was my original intention to omit the more intimate passages, but as Claire's only comment on this suggestion was a blank "Why?", I have left them in.

> HOTEL PARIGI,
> MILANO,
> *Tuesday.*

Dearest Claire,

Already, I am gripped by the most excruciating pangs of nostalgia. It is, I find, just four days since I saw you. It seems like four months. Trite, I know; but then the plain, ordinary, human emotions nearly always do seem trite when you put them down on paper. I don't know whether or not triteness increases in direct proportion to the number and intensity of the plain, ordinary, human emotions experienced. It probably does. My present P.O.H.E.'s are (a) a profound sense of loneliness and (b) the growing conviction that I was a fool to leave you no matter what the circumstances. No doubt I shall feel a little better about item (a) in a day or two. As for item (b), I'm not quite sure if a conviction, even a growing one, can possibly be described as an emotion. In any case, if I start talking about it now I shall end by running amok, and I don't think that the management of the Parigi would care much for that.

I remember that at this point I stopped and read the paragraph through. What nonsense it sounded! a ghastly attempt to smile through imaginary tears. Claire would despise it. The smile was an arch grin. The tears were crocodiles'. And that bit about emotions and convictions. Piffle! I screwed it up and threw it in the wastepaper basket and then, when I had made one or two desultory attempts to start again, I retrieved it from the basket and copied it out on a fresh sheet of paper. Hang it all, it expressed what I felt. I went on.

You are probably wondering why on earth I am staying here and whether, for Pity's sake, I propose to go on staying here. It is a long story.

It wasn't a long story. It was quite a short one. However . . .

I arrived yesterday afternoon at about four o'clock (3 p.m. to you in England, my love), and was met at the Centrale Station by Bellinetti, who was, you may remember, my predecessor's assistant.

He is rather older than I had expected from the way Pelcher and Fitch talked about him. Picture a small, stocky Italian of about forty with incredibly wavy black hair, greying at the temples, and the sort of teeth that you see in dentifrice advertisements. He is a very natty dresser and wears a diamond (?) ring on the little finger of his left hand. I have a suspicion, however, that he doesn't shave every day. A pity. He is an enthusiastic reader of the Popolo d'Italia, and has a passion for Myrna Loy ("so calm, so cold, such secret fires"), but I have not yet discovered whether he is married or not.

I considered this description of Bellinetti for a moment. It wasn't quite right. It was accurate enough as far as it went, but there was more to the man than that. He wasn't so theatrical. He had a way of leaning forward towards you and dropping his voice as though he were about to impart some highly confidential tit-bit. But the tit-bit never came. You received the impression that he would have liked to talk all the time of momentous and very secret affairs, but that he was haunted by the perpetual triviality of real life. His air of frustration was a little worrying until you became used to it. But I couldn't put all that in a letter. I lit a cigarette and went on again.

As I told you, I wasn't anticipating a great deal of active co-operation from Arturo Bellinetti. After all, he was expecting that Ferning's death would mean that he got Ferning's job. Fitch told me that in a weak moment and to encourage the man, Pelcher had hinted that he might possibly be appointed. It was scarcely to be expected that he would fall on the neck of the Sporco Inglese with cries of enthusiasm. But I must say that he has been extraordinarily helpful, and I shall tell Pelcher so.

As soon as we had got over the preliminary politenesses, we went to a caffè (two f's and a grave accent here, please), where he introduced me to his pet tipple which is a cognac with a beer chaser. I wouldn't like to try it with English bitter, but here it doesn't seem too bad. At all events it took the edge off that interminable journey. The next thing was to make my living arrangements. Bellinetti suggested that I might like to take over Ferning's old place which was in an apartment house near the Monte di Pieta. This seemed to me a good idea, and we piled my luggage into a taxi and drove there. Little did I know, as they say in books, what was in store for me.

Imagine the Ritz, the Carlton and Buckingham Palace rolled into one, a dash of rococo and a spicing of Lalique, and you will have some idea of what I found. Not a very large building, it is true, but decidedly luxurious. Manager in attendance, we went up to the second-floor front. This, said the Manager, had been signor Ferning's apartment. A very liberal and sympathetic Signore had been the signor Ferning. His death was nothing short of a tragedy. But he would be delighted to serve the so sympathetic signor Marlow. The price of the apartment was only six hundred lire a week.

Well, darling, it was probably worth the money. In fact, I should say that it was cheap. But six hundred lire a week! Either the manager was trying it on (it is still a popular illusion here that all Americans and English are millionaires), or the late lamented and so sympathetic signor Ferning had made a better bargain with Spartacus than I had. The Manager was dumbfounded when I turned it down so promptly and, with a hearty misunderstanding of the situation, tried to show me something even more luxurious and expensive on the first floor. We retired in disorder. I shall have to get Fitch to tell me more about Ferning when he writes.

I did not tell Claire of the suspicion I had entertained that my assistant might have arranged to take a commission on the deal. The idea had crossed my mind as soon as the Manager mentioned the price; but as Bellinetti had not seemed at all put out when I had refused the offer and as, on reflection, I had not seen how even a generous commission could account altogether for such a price, I had quickly abandoned the notion.

By this time, the effects of the brandy and beer were beginning to wear off and I was feeling rather tired. Bellinetti, bounding with energy, was all for going on an intensive apartment hunt; but I decided that the best thing I could do was to put up at a hotel for a day or two and find a place at my leisure. Bellinetti knows the management here, so here I came.

It is not quite as expensive as the note-paper might lead you to think. It appears that the present vogue is for "modernity" à la Marinetti. The only really modern aspect of the Parigi is the hot-water system which gurgles a great deal and makes the place like an oven. The rest is, I should say, a relic of Milan under Napoleon. The corridors are shadowy, the ceilings are high, there is much green plush and dull gilt plaster work. In the restaurant (nearly always two-thirds empty), there are long mirrors with the silvering turning black near the edges. My bed is an enormous mahogany structure with a plush canopy impressively edged with tarnished gold braid, while the chair in which I am sitting now is more uncomfortable than I should have thought possible. The Parigi is not, I should say, a very paying proposition for the owners. But then I haven't yet seen the extras on the bill.

Milan, as a whole, has proved something of a surprise. I don't know why it should have done so; but you know how it is. You get an imaginary picture of a place in your mind, and then are upset when the reality doesn't fit. I had always pictured it as a collection of small houses in the Borghese manner grouped round an enormous rococo opera house peopled by stout, passionate tenors, sinister-looking baritones and large mezzo-sopranos with long pearl necklaces. Vociferous international audiences thronged the streets. Actually, it is nothing more nor less than an Italian version of Birmingham. I haven't yet set eyes on La Scala, but a poster told me that they are doing ballet there—not even opera. The only "sight" I have seen so far is the offices of the Popolo d'Italia, from which Mussolini is said to have set out on the March to Rome. Bellinetti pointed them out to me. He is an enthusiastic adherent of Fascismo and tells me that Italy will "wade through blood to an Empire." He didn't tell me whose blood, but I gather that he does not expect to be called upon to supply any part of it.

I was afterwards told that Mussolini's participation in the glorious March on Rome was confined to arriving in the Eternal City three days later in the luxury of a *wagon-lit.* But it is quite true that he set out from the offices of the *Popolo.* That, however, is by the way.

I have spent most of to-day looking into things at the Via San Giulio. The offices themselves are on the fourth floor of a comparatively recent building and, although small, are quite clean and light. My staff consists of Bellinetti and two typists, one male and one female. The male is aged about twenty-two, fair, very self-conscious. His Christian name is Um-

berto, but so far I have not discovered the surname. Bellinetti says that he reads too many books. He looks to me as
though he needs a square meal. It is possibly only my imagination but I fancy, too, that Bellinetti may be a bit of a
bully.

The female help is astonishing. Her name is Serafina, and
she has two dark pools of mystery where her eyes ought to be,
a complexion like semi-transparent wax and clothes that
would make your mouth water. Unfortunately she is also
very stupid. A protégée of Master Bellinetti's, I fear. The
girl cannot even type. The sight of her blood-red finger-nails
twitching uncertainly over the keyboard of her typewriter,
I found irritating. Our Serafina must be discussed in the near
future. I haven't really had a chance yet to go very far into
the actual business workings of the office. I had a long
memorandum from Fitch on the subject. I shall begin the
inquest to-morrow. Bellinetti assures me that everything is
fine. I hope he's right.

The only extra-office contact I've made so far was with an
American, whose name I don't know, but who has an office
on the floor below us. He is an odd-looking blighter with a
large, pugnacious nose like a prize-fighter's, brown, curly hair
that stands up at an angle of forty-five from his forehead, sur-
prisingly blue eyes, and a pair of shoulders that look all the
heftier because he's slightly shorter than I am. Sorry to be so
pernickety about what he looks like, but he impressed me
rather. We met on the stairs this morning. He stopped me
and asked if I wasn't English. He explained that it was my
clothes that had given him the idea. We made a vague arrangement to have a drink together some time. He says he
knew Ferning.

If I had known just how much of an impression this
"American" was going to make on me in the very near
future, I doubt very much whether I should have dismissed
him quite so easily from my thoughts. But I was feeling very
tired. I decided to finish.

Well, darling, I'm going to stop this letter-writing now.
It's too long, anyway, and, even though it's only nine o'clock,
I can hardly keep my eyes open. I haven't said any of the
things I meant to say and very little of what I'm really thinking—about you and me, I mean. Possibly you can guess all
that. I hope so, because, with all this replanting of roots going on, all I seem to be able to get down on paper is something between an inter-departmental memo and a particularly
dull book of memoirs. I shall go now and soak myself in a

hot bath and then go to bed. Good night, and a sweet sleep to you, darling. Write to me as soon as you can. I keep consoling myself with the thought that you'll be coming here for your summer vacation, but it's a terribly long time to wait. Let me know as soon as may be when it will be. Bless you.
Nicky.

I looked it through. It took up six sides of the hotel notepaper. Far too long and far too plaintive. Still, it was the best I could do under the circumstances and Claire would understand.

I had stuck down and addressed the envelope when I remembered that I had meant to add a postscript. There were no more envelopes in the rack. Then I did something which I was to remember later. I turned the letter over and wrote the postscript across the back of the envelope.

P.S.—Do you mind sending me a copy of Engineering each week? We get it here but not until Fitch has finished with it. Love. N.

That was that. I would post it in the morning. I yawned and wondered whether to turn the bath on straight away or smoke a final cigarette.

The question was decided for me. The telephone by the bed rang sharply and the voice of the reception clerk informed me that a signor Vagas was asking to see me.

My first impulse was to say that I was in bed and unable to see anyone. I did not know a signor Vagas, I had never heard of a signor Vagas and I was feeling too tired to do anything about it now. But I hesitated. The fact that I personally did not know the name of Vagas was beside the point. I knew nobody in Milan. The man might conceivably be an important buyer, a Spartacus customer. I ought not to take any risks. I ought to see him. The name did not sound particularly Italianate, but that was beside the point. I certainly *ought* to see him. What on earth could he want? With a sigh, I told the clerk to send him up.

I have wondered since what would have happened subsequently if I had yielded to my aching desire for a hot bath and refused to see him. Probably he would have called again. Possibly, on the other hand, he might have made other arrangements. I don't really know enough about what went on behind the scenes to say. In any case, such speculations are unprofitable. My only reason for raising the point is that it seems to me that a state of society in which such trivialities as the desire of one insignificant engineer for a hot bath are capable of influencing the destinies of large numbers of his fellow-creatures, has something radically wrong with it. However, I *did* postpone my bath and I *did* see General Vagas. But if I had known then what the consequences of that piece of self-denial were going to be, I should, I am afraid, have been inclined to let my fellow-creatures go hang.

He was a tall, heavy man with sleek, thinning grey hair, a brown, puffy complexion and thick, tight lips. Fixed firmly in the flesh around his left eye was a rimless monocle without a cord to it. He wore a thick and expensive-looking black ulster and carried a dark-blue slouch hat. In his other hand he held a malacca stick.

His lips twisted, with what was evidently intended to be a polite smile. But the smile did not reach his eyes. Dark and small and cautious, they flickered appraisingly from my head to my feet. Almost instinctively my own eyes dropped to the stick in his hand, to his fat, delicate fingers holding it loosely about a third of the way down. For a minute fraction of a second we stood there facing one another. Then he spoke.

"Signor Marlow?" His voice was soft and husky. He coughed a little after he had said it.

"Yes, signor Vagas, I believe? *Fortunatissimo*."

The small eyes surveyed my own. Slowly he drew a card from his pocket and presented it to me. I glanced at it. On it was printed: *"Maggiore Generale F. L. VAGAS,"* and an address in the Corso di Porta Nuova.

"I beg your pardon, General. The clerk did not give me your name correctly."

"It is quite unimportant, Signore. Do not concern yourself, I beg you."

We shook hands. I ushered him in. He walked with a slight limp over to a chair and put his coat, hat and stick carefully on it.

"A drink, General?"

He nodded graciously. "Thank you. I will take cognac." I rang the bell for the waiter.

"A chair?"

"Thank you." He sat down.

"A cigarette?"

He looked carefully at the contents of my case.

"English?"

"Yes."

"Good, then I will smoke one."

I gave him a match and waited. His eyes wandered for a moment or two round the room, then they returned to me. He adjusted the monocle carefully, as if to see me better.

Then, to my surprise, he began to speak in tolerably accurate English.

"I expect, Mr. Marlow, you are wondering who I am and why I have come here to visit you."

I murmured something about it being, in any case, a pleasure. He smiled. I found myself hoping that he would not consider it necessary to do so a third time. It was a grimace rather than a smile. Now that I knew him to be a General it was easier to sum him up. He would look better in uniform. The limp? Probably a war wound. And yet there was a quality of effeminacy about the way he spoke, the way he moved his hands, that lent a touch of the grotesque to the rest of him. Then I noticed with a shock that the patches of colour just below his cheekbones were rouge. I could see, too, on the jaw line just below his ear the edge of a heavy and clumsily applied *maquillage*. Almost at the same moment as I made the discovery he turned slightly in his chair. In the ordinary way I should have seen nothing in the movement but a desire for greater comfort; now I knew that he was avoiding the light.

In answer to my polite disclaimer he shrugged.

"How odd it is, Mr. Marlow. We on the Continent spend half our lives in the belief that all Englishmen are boors. And yet, in truth, how much more polite and sympathetic they are." He coughed gently. "But I must not take up too much of your time. I come, so to speak, in a spirit of friendliness and to give myself the pleasure of meeting you." He paused. "I was a friend, a great friend, of Mr. Ferning."

I said "Oh" rather foolishly and then expressed my sympathy.

He inclined his head. "His death was a great tragedy for me. Poor man. Italian drivers are abominable." It was said smoothly, easily and entirely without conviction. Fortunately, the arrival of the waiter made it unnecessary for me to reply to this. I ordered the drinks and lit a cigarette.

"I am afraid," I said, "that I never had the pleasure of knowing Mr. Ferning."

For some reason, he chose to misinterpret the statement.

"And neither did I, Mr. Marlow. He was my dear friend, it is true, but I did not know him." He gestured with his cigarette. "It is, I think, impossible to know any man. His thoughts, his own secret emotions, the way his mind works upon the things he sees—those things are the man. All that the outsider sees is the shell, the mask—you understand? Only sometimes do we see a man and then"—his eyes flickered towards the ceiling—"it is through the eyes of an artist."

"There is probably a lot in what you say," I pursued stolidly; "I meant, however, that I had never even met Ferning."

"How unfortunate! How very unfortunate. I think you would have liked him, Mr. Marlow. You would, I think, have had sympathies in common. A man—how do you say? —sensible."

"You mean sensitive?"

"Ah, yes, that is the word. A man, you understand, above the trivialities, the squalor of a petty existence—a man, Mr. Marlow, with a philosophy."

"Indeed?"

"Yes, Mr. Marlow. Ferning believed, as I believe, that in such a world as this, one should consider only how to secure the maximum of comfort with the minimum of exertion. But, of course, that was not all. He was, I used to tell him, a Platonist *malgré lui*. Yes he had his ideals, but he kept them in the proper place for such things—in the background of the mind, together with one's dreams of Utopia."

I was getting tired of this.

"And you, General? Are you too interested in machine tools?"

He raised his eyebrows. "I? Oh yes, Mr. Marlow. I am certainly interested in machine tools. But then"—something very nearly approaching a simper animated him—"but then, I am interested in everything. Have you yet walked through the Giardini Pubblici? No? When you do so you will see the attendants wandering round like the spirits of the damned, aimless and without emotion, collecting the small scraps of waste-paper on long, thin spikes. You understand me? You see my point? Nothing is too special, too esoteric for my tastes. Not even machine tools."

"Then that was how you met Ferning?"

The General fluttered a deprecatory hand. "Oh dear, no, no. We were introduced by a friend—now, alas, also dead— and we discovered a mutual interest in the ballet. Do you care for the ballet, Mr. Marlow?"

"I am extremely fond of it."

"So?" He looked surprised. "I am very glad to hear it, very glad. Between you and me, Mr. Marlow, I have often wondered whether perhaps poor Ferning's interest in the ballet was not conditioned more by the personal charms of the ballerinas than by the impersonal tragedy of the dance."

The drinks arrived, a fact for which I was heartily thankful.

He sniffed at his cognac and I saw his lips twist into an expression of wry distaste. I knew that the Parigi brandy was bad, but the grimace annoyed me. He put the drink down carefully on a side table.

"Personally," he said, "I find this city unbearable except for the opera and ballet. They are the only reasons for which I come. It must be lonely here without any friends, Mr. Marlow."

"I have been too busy so far to think about it."

"Yes, of course. Have you been to Milan before?"

I shook my head.

"Ah, then you will have the brief pleasure of discovering a new city. Personally I prefer Belgrade. But, then, I am a Yugo-Slav."

"I have never been to Belgrade."

"A pleasure in store for you." He paused. Then: "I wonder if you would care to join my wife and I in our box to-morrow night. They are reviving Les Biches, and I am always grateful for Lac des Cygnes. We might all three have a little supper together afterwards."

I found the prospect of spending an evening in the company of General Vagas singularly distasteful.

"That would be delightful. Unfortunately, I expect to be working to-morrow night."

"The day after?"

"I have to go to Genoa on business." This, it afterwards turned out, was perfectly true.

"Then let us make it next Wednesday."

To have refused again would have been rude. I accepted with as good a grace as possible. Soon after, he got up to go. There was a copy of a Milan evening paper lying on the table. Splashed right across the front page was a violent anti-British article. He glanced at it and then looked at me.

"Are you a patriot, Mr. Marlow?"

"In Milan, I am on business," I said firmly.

He nodded as though I had said something profound. "One should not," he said slowly, "allow one's patriotism to interfere with business. Patriotism is for the *caffè*. One should leave it behind with one's tip to the waiter."

There was a barely perceptible sneer in his voice. For some reason I felt myself reddening.

"I don't think I quite understand you, General."

There was a slight change in his manner. His effeminacy seemed suddenly less pronounced.

"Surely," he said, "you are selling certain machinery to the Italian Government? That is what I understood from my friend Ferning."

I nodded. He gazed at my tie.

"So. That would seem to raise a question in the mind." He raised his eyes. "But, of course, I appreciate the delicacy of these affairs. Business is business and so logical. It has no

frontiers. Supply and demand, credit and debit. I have myself no head for business. It is a ritual which I find be-
wildering."

He had lapsed into Italian again. We moved towards the
door and I picked up his coat to help him on with it. We
both bent forward simultaneously to pick up the hat and
stick; but he was still settling his overcoat on his shoulders
and I forestalled him. The stick was fairly heavy and as I
handed it to him my fingers slid over a minute break in the
malacca. He took the stick from me with a slight bow.

"On Wednesday then, Signore."

"On Wednesday, General."

At the door he turned. By the hard light of the electric
chandelier in the corridor, the rouge on his cheeks was ridic-
ulously obvious.

"Shall you be remaining here at the Parigi, Mr. Marlow?"

"I don't think so. It is a little too expensive for me."

There was a pause. "Mr. Ferning," he said slowly, "had
a very charming apartment."

"So I believe. Mr. Ferning could probably afford it. I cannot."

His eyes met mine. "I wouldn't be too sure of that, Mr.
Marlow." He coughed gently. "To a man of intelligence, a
business man, there are always opportunities."

"No doubt."

"It is a question only of whether he has the will to take
them. But I must not take up any more of your time with
these ideas of mine. Good evening, Mr. Marlow, and thank
you for a pleasant meeting. I shall look forward to seeing
you again next Wednesday." He clicked his heels. *"A rivederci, Signore."*

"Good evening, General."

He went. I returned to my room but, for the moment, I
had forgotten about my bath.

General Vagas puzzled me. I had, too, an uncomfortable
feeling that there had been a point to his conversation that I
had somehow missed. I found myself wishing that I had
known more about Ferning. There had obviously been something odd about him. His apartment, Vagas' veiled hints . . .
but Ferning was dead, and I had more important things to
think about than effeminate Yugo-Slav generals. In a day or
two I would write to the man and tell him that a business
engagement prevented me from meeting him and his wife
on the Wednesday. It would probably be true, anyway. I
should have to present the letters of introduction that Pelcher
had given me and make myself agreeable to the company's
excellent customers. Yes, that was my job—to make myself

agreeable. If Spartacus were willing to sell shell-production machinery and someone else were willing to buy it, it was not for me to discuss the rights and wrongs of the business. I was merely an employee. It was not my responsibility. Hallett would probably have had something to say about it; but then Hallett was a Socialist. Business was business. The thing to do was to mind one's own.

I had turned my bath on and was beginning to undress when there was a knock at the door.

It was the Manager of the Parigi in person.

"I must apologise profoundly for disturbing you, signor Marlow."

"That's all right. What is it?"

"The police, Signore, have telephoned. They understand that you intend to stay in Italy for some time. It is necessary to deposit your passport for registration purposes. The passport is retained for only a few hours and then returned to you."

"I know. But I gave you my passport. You said that you would arrange these formalities."

He fluttered uneasily. "Quite so, Signore. In the ordinary way—in the case of a tourist—but in the case of the Signore it is different. I have your passport here, Signore. If you would be so kind as to present yourself personally at the *Amministrazione* in the morning, the matter will arrange itself."

"Oh, very well." I took the passport. "I suppose this is usual?"

"Yes, yes, Signore. Certainly it is usual. The regulations, you understand. If the Signore were a tourist then it would be simple. In the case of a resident there are certain formalities. Quite usual, Signore, and according to the regulations. Good night, Signore."

"Good night."

He went and I put the matter out of my mind.

It was not until I was soaking blissfully in the steaming water that it occurred to me to wonder why General Vagas thought it necessary to carry a sword-stick.

Chapter IV

BLACK WEDNESDAY

IT USED to be the custom to commemorate moments of national humiliation or disaster by applying the adjective "black" to the day of the week concerned. The pages of European history are, so to speak, bespattered with the records of Black Mondays and Black Thursdays. It may be that, in this twentieth century, almost daily acquaintance with large-scale catastrophe has deprived the custom of its point. Black and white have tended to merge into a drab grey.

Yet, for me, there is a Wednesday which, in its sooty blackness, is easily distinguishable from the grey. It is the day following that upon which I met General Vagas.

It began with a visit to the *Amministrazione della Polizia.*

I presented myself, passport in hand, shortly after nine o'clock. After surrendering the passport to a policeman wearing a Monagesque uniform and a huge sword, I was ushered into a waiting-room. Except for a row of greasy wooden armchairs and an ink-stained table it was bare of furniture. From one wall glowered a large fly-blown photograph of Mussolini. Facing it on the opposite wall was a companion representation of King Victor Emmanuel. The frames of both portraits were draped, rather carelessly, with Italian flags. When I arrived, one of the chairs was occupied by an old woman in mourning, eating a cold compress of spaghetti out of an American-cloth bag. After about ten minutes she was beckoned out by the policeman and I was left alone to study the Duce's apoplectic glare.

I waited for an hour and a quarter. Shortly after the forty-five minutes mark I went to the door and complained to the policeman. I had, I protested, work to do. His only response was a shrug and a vague assurance that my case was receiving attention. I retired once more to the waiting-room. By the time he appeared at the door and beckoned to me, my temper was already a trifle frayed. What followed did nothing to improve it.

I was shown into a room occupied by a man in a dark-green uniform. He was lolling back in his swivel chair flipping over the pages of an illustrated magazine. One gleaming, booted leg was cocked over an arm of the chair which he had swung round, so that all I could see of him was the back of his neck. Beyond affecting a slightly more intense preoccupation with the magazine, he took no notice of my entrance. With rising irritation, I studied the neck.

It was plump and brown and bulged over the narrow line of white stiff collar above the uniform collar. I took an immediate dislike to the neck and to its owner. He flipped over the last of the pages, dropped the magazine on his desk and swung round to face me. My dislike was promptly confirmed. His face was small, smooth, round and spiteful. He scowled at me.

"Yes? What do you want?"

"My passport."

"And why should I have your passport? Get out!"

Deciding that the fool of a policeman had probably shown me into the wrong room, I turned to go.

"Wait."

I stopped.

"What is your name?"

"Marlow."

"English?"

"Yes."

"Ah!" He turned to his table, picked up my passport from under the magazine and looked at the name on it. "Ah, yes! Signor Marlow, the Englishman." He smiled unpleasantly.

"Precisely, Signore," I burst out angrily. "And I should like to know why I have been kept waiting for an hour and a quarter." I nodded towards the magazine. "I, at any rate, have something to do with my time."

It was perhaps unwise of me, but I could not help it. The prospect of carrying out my intention of putting in a good day's work at the office was receding rapidly. I was thoroughly angry. Nevertheless, as soon as the words were out of my mouth, I knew that I had blundered.

His lip curled viciously.

"Be more respectful in your manner, please," he snapped; "and be so good as to address me as *signor Capitano*."

I glared at him in silence.

"*Allora*." He turned to the passport and drew a sheet of paper towards him. "You will answer the questions I put to you."

"Very well." I carefully omitted the "*signor Capitano*."

With great deliberation he put his pen down, fitted a cigarette into a holder and produced a jewelled lighter. His obvious intention was to waste time. I could have hit him.

"Now," he went on at last, "we will begin. Where were you born?"

"You will find the place and date in my passport."

"I did not ask you what is in the passport, you fool, I asked you where you were born."

"London."

"The date?"

I gave him the date. The questions went on. What nationality was my father? British. My mother? British. My grandfathers? British. My grandmothers? British. Was I married? No. Had I any brothers or sisters? A brother. Was he married? Yes. What was the nationality of his wife? British. Had I ever been in Italy before? No. Where had I learned

Italian? From a friend in London. What was the friend's name? Carmelo. Where was he now? I did not know. Had I known Signor Ferning? No. Had I ever had any other profession but that of engineer? No. Why had I come to Italy? To act as my employer's representative. How long did I hope to stay? Indefinitely. Was I a member of any political party? No. Was I a Socialist? No. Was I a Marxist? No.

By now I had my temper well under control. He sat back and surveyed me sullenly. I waited. Then he stood up. I was interested to see that he wore corsets.

"Permission will be given for you to remain in Italy providing that you report here every week to have your permit stamped. You have brought the regulation photographs? Very well. Report here to-morrow for your permit. You may go."

"Thank you. My passport, please."

He scowled. "Your passport will be retained until to-morrow for official purposes."

"But—"

"There is no argument. You are in Italy now and Italian regulations must be obeyed. And"—he put one hand on his hip in the authentic Mussolini pose and tapped me threateningly on the chest—"I should advise you to be careful about the acquaintances you make."

"I am always careful about my acquaintances."

"Very likely. But there are some persons with whom it is unhealthy to associate."

I stared hard at him. "I can quite believe you," I said deliberately.

His lip curled again. "A little Fascist discipline would do you good, signor Marlow," he said slowly. "Let me advise you once more to be discreet." He turned his back on me and sat down.

I went, seething. On the way to the Via San Giulio I called at the British Consulate. I was interviewed by a very polite young man in a Savile Row suit. He listened to my tale of woe in silence. Then:

"Well, of course, Mr. Marlow, it is very unusual of them to behave like that, and I've never heard of them retaining a British passport like that. But you were probably just unlucky. And they *are* inclined to be a little touchy at the moment. I'll have a word with the Consul about it. But I shouldn't worry. If you don't get your passport back, let us know. By the way, what did you say your business was?"

"My company is supplying machinery to the Government."

"What sort of machinery, Mr. Marlow?"

"For making munitions."

"Oh quite. Well, I expect that that might have something

to do with it. Let me see, Mr. Ferning was your predecessor, wasn't he?"

"Yes."

"Did you know him?"

"No. I have only just left England."

"Ah, just so. Charming fellow, of course. Well, good morning, Mr. Marlow. Let us know if you have any trouble."

I went on my way. That was the third time in twenty-four hours that I had been asked whether or not I had known Ferning. Vagas, the *signor Capitano,* and now the Consulate. It was, I supposed, only to be expected. A man who dies in a street accident in a foreign city is not immediately forgotten by all his associates there.

Bellinetti greeted me cordially and informed me with pride that he had done most of the work for the day.

"The Signore," he added, "need never trouble to attend the office until after luncheon. I, Bellinetti, will see that all goes well." He smacked his lips and flashed a smile in the direction of Serafina, who looked up from the book she was reading to nod graciously.

I scowled at them and strode into my office. Bellinetti followed me.

"There is something wrong, Signore?"

Impatiently, I told him how I had spent the morning.

He pursed his lips. "That is bad. I will speak to my brother-in-law on the subject. He is most sympathetic, and he has a friend who knows an important personage in the *Amministrazione.* There is, however," he went on gaily, "no need for you to worry. The business is all in good order. Everything arranges itself admirably."

It took me exactly four hours to find out just how admirably everything in the Milan office of the Spartacus Machine Tool Company did, in fact, arrange itself. The knowledge was profoundly depressing. Everything had arranged itself into the most disgusting muddle.

Hidden away in drawers and cupboards I found stacks of correspondence.

"Our files," explained Bellinetti proudly.

I went through one pile with him. Roughly one half of it consisted of unanswered requests for information of various kinds, the other of accounting records that should have been sent to Wolverhampton over six months previously.

The latter I flourished in his face. "You might not have known how to deal with the letters," I snapped, "but at least you should have known that these go to England."

He eyed me apprehensively and flashed an uneasy smile.

"Signor Ferning said to keep them here, Signore."

It was a palpable lie; but I said "Oh," and went on to the next cupboard. This was a mistake, for, imagining, evidently, that he had found a formula that would silence my criticisms, he proceeded to invoke the name of my predecessor as every fresh defection came to light. He, Bellinetti, had known that it was wrong but—here a shrug—signor Ferning had said . . . It had not been for him to dispute with signor Ferning. Signor Ferning had had the confidence of those at *Volver' ampton*. He, Bellinetti, had done his best, but his services had not been recognised. I soon gave it up, and went back to my room to sit down behind the mountains of "files" now reposing on my desk. Bellinetti, a Daniel come to judgment, followed me.

For five minutes I talked without stopping. He smiled steadily through it all. By the time I had finished, however, the smile had changed considerably in quality. I saw, to my satisfaction, a new Bellinetti shining through it—a Bellinetti who would gladly have knifed me.

He shrugged, at last, disdainfully. "These things," he said, "are not my responsibility, but that of signor Ferning."

"Signor Ferning has been dead over two months."

"Without assistance I can do nothing. Umberto is a cretin."

I let this pass. I had, during the afternoon, formed my own opinion of Umberto.

"Who," I pursued, "engaged the Signorina?"

I had already ascertained that she had been engaged since Ferning's death, and he knew that I knew.

"I did, Signore. It was essential that I had some assistance. The Signorina has been a great help while I was here alone bearing the responsibilities for your English company."

"The Signorina cannot even type."

"She is my secretary, Signore."

"You have no secretary, Bellinetti. The Signorina must go. You can tell her yourself or I will do so. Now be good enough to ask Umberto to come in. You need not stay any longer to-day. I shall expect to see you at nine o'clock to-morrow morning to go through these files of yours."

"The office does not open until ten o'clock, Signore."

"From now on, it opens at nine."

The smile had deteriorated into a show of teeth. He retired, slamming the door after him. A moment or two later a terrified Umberto appeared.

"You wished to see me, Signore?"

"Yes, Umberto. How much do you earn a week?"

"Eighty lire, Signore."

"Beginning this week you will receive a hundred lire a week."

For a moment he goggled at me. Then, to my horror, he burst into tears. After a bit he began to stammer his thanks. He lived with his grandfather who was bed-ridden. His brother was doing his military service. His mother had died when he was born. His father had been killed by the Squadristi in nineteen-twenty-three. I was, he sobbed, his benefactor.

I got rid of him as soon as I could, and began the assault on Ferning's desk.

The drawers were stuffed with blue-prints, specifications, German machine-tool catalogues and memoranda from Pelcher and Fitch. But there was a certain amount of order in the way in which it had been put away. I guessed that the desk had not been touched since Ferning's death. The tone of the Wolverhampton correspondence was cordial and businesslike. I found also a set of false teeth in a thick cardboard box, two dirty handkerchiefs, a piece of soap, a razor, a slide-rule, an empty Strega bottle and a small loose-leaf notebook. I put these objects aside and began to sort the papers.

I became so immersed in the task that it was eight o'clock when I glanced at my wrist-watch and decided to finish for the day. I had told Bellinetti that he was to be in the office at nine. I should have to see that I was on time myself. Besides, except for some fruit that I had sent Umberto for during the afternoon, I had had nothing to eat since breakfast. It was time that I had dinner.

I rose and got my coat. As I was putting it on it brushed against the desk and knocked the note-book on to the floor. I picked the note-book up. It had fallen open and one of the leaves had come adrift. Almost automatically I patted it back into place and refastened the loose-leaf catch. Then I stopped and looked at it again. The page was covered with minute pencil notes. But it was not the notes that had made me look twice. Roughly printed in pencil at the head of the page was the word "VAGAS."

I carried the book to the light and began to read. This, I remember, is how it began:

VAGAS

Dec. 30

S.A. Braga. Torino. 3 specials. adapt. 25 + 40 m.m. A.A.A. L.64, L.60. Borfors 1,200 plus. 1 stand. 10.5 c.m.N.A.A.150 plus 40 m.t.bp. Spez. rept. 6 m. belt mg.s.a. 1.2 m. 14 mths. 6 x 55 c.m. 30° el. Mntgs. Gen.

The rest of the page was filled with similar hieroglyphics. I examined them carefully. It could, of course, be that the name and the date referred to an appointment and were nothing to do with the rest of the page; but that was unlikely. The whole page had the appearance of having been written at the same time. I looked at the other pages. They were all blank. A man didn't write an appointment down in a book that he didn't use fairly constantly. Well then, supposing Vagas and December the thirtieth *were* part of the rest of the page, who was S.A. Braga of Turin, and what did the rest of it mean? It looked as though Ferning had had some sort of business dealing with Vagas. That possibility didn't quite fit in with the impression I had received from Vagas concerning his relationship with Ferning.

I folded the page and put it in my wallet. After all, it was nothing to do with me. I could enclose the page when I wrote to Vagas to put off our appointment for the following Wednesday. All the same, those notes *were* curious. I found myself wishing that I knew more about Ferning. I had only the vaguest picture of the man in my mind. According to Pelcher he had been nervous and sensitive. According to Vagas he had been a "Platonic realist," with a penchant for ballet girls. The British Consulate had described him as "charming." No doubt it didn't matter what he had been like; but I still felt curious. I wished that I could have seen a photograph of him.

I switched off the lights, locked up and began to walk down the stairs. They were in darkness, but from a half-opened door on the third floor a shaft of light cut across the landing. I crossed it and was about to start down the next flight when the door swung open and a man came out. I half turned. He had his back to the light, and for a moment I did not recognise him. Then he spoke. It was the American.

"Hullo, Mr. Marlow."

"Good evening."

"You're working late."

"There's rather a lot to be done just now. You're none too early."

"It's not so good as it looks. I've been waiting for a long-distance call. What about a drink?"

I had a sudden desire for the company of someone who spoke English.

"I was just going to have some dinner. Will you join me?"

"Glad to. I'll just lock up if you don't mind. Not," he went on as he turned to do so, "that it matters a row of canned beans whether you lock or don't lock here. The *portinaia* has a duplicate key. But it preserves the illusion. The great thing is not to leave anything private or valuable where she can lay her hands on it."

I had been trying to read the name of his firm on the

door, but he had switched the light out. But I knew there would be a name panel on the wall by the stairs. Under cover of lighting a cigarette I looked at it by the light of the match.

"Vittorio Saponi, Agent," said a voice in my ear; "but my name is Zaleshoff, Andreas P. Zaleshoff. It's a Russian name, but that's my parents' fault, not mine. It's no use asking me where old Mister Saponi is, because the guy's dead and I wouldn't know. I bought the business off his son. Shall we go and eat?"

By the dying flame of the match I could see his blue eyes, shrewd and amused, on mine. I grinned back at him. We groped our way downstairs.

At his suggestion we went to a big underground restaurant near the Piazza Oberdan. The ceiling was low and the air was thick with tobacco smoke. The sound of an orchestra playing energetically in one corner was lost in the din of conversation.

"It's noisy," he acknowledged, "but the food's German and pretty good. Besides, I thought you might like to know of the place. It's convenient, and when you're as tired of *pasta* as I am, it's a godsend. You've only been here three days, haven't you?"

"Yes, I got here Monday. By the way—sorry to be inquisitive—what are you agent for?"

"Moroccan perfumes, Czech jewellry and French bicycles."

"Business good?"

"There isn't any." I did not know quite what to say to this but he went on. "No, Mr. Marlow, there isn't so much as a smell of business. I was drilling for oil in Yugo-Slavia before I came here. I'd tapped a lot of gas and got the usual indications but I decided eventually to give it up as a bad job and the Government there took over. Three weeks later they struck it good and hard—gushers. When Fate makes a dirty crack like that, Mr. Marlow, it's apt to jaundice a man's outlook. I came here and bought this outfit off the executors of the late V. Saponi. The books looked pretty good. It wasn't until I'd actually paid over my good dollars that I found that all the goodwill in the agency had died with old Saponi and that young Saponi had side-tracked what pickings were left into his own pants' pocket."

"That's bad."

"Bad enough. Fortunately, I've got other contacts. All the same, I've promised myself a good five minutes with young Saponi one of these days." His jaw jutted forward. He regarded me with an expression of amiable ferocity. "I suppose you wouldn't like to buy a French bicycle, Mr. Marlow? I've got the sample somewhere."

I laughed. "I'm afraid I shan't have much time for cycling. There's a lot to be done on the fourth floor."

He nodded. "I thought there might be. Your people in Wolverhampton were rather long about appointing someone."

"You knew Ferning, didn't you, Mr. Zaleshoff?"

He nodded and began to roll himself a cigarette.

"Yes, I did. Why?"

"Oh, nothing in particular. Except that I've no idea what he looked like."

"I shouldn't think that would worry you."

"It doesn't. I'm just curious."

"Any special reason for the curiosity?" It could not have been said more casually.

"No. Only so many people seem to want to know if I knew Ferning. Even the police seem interested."

"The police! You don't want to take any notice of *them*."

"It's difficult not to take notice. I spent practically the whole morning at the *Amministrazione*." I launched into a somewhat spiteful account of my encounter with the *signor Capitano*. He listened but made no comment. By the time I had finished, the food had arrived.

We ate in comparative silence. I was, quite frankly, more interested in my food than in conversation. This seemed to suit my companion. His thoughts seemed to have strayed. Once I noticed him gazing moodily at the table-cloth, his fork poised in mid-air. His eyes met mine and he grinned. "There's a soup stain on the cloth that looks exactly like South America," he said apologetically. But it was obvious that his mind had not been on the soup stain which was, in any case, shaped more like the Isle of Wight. I put it down to the late Vittorio Saponi.

"I think," I said when I had finished, "that I'll have a brandy with my coffee."

"Have you tried Strega yet, Mr. Marlow?"

"No, but I think I'll postpone that pleasure. I feel like brandy. Will you join me?"

"Thanks." He looked at me for a moment. Then:

"Who else has asked you about Ferning, Mr. Marlow?"

"A man who calls himself General Vagas. Do you know him?"

"The guy that gets himself up like a rocking horse?"

I laughed. "That sounds like him. Apparently he's a Yugo-Slav. He wants me to go to dinner with him and his wife next week. Do you know anything about him?"

"Not very much." His expression had become quite blank. He was scarcely listening to me. Suddenly, he snapped his fingers and his face lit up in triumph. "Got it!" He beamed at me. "You know how it is, Mr. Marlow, when you kind of feel you've lost something somewhere and can't quite think what? Well, that's how I felt. But I've just remembered. In my office, I've got a photograph of Ferning. Would you like to see it?"

I was rather disconcerted by this sudden interest.

"Well, yes. I would. Perhaps I could look down some time to-morrow."

"To-morrow?" He looked at me incredulously. "To-morrow nothing. We'll call back in the office when we leave. I've got a bottle of brandy there. The real stuff. Not like this."

"I shouldn't dream of bothering you." I did not, in any case, feel like toiling back to the Via San Giulio at that time of night.

But he was adamant. "It's no bother at all, Mr. Marlow. Glad to be of assistance. I can't think why I didn't remember before. It's only a snap, mind you, and not particularly good of him. He wanted some photographs for his identity card and I had a Kodak. I'd forgotten all about it until just now." He changed the subject abruptly. "How are you getting on with Bellinetti?"

"Not too badly," I said cautiously. "He probably resents me a little."

"Sure, sure"—he nodded sagely—"only natural for a guy in his position." He summoned the waiter and asked for the bill, which he discomforted me by insisting on paying.

On our way back to the offices, however, he fell silent again. I concluded that he was regretting his earlier enthusiasm and suggested again that to-morrow would do just as well. The response was a stream of reassurance. He would not hear of my waiting. Besides, there was the cognac. He had been trying to remember exactly where he had put the photographs, that was all. We walked on. He was, I decided, a very curious man; not at all my idea of an American. But, then, the Englishman's idea of what an American ought to look like and how an American ought to behave was notoriously wide of the mark. Still, he *was* odd. And there was a quality about him that attracted you. It wasn't so much in *what* he said, but in the manner in which he said it. He had a way of disconcerting you with a gesture, with the way he timed his phrases. Yet you could not quite discover just why you had been disconcerted. You received the impression that you were watching a very competent actor using all the technical tricks in his repertoire in an effort to make something of a badly written part. There was something about him which cried out for analysis and yet defied it. I glanced sideways at him. His chin was tucked inside the thick grey muffler that he wore coiled twice round his neck; and he was staring fiercely at the ground in front of him as though he suspected the presence of a man-trap in the pavement. It was a portrait of a man with something on his mind.

In his office, he switched on the desk lamp.

It was a large room, larger than mine, and very neat and tidy, with a row of steel filing cabinets along one wall and a green steel desk to match. But on the wall behind the desk was a dreadful tinted photograph of the Venus de Medici. He saw me looking at it.

"It's a honey, isn't it, Mr. Marlow? I keep it in memory of Mister Saponi. One day I'm going to give her a moustache and a monocle. Sit down and make yourself at home."

He got out a bottle of cognac, half-filled two wine glasses with it and pushed a box of cigarettes towards me. Then he went to one of the cabinets and began to go through the files in it.

"By the way," he murmured over his shoulder, "have you decided to accept Vagas' invitation?"

The question irritated me. "I really haven't thought about it. Why?"

But at that moment he gave vent to an exclamation of satisfaction. "Ah! here it is." He drew a large card out of the file and brought it over to the light. "There you are. The late Mr. Ferning."

I took the card. Gummed in the top right-hand corner was a hard, flat head-and-shoulders photograph of a middle-aged man. Except for a fringe of hair above his ears, he was quite bald. The face was round and podgy with small anxious eyes and an indeterminate mouth that seemed on the point of framing a protest. It was a weak and ordinary face. I looked at the rest of the card. In the top left-hand corner was written "F326." The lower half was taken up by a strip of typewritten paper pasted on by the corners.

Sidney Arthur Ferning (I read). *Born London* 1891. *Engineer. Representative of Spartacus Machine Tool Co. Ltd. of Wolverhampton, England, in Milan. Killed in street, Milan.* (Here followed the date.) *See V.18.*

I read it through once more, then I looked at the photograph again. One corner of it had come adrift from the card. Without thinking I pressed it back into position. As it did not stick, I lifted it to moisten the gum.

It was done almost subconsciously; to play for time. There was very obviously nothing casual, nothing unpremeditated about this formidable card. My mind went back to the restaurant. So he had forgotten all about the photograph. A few minutes ago he had been "trying to remember" exactly where it was.

Then I had my second shock. As I lifted the corner of the photograph I saw that there was a red rubber stamp mark on it. The stamp consisted of the name and address of a London passport photographer. I put the card down. So much for the "Kodak snap."

I looked across the desk. Zaleshoff was watching my face and on his lips was a faint smile. I had a sudden desire to go. There was something here that I did not understand, that I did not want to understand. I got to my feet.

"Well, thank you, Mr. Zaleshoff. It's good of you to take so much trouble to satisfy my curiosity. But now, if you'll excuse me, I'll be going. I have to be up early in the morning."

"Yes, of course. You have an appointment with the police, you said."

"I have also some work to do."

"Naturally. But don't forget your brandy, Mr. Marlow." I glanced at the glass. I had not touched it. I picked it up.

"Have another cigarette while you're drinking it." He held the box out. I hesitated. I could not very well swallow the brandy at a gulp and leave. To leave it untouched would be rude. I took a cigarette and sat down again. He blew the match out and examined the stalk. "You know," he said pensively, "I wouldn't, if I were you, bother to go to the police to-morrow."

"They have my passport."

He dropped the match. "I'll make a bet with you, Mr. Marlow. I'll bet you a thousand lire to a cake of soap that the police have mislaid your passport."

"Good Heavens, why?"

He shrugged. "It's just a hunch."

"A bad one, I hope. I won't take your bet. It would be sheer robbery. By the way"—I glanced at the card lying on the desk—"do you card-index all your acquaintances?"

He shook his head. "No, not all of them, Mr. Marlow. Only some of them. It's a sort of hobby with me, you see. Some people collect sea shells. I collect photographs."

He leaned forward suddenly, his jaw thrust out pugnaciously. "Mr. Marlow, this evening is, to all intents and purposes, the first time we've met and I've spent most of it so far in telling you a pack of lies. You've probably guessed that already, because you've caught me out in one that I hadn't meant you to catch me out in. I didn't know that that photograph wasn't fixed properly. Well, all right. That's about as bad a way of starting up a life-long friendship as I can think of off-hand. There's a nice atmosphere of skulduggery and mistrust about it. You realise that you don't know who the Hell I am and decide that you don't want to know. You're probably thinking that I must be some sort of crook. Splendid! And now I'm going to ask you to let me give you a piece of advice. I'm going to tell you that it won't cost you a cent, that, on the contrary, you stand to make big money by taking the advice, and you're going to wonder what my game is. And now, the whole thing is sounding to you about as phoney as a glass eye, isn't it?"

"It is," I said firmly; "what is it to be, a vacuum cleaner or a refrigerator? I don't need either."

He frowned. "Do you mind being serious for a moment, Mr. Marlow?"

"I'm sorry. All this disarming candour has been a little too much for me."

"Well now, I'm going to ask you to trust me and take the advice."

"I'm always ready to listen to advice."

"Good. Then my advice to you is to accept General Vagas' invitation. He might have a proposition for you."

I faced him squarely. "Now look here, Mr. Zaleshoff. I don't know what you've got in the back of your mind and I really am not interested. Furthermore, I quite fail to see what on earth an invitation issued to me has to do with you."

"I still ask you to accept it."

"Well, it may interest you to know that I have already decided to refuse it."

"Then change your mind, Mr. Marlow."

I rose. "I feel sure you will excuse me, Mr. Zaleshoff. I've had a tiring day and I'm not very fond of round games, even in the morning. Thank you for your dinner and for your very pleasant brandy. Perhaps you will allow me to return your hospitality some time. At the moment I'm afraid I must go. Good night to you."

He stood up. "Good night, Mr. Marlow. I shall look forward to seeing you again soon and having another chat."

I went to the door.

"Oh, by the way."

I turned. He picked the card up from his desk and flicked it with a finger-nail. "You may have noticed," he said slowly, "that at the foot of this card there is a note. It says: 'See V. 18. Card V. 18 is in one of those filing cabinets. If, after you see General Vagas next time, you would like to inspect that card, I shall be delighted to get it out for you."

"Why should I want to inspect it?"

"The V, Mr. Marlow, stands for Vagas."

"That's very interesting; but as I shan't be seeing General Vagas . . ." I shrugged. "Good night."

"Pleasant dreams, Mr. Marlow."

I went.

My dreams that night were far from pleasant. I remember waking up at about half-past three from a nightmare in which Bellinetti was smothering me with huge stacks of photographs of General Vagas. But when I finally went to sleep again I was thinking of Claire. It was, after all, only a question of a month or two before I would see her again. Dear Claire.

Chapter V

DIPLOMATIC EXCHANGES

I DID not see Zaleshoff again for over a week.

The gods, like most other practical jokers, have a habit of repeating themselves too often. Man has, so to speak, learned to expect the pail of water on his head. He may try to sidestep, but when, as always, he gets wet, he is more concerned about his new hat than the ironies of fate. He has lost the faculty of wonder. The tortured shriek of high tragedy has degenerated into a petulant grunt. But there is still one minor booby-trap in the repertoire which, I suspect, never fails to provoke a belly-laugh on Olympus. I, at any rate, succumb to it with regularity. The kernel of the jest is an illusion; the illusion that the simple emotional sterility, the partial mental paralysis that comes with the light of the morning, is really sanity.

The morning after that first curious evening with Zaleshoff was fine. It was cold, but the sun was shining and lighting up the faded green plush hangings of my room so that they looked more tawdry than they really were. The effect heightened the deception, coloured the illusion that now I was seeing clearly. Over my coffee I cheerfully pooh-poohed my sneaking apprehensions of the night before. The card index, this American's mysterious hintings—what a lot of nonsense! I must have been crazy to think of taking it seriously. It was all, I assured myself, due simply to my ignorance of the Continental business atmosphere. I must not forget to make allowances for that factor. Fitch had warned me of it. "Over there," he had said, "they approach business as if it were a particularly dirty game of politics. They'd sooner play politics really; but if they can't do that they play business in the same spirit." Zaleshoff the American had evidently caught the infection. He was probably working up to a proposal that Vagas should introduce me to a man with an order to place, and that a substantial commission (payable in advance) would secure adequate representation of Spartacus' interests. Well, he wouldn't get the chance. I had too much real work to do to permit me to waste time with such childish nonsense.

I see now that it was a piece of self-deception that was very nearly conscious; but semi-conscious or not, it was thoroughly effective, almost too effective, for I forgot General Vagas and the fact that I had to put off my appointment with him until practically the last minute.

After an acrid morning with Bellinetti and his files, I went to the *Amministrazione* to collect my passport. After half an hour in the waiting-room, I wrung an admission from the attendant policeman that the *signor Capitano* was not in the building, and that he had left no instructions about either my identity card or my passport. If I would return later, all would arrange itself. I returned later and waited for a quarter of an hour. This time the policeman was more helpful. The *signor Capitano* had not returned, but he himself had made inquiries. The passport had been sent to the Foreign Department. It would, doubtless, be available on the following day. If I could call in then . . .

But I did not call in on the following day. I did not call in until the following Tuesday. The reason for this was that on the Thursday night I went to Genoa.

As Pelcher had explained, one of my principal duties was to maintain personal contact with the users of Spartacus machines. Thursday's post had brought a letter from one of these users, a big engineering firm with works near Genoa, and, as the letter raised points of technical importance, I had decided to make it an excuse to visit them. I should, in any case, have gone, as I had found that my Italian, though equal to most ordinary demands upon it, was as yet far too sketchy to permit me to commit my thoughts on technical subjects to paper.

I spent Friday, Saturday and Monday in the customer's works, and arrived back in Milan early on the Tuesday morning.

It had been my first direct contact with a customer, and I had been impressed by the evidence I had had of Mr. Pelch-

er's earlier activities. There had been some trouble over Bellinetti's lack of attention to their interests, but they had been
notified by signor Pelcher of my arrival and all was now
well. On Sunday the works manager had driven me to Porto-
fino in his car, and had permitted me to buy him a very
expensive lunch. There had been talk of an order for six more
S2 machines. I had received veiled but precise instructions
concerning the method of paying the secret commission, and
learned that my German competitors were obtuse and parsimonious when it came to the arrangement of such affairs.
It was understood, however, that Spartacus were a sympathetic company to deal with. Their machines, too, were
of the best. The Government inspectors would be in the
works on the Monday. If I could spare the time to meet
them, it would be to my advantage. I *had* spared the time,
and found the inspectors as tractable as, if rather more discreet than, the works manager.

I was both pleased and disgusted by my week-end's work.
Fitch had warned me what to expect, and had, indeed,
coached me carefully in the order-taking ritual; but the reality
was disconcerting none the less. It was one thing to talk
glibly of bribery and corruption; it was quite another thing
actually to do the bribing and corrupting. Not, I reminded
myself, that my part in the proceedings was anything but
passive acquiescence. These people were already corrupt. It
was merely a question of who paid—the German firm or
Spartacus. *"Chi paga?"* was, after all, a favourite gibe in
Italy. "When in Rome . . ." Perhaps there was more to that
old saw than met the eye.

With such things on my mind it was scarcely surprising
that I should have forgotten that such persons as Zaleshoff
and Vagas existed.

I was soon to be reminded of the fact.

The first reminder was contained in a long postscript to a
letter from Claire that was waiting for me at the Hotel Parigi
on my return. Here it is:

*P.S.—By the way, Nicky my sweet, I think you'll have to do some-
thing about the chambermaid or whoever it is who has access to your
room. You may remember that you asked me to send you the Engineer
each week (matter attended to, by the way), and that you wrote about
it across the back of the envelope. Well, dear, in your little Miss Sher-
lock's opinion, the envelope was steamed open after that. What made
me notice it particularly was a slight kink in the writing (you know how
you run all the words together?), and when I looked at the envelope
closely I could see a thin ridge of gum running round the edge of the
flap and approximately .05 c.m. from it. I think that research grant they
gave me years ago must have had a bad effect on me, because what
must I do but rush out there and then and buy five different kinds of
envelopes with which to experiment. First I sealed the five envelopes,*

then, after a two hours' interval, I steamed them open again. Immediately after opening them I re-sealed them and left them until the morning when I compared the results with your envelope. All revealed the ridge of gum which (note the scientific mind at work) may, I suggest, be produced partly by the shrinkage of the paper flap following the steam treatment, and partly by the surface tension of the gum while it is in a liquid state. I am aware (O Shades of Socrates!) that there is nothing proved here, and that I ought to have kept quiet about it until I had tested at least five hundred sample envelopes, but I can't spare the time to do so and, in any case, prolonged steaming operations take the wave out of my hair. All the same, I thought I'd better report. She's probably jealous, my sweet. I advise prompt posting to avoid the crush. Love. Claire.

I thought carefully. It could not possibly have been the chambermaid. As soon as I had finished writing the letter, I had put it in the pocket of the suit I had been going to wear the following day. I had posted it in the hotel letter-box on my way out in the morning.

Then an unpleasant idea flashed through my mind. I examined the back of the envelope in which Claire's letter to me had arrived. There, unmistakably, was the ridge of gum to which she had referred. There was no longer any doubt in my mind. My correspondence was certainly being read. The question was: by whom?

It might, of course, be one of the hotel employees; but there was an objection to that solution. The hotel letter-box was opened and cleared by the postman. I had seen him do the job. Probably, none of the hotel employees would have access to the contents of the box. In any case, it was located in full view of everyone near the reception counter. Very odd!

I bathed, changed, had some breakfast and went to the office. Bellinetti welcomed me effusively. Everything had arranged itself admirably while the Signore had been away. Umberto smiled shyly. Serafina was not there. I went to my room.

"Who opened the post this morning, Bellinetti?"

"I did, Signore, as you instructed."

"Good. I want to see the envelopes in which the letters came."

"The envelopes, Signore?" He smiled condescendingly. "You mean the letters?"

"No, I mean the envelopes."

His eyebrows nearly touching his scalp, he retrieved the envelopes. I went through them one by one. The ridge of gum was evident in every case. I dropped the envelopes back into the wastepaper basket. He was watching me in mystified silence.

"Can you think of anyone who would have either a reason

for or an opportunity of steaming open and reading our correspondence, Bellinetti?"

He blinked. Then his face became blank. "No, Signore."

"You haven't an idea?"

"No, Signore."

"Did you know that it was happening?"

"No, Signore."

I gave it up. Obviously, the news was no surprise to him. Equally obviously, he did not propose to discuss it. Grimly, I got on with my work.

After lunch, I went to the *Amministrazione*.

This time I was kept waiting for only five minutes. Then I was shown into the *signor Capitano's* office.

He nodded curtly.

"Yes, your identity card is ready." He handed it to me. "I will remind you again that it must be presented here each week for stamping."

"I have to travel about the country a good deal on business. It is possible that I shall not be in Milan every week."

"In such cases you will notify us here in advance."

"Thank you. And my passport, please?"

He frowned. "But that matter has already been explained to you."

For some reason, my heart missed a beat.

"Nothing has been explained to me. I was told last week that it was in the hands of the Foreign Department."

"That is so. Unfortunately," he said blandly, "it has been mislaid. We expect it to be found at any moment. When it is found it will be restored to you immediately. Until then, you have your permit."

"But . . ."

"You do not wish to leave Italy at present, do you?"

"No, but . . ."

"Then your passport is unnecessary."

I swallowed hard.

"But it is a valuable document. It cannot be mislaid."

He shrugged irritably. "These things happen."

"I shall report the matter to the British Consul immediately."

"It has already been reported to your Consul."

This, as I soon found, was correct. I was interviewed at the Consulate by the same exquisite suit.

"Bad luck, of course," agreed its owner amiably, "but we can't do anything much about it, you know. We shall have to give them every chance to find it. Still, you're not wanting to leave the country at the moment, are you?"

"Not at the moment," I said reluctantly.

"Then we'll see what happens. Very serious matter, you know, a lost passport. We'll have to be very careful. Of course, if you did want to leave we could issue you with papers that would get you home. But then, that doesn't clear up the question of the passport. We'll let you know as soon as we hear."

Back in the office, I lit a cigarette and sat down to think things over.

It may have been that, as I had spent the previous night dozing fitfully in a railway carriage, my powers of self-deception had fallen off a little; for now I began, for the first time, to allow myself to take Zaleshoff seriously. Zaleshoff had said that my passport would be mislaid. He had been right. A coincidence perhaps? No, that just would not do. It was too much of a coincidence. People didn't lose passports like that. And my comfortable explanation about commissions and introduction wouldn't do either. It didn't fit. My thoughts went back to the evening I had spent with him. There were a lot of things about that evening that needed explanation. Was it, for instance, pure coincidence that had led Zaleshoff to leaving his office at precisely the same time as I? I began to wonder. Then there was Vagas, with his obscure hintings, and Zaleshoff's curious insistence on my seeing the General again. Ferning came into it somewhere, too. I remembered that in my wallet was the page out of Ferning's loose-leaf note-book. S.A. Braga of Turin was still unaccounted for. Card indexes . . . V.18 . . . "as phoney as a glass eye . . ."

I crushed my cigarette out impatiently. Ferning's business was not my business. General Vagas sent cold shudders down my spine. Zaleshoff irritated me. The best course was to ignore the whole thing. It was absurd for a man of my age to take any notice of such childish nonsense. And then I remembered again about my passport. That was something I could not ignore. And there was this wretched business of the letters. Perhaps Zaleshoff knew something about *that* . . .

I should probably have continued to think in this sort of circle if Umberto had not come into the room at that moment and put some papers on my desk. I looked up.

"The list, Signore."

"Oh yes. Thank you."

I had instructed Umberto to prepare for me a complete up-to-date list of all the Italian firms on the Spartacus books, together with the amount spent by each during the past year. I glanced at it. It was in alphabetical order. The fourth name down caught my eye. The reason was that the initial letter which determined its place in the list belonged to the third word in the title of the concern and for a moment I had thought that Umberto had made a mistake. Then, I looked again. Yes, there it was in black and white—Società Anonima BRAGANZETTA, Torino. I had found S.A. Braga of Turin!

For a minute or two I sat looking at the name. There was no doubt about it. "Braga." was simply Ferning's abbreviation. I looked at the figure entered against the name. S.A. Braganzetta had spent a lot of money with Spartacus. I rang for Umberto.

"Signore?"

"Bring me the records of all our transactions with the Braganzetta company of Turin."

He returned a few minutes later with a thick wad of papers. I went through them carefully. Soon I had learned all I wanted to know. I retained a series of specifications and returned the rest to Umberto. Then I took Ferning's page of notes from my wallet and went through it item by item.

The first two lines were easy.

In December, Spartacus had delivered to the Braganzetta works three special high-production shell machining units. That accounted for the "3 specials." What followed immediately after that was just as obvious. The special feature about these machines had been, I saw from the specifications, the fact that they were adapted for producing a very much smaller class of shell than that for which the standard S2 range allowed. The shells in question were those for the twenty-five and forty millimetre automatic anti-aircraft guns, types L/64 and L/60, made by the Swedish firm of Borfors. "1 stand. 10.5 c.m.N.A.A." was a reference to a fourth and standard machine supplied for machining ten-point-five centimetre naval anti-aircraft gun shells. The "1,200 plus" and "150 plus" were references to the output potentialities of the machines in question.

Beyond that point, however, I could make nothing of it. What did "Spez." and "6 m. belt" and the rest of the page mean? I could trace no connection between it and any Spartacus dealings with Braganzetta. I puzzled over it for a bit and then put the paper back in my pocket. This much was clear. Ferning's dealings with Vagas had had something to do with Spartacus. Therefore—I forced myself to face the conclusion with some reluctance—I, as the present representative of Spartacus in Milan, had more than my curiosity to satisfy. It was (I boggled at the word) my *duty* to keep my appointment with Vagas for the following evening—if only to hear his proposition.

The next moment I cursed myself for a fool. Vagas had said nothing about having any proposition to put to me. That was Zaleshoff's idea. Blast Zaleshoff! I was getting the man on the brain. And then I thought again. One of Zaleshoff's ideas had been right. This one might be. It would be wiser to see Vagas. Yes, that was the word—"wiser." It could do no harm, anyway, and an evening at the ballet would do me good. There was this to be considered too: if I did not see him I should probably worry over the affair and wish that I had done so. Better get it over.

Having made this decision, I felt better. For the rest of the day I put the whole thing out of my mind and got on with the work in hand. My trip to Genoa had cost me time that I could ill afford at the moment, for, quite apart from the current work which had accumulated in my absence, there was the pressing business of a complete office reorganisation. As far as Bellinetti was concerned, I had come to a definite conclusion. His activities during my absence had confirmed me in my earlier opinion that he was thoroughly incompetent to organise the work of the office. His technical knowledge was non-existent. Ferning, I decided, must have been mad to engage him. Before I left the office that night and when the others had gone, I sat down at Umberto's typewriter and composed a confidential memorandum to Pelcher. I concluded by asking for permission to give Bellinetti notice. I added that I proposed to promote Umberto and engage a good typist, thus saving money and securing a more efficient organisation. This done, I went to the restaurant near the Piazza Oberdan, had some dinner and decided to walk back to the hotel and go straight to bed.

It was a cold night, but as it was fine, and as I needed the exercise, I took the slightly longer route through the Public Gardens.

A faint ground mist was rising and the electric lights glowed yellowly among the trees. Couples sat huddled on the benches or stood in the shadows or walked sedately arm-in-arm along the stone paths. But towards the centre of the gardens, where the lakes made the mist thick and dank, there were fewer persons about. I turned into a tree-shadowed path that ran parallel to one of the main avenues. It was then that I noticed the man behind me.

I had been thinking that, so far, I had been able to do nothing about moving from the Parigi, that every day I stayed there was a waste of money, and that, at the earliest possible moment, I must make a real effort to find a *pensione*. Something must be done, too, about my passport. Was it, I wondered vaguely, any use asking Fitch or Pelcher to try to press at the Foreign Office in London for action. The next moment, I tripped over one of my shoe laces.

I bent down near the railings to retie the lace. As I did so I saw out of the corner of my eye a slight movement near the railings about twenty yards back.

If I had not moved close to the railings with the idea of leaning against them while I tied the shoe, I should not have seen him. It was very dark beneath the trees. But the railings were in a direct line with a lantern over a gateway about a hundred yards along and, from where I stood, I could see, in faint silhouette, his head and shoulders.

I took no notice at first and finished tying up my lace. Then I glanced back again. The man had not moved. Mentally I shrugged. I walked on. A second or two later I heard a slight *click* behind me. I recognised the sound. A few yards back I had trodden on a loose drain cover. The man behind me had done the same thing. And then I stopped again. I don't quite know why I did so. It may have been the half-formed suspicion in my mind that the man behind me might be some sort of footpad. There had been something odd about the way he had remained motionless while I had retied my shoe. I went to the railings again and pretended to adjust the knot. I could no longer see him, but there was not a sound of footsteps, only the distant hum of traffic along the Corso Venezia. He must, I knew, still be there. I walked on quickly and cut across by the shortest possible route out of the gardens.

There was light now and I could see him, a short, stocky, overcoated figure with a high-crowned soft hat. He had dropped back a little, and was sauntering along with his hands in his pockets and his collar turned up. There was, I thought, something familiar about that hat. But I did not look back again. There was no doubt about it. I was being followed. Obviously, the motive could not be robbery. The opportunity for that had passed. The man might be a pimp who had marked me down as foreign, and therefore a sound business prospect; but it was unlikely. Pimps did not have the sort of staying power this man seemed to possess. A pimp would have tackled me before.

I turned off the main road and threaded my way quickly through a series of back streets to the Via Alessandro Manzoni. Then I looked back again. He was still there, a shadowy figure keeping close to the shadow of the wall.

I decided on action. I walked on rapidly until I came to a fairly quiet side street. On the corner I hesitated as though I were uncertain as to my whereabouts, then turned down the side street. A few yards along it I stopped and moved into the darkened entrance to a shop. A second or two later I heard the footsteps of the man behind me approaching. He was almost level with the shop when I stepped out and stood in the middle of the pavement. Facing me and looking as though he would have given anything to be able to turn tail and run, was Bellinetti.

He made a gallant effort to carry off the situation.

"I thought I recognised you, Signore, but I could not be sure. I was alone. I thought that we might drink a cognac together."

"With pleasure." We began to walk back to the main road. "Do you often walk in the Gardens at night, Bellinetti?"

"On fine evenings, yes. You walk very fast, Signore."

There was a note almost of insolence in his voice. He had clearly recovered his composure. I took up the challenge.

"Then, Bellinetti, I advise you not to try to keep up with me. Who knows what may happen to a man in your state of health."

"My state of health, Signore?"

"You might be seriously injured at any moment," I said blandly.

He frowned. "I am always very careful, Signore."

"I am glad to hear it." We were passing a *caffè*. "Shall we have our drink here?"

Ten minutes later I resumed my walk back to the hotel. It would, I decided, be a distinct relief to be rid of signor Bellinetti. It was bad enough to have an inefficient assistant. An inefficient assistant who supplemented his office work by spying upon one's movements outside the office was intolerable.

There were two letters waiting for me when I got back to the hotel.

One was from my bank in London and concerned facilities for my drawing on their Milan agents. It was unimportant except for one thing. It was from England, and it had not been steamed open. Claire's postscript had evidently been taken to heart by the unknown censor.

The other letter had been posted in Milan that afternoon. The envelope contained a small slip of paper with a single sentence typed on it:

ETHICALLY SPEAKING, YOU OWE ME A CAKE OF SOAP!

—that was all. There was no signature.

Chapter VI

ENTRECHAT

AT HALF-PAST eight the following evening, I presented myself at the Opera House.

Madame Vagas' greeting was, I thought, a trifle cold.

She was a thin, imposing woman with greying black hair, small haggard eyes and an air of fighting off an almost overpowering lassitude. There was a hint of strain at the corners of her mouth, and the movements of her hands were sudden and awkward, as though she were consciously directing their activities.

It was in the ante-room of his box that the General introduced me to her. "My wife, Mr. Marlow," he said. I had bowed and now we stood looking at one another while a waiter spread caviar and opened a bottle of Asti Spumante.

She examined me for a moment or two. Then: "Are you sympathetic to the ballet, signor Marlow?"

She spoke a thick, guttural Italian. The words seemed to be forced from her lips. I was irresistibly reminded of the involuntary grunt of a person hit in the solar plexus.

The General replied for me.

"Signor Marlow is a devotee, Elsa, my dear. Otherwise I should not have asked him to join us here." His tone was smooth enough, but I thought he smiled at her a little malignantly. In the subdued yellow light of the ante-room, his make-up was less obtrusive than when I had first seen him; but the points of his dress collar, where they touched the neck, were already smeared with grease and sun-tan powder. He transferred the smile to me. "How are you finding Milan, signor Marlow?"

"I can't say that I've seen anything of it, General. I've been away in Genoa for the last few days. I only returned yesterday."

"So? A glass of champagne?"

"Thank you."

"You must have found Genoa very dull." He turned to his wife. "Elsa, my dear, you remember that we found Genoa unspeakable?"

She took her glass of Asti. "That is the place with the

large cemetery, isn't it, signor Marlow?" Her eyes surveyed me. I had a feeling that my tie must be crooked. It was with difficulty that I prevented myself from fingering it.

"I was told so. The Genoese seem very proud of their cemetery."

Vagas laughed politely. "I don't suppose signor Marlow had much time for cemeteries. Let me see," he added, "poor Ferning used to mention the Grigori-Sforza works at Genoa. I suppose, by any chance, you . . . ?"

"Yes, it was the Grigori-Sforza works that I visited."

He turned suddenly and spoke to Madame Vagas in a language that sounded like German. "I must apologise," he went on to me; "I was just explaining to my wife that you are Mr. Ferning's successor." He put his glass down. "I think the overture is nearly finished. Shall we go in?"

The first ballet was Lac des Cygnes. From where I sat Vagas' head was sharply outlined against the glare of the stage. Almost against my will my eyes kept wandering from the tremulous flutterings of the *corps de ballet* to watch his face. With the rise of the curtain his expression had changed. His lips had parted slightly, and he was breathing slowly and deeply. Every now and again he would swallow and clear his throat. It was like watching a man asleep. There was about him the same quality of unawareness, of preoccupation with dreams. Beyond him, in the shadows, I could see Madame Vagas, her face a smudge of grey against the curtains of the box, her body motionless. I looked down into the house upon the rows of white, still faces. It was as if they belonged to the dead, and only the figures on the stage were alive. A green light flickered in the wings and the Prince staggered back miming dread and horror, his body taut, his ridiculous crossbow jerking with the staccato movements of his arms. I saw the General raise a handkerchief and dab his lips. Madame Vagas yawned. The faces below did not move. The ballet approached its climax. At last the curtain fell. There was a roar of applause. The curtain rose, fell, rose again. More bows. Bouquets were carried on to the stage. The Prince kissed his hands to the Swan. The conductor took a bow. The curtain fell. The applause died away into a hum of conversation as the house lights went up.

The General sighed and put his monocle back in his eye.

"There is only one Fokine," he said. "Did it please you, Mr. Marlow?"

"Very much."

"The best is yet to come. Shall we smoke? Are you coming, Elsa, my dear?"

She shook her head slowly. "I think that the Contessa Perugia is on her way here."

He frowned. "Please make my excuses to the lady. I think we might walk round to the cigar stall, Mr. Marlow."

We made our way to the top of the main staircase. The place was packed. I could hear German, French and Spanish being spoken in my immediate vicinity. I could see a Hindu, a Chinese, two Japanese and a grey-faced man wearing a tarboosh.

"You see, Mr. Marlow," murmured the General in my ear, "at La Scala, ballet recognises no frontiers." He inclined his head gracefully but repressively to a man with a pointed white beard who seemed about to accost us, and led the way to the cigar stall.

"That man," he explained, "is a member of a drug syndicate. Very charming, but his confidences are apt to be embarrassing. A match, Mr. Marlow?"

But I was no longer paying any attention to him. Weaving their way towards us through the crowd were a man and a woman. I gaped at them. The woman was young, almost a girl, and she was beautiful. It was a curious, nearly masculine beauty. The cheek-bones were high and drew the flesh smoothly away from the red lips in a way which gave her an oddly impassive expression. Her hair gleamed a very dark brown. Her hands were exquisite. Yet it was not so much she who had attracted my attention as the fact that beside her, his hand on her elbow and looking in his evening clothes more like a prize-fighter than ever, was Zaleshoff.

He saw me at the same moment that I saw him. Our eyes met. I prepared for a greeting. But, without a flicker of recognition in his eyes, he looked straight through me. Another second and he was past. I recovered myself quickly.

"I beg your pardon, General."

He smiled and struck another match.

"Don't apologise, Mr. Marlow. She is, I agree, quite lovely here."

"Here?"

"A common Slav type, Mr. Marlow. In Belgrade you could take your choice. The man with her is her brother. Haven't you seen them before?"

"No."

He attended to his cigar. "The man is called Zaleshoff, Andreas Prokovitch Zaleshoff. Her name is Tamara Prokovna. Russian, of course; but they were both, I believe, brought up in the United States. I'm afraid," he added gravely, "that I cannot recommend you to pursue your interest in the lady. The man is an agent of the Soviet Government, and it is highly probable that his sister is also."

I managed a light laugh.

"That sounds very sensational, General. But I assure you that I hadn't the least intention of pursuing my interest. I have a fiancée in England." The words sounded to me appallingly pompous and unreal, but he nodded as if satisfied.

"A foreigner in Italy," he said, "does well to be discreet. Excuse me."

To my relief, he turned aside to speak to some people who were passing. I had time to collect myself. Either Vagas was making a clumsy effort to impress me or I was moving in rather deeper waters than I had thought. What was it Zaleshoff had said? "Fortunately, I've got other contacts." But it was ridiculous. In any case, I was wishing very earnestly that I had not come. I passed in quick review the possible excuses I might make for leaving at the next interval. I might plead illness, or a forgotten business engagement. I might . . .

Vagas touched me on the arm.

"I want you to meet the signora Bernabò, Mr. Marlow." He turned to the fat, shrill-voiced woman by his side. *"Le voglio presentare il signor Marlow, Signora."*

"Fortunatissimo, Signora."

"Fortunatissimo, Signore."

"E Commendatore Bernabò." He indicated a moustachioed gentleman wearing the insignia of the *Ordine della Corona d'Italia.*

"Fortunatissimo, Commendatore."

There was a great deal of hand shaking. The ballet was discussed. Signora Bernabò breathed heavily in the background.

"I only come here," she announced after a while, "to see the gowns."

The Commendatore laughed heartily and twirled his moustaches. To my surprise, Vagas laughed too. Later, however, as we were returning to the box, I was given an explanation for this.

"That woman," he said viciously, "is an imbecile, a cretin. Bernabò himself, however, is in the purchasing section of the Ordnance Department, and an important man. I wouldn't have bored you with them, but I thought you might find him useful. I mentioned your business to him. You need have no qualms about pursuing the acquaintance. He will not rebuff you. It might be worth your while to cultivate him. A little dinner would be sufficient to begin with. The rest will follow naturally."

I did not need to ask what "the rest" consisted of. My experience at Genoa had taught me something.

"It's very good of you, General."

"Not at all." He paused for a split second and glanced at me. "There are probably all sorts of ways in which I can help you, Mr. Marlow."

I thanked him again. We had reached the box.

"Milan," he said as we went in, "is a city in which it is wise to have good friends. By the way, I suggest that we leave after the next ballet. The last on the programme tonight is a local product, and will, I fear, be quite dreadful."

"Then I should prefer to leave."

"I anticipated that you might. I have ordered supper for ten o'clock."

It was actually after ten o'clock when eventually we left La Scala for the Corso di Porta Nuova.

It was a small house; but the interior was fantastically grandiose. It was decorated in a sort of baroque-Gothic manner with huge swagged hangings of dark red velvet, heavy Cinquecento furniture and painted walls. The lighting was by candelabra. Except for a faint smell of incense in the air, the effect was fantastically like that of a piece of ballet décor. A pale, dainty-footed young manservant in blood-red satin knee-breeches helped the illusion considerably.

He tripped forward, took our coats and was gliding away into the shadow of the stairs when Madame Vagas called after him.

"Ricciardo."

He stopped with evident reluctance. "Signora?"

"You have been burning incense again."

He pouted. "Only a little, Signora."

Her voice suddenly became shrill. "You are not to burn it, you understand? You are not to burn it."

Ricciardo's lip trembled. He was, it was clear, about to burst into tears.

"My dear Elsa," murmured the General repressively, "we have a guest." He raised his voice. "Ricciardo, come here."

The youth advanced a few steps. *"Si, Eccellenza."*

"Go and put some colour on your cheeks and then serve supper. And remember that there must be no flowers on the table."

"Si, Eccellenza." He flashed a smile at us, bowed low and retreated.

The General turned to me. "I insist on the servants looking decorative." He fluttered a hand towards the walls. "Do you like it, Mr. Marlow? The Loves of Mejnôun and Leilah. I had it copied from some tapestries."

"Yes, signor Marlow," echoed Madame Vagas with a thin, malicious smile; "do you like it?"

"It is charming."

"Charming!" She repeated the word with polite derision. "You may be right."

There was no doubt that I had said the wrong thing. I was feeling distinctly embarrassed.

"My wife," said Vagas, "detests the place."

"My husband, signor Marlow, has a weakness for the macabre."

It was said most amiably. Both of them were smiling at me; but the atmosphere was suddenly deadly with hatred. More than ever I wished that I had not come. There was, I knew, something inexpressibly ugly about the two Vagas. They were both grotesque, as grotesque as their house and as their manservant.

Vagas took my arm.

"Come, my friend; supper is waiting."

It was served in an alcove leading off the main room. The glass was exquisite, the china was beautiful, the dishes were perfectly presented. The General and I drank Tokay. Madame Vagas sipped a glass of Evian water. To my relief, for I had nothing to say, the General monopolised the conversation with a monologue on the subject of the ballet.

"I feel sure," said Madame Vagas after a while, "that signor Marlow is not so interested in the ballet."

The General raised his eyebrows. "My dear Elsa, I was forgetting. I am so sorry, Mr. Marlow."

I mumbled my protest.

"You must forgive me, Mr. Marlow," he went on; "the ballet interests me enormously. It is, I believe, the final expression of a disintegrating society. The idea of the dance, you know, and the preparation for death have been inseparable since the human animal first crept through the primæval forest. Ballet is merely a new rationalisation of society's instinctive movement towards self-destruction. A dance of death for the Gadarene swine. It has always been so. Catherine de' Medici's musician, Baltazarini, invented the ballet as we know it. It has remained the prophet of destruction. In the years before nineteen-fourteen it drew larger audiences than ever before. In the early nineteen-twenties, when Diaghilev was doing his best work, it became a more esoteric pleasure. Now it is popular again. If I never read a newspaper, Mr. Marlow, one evening at the ballet would tell me that once again society is preparing for death."

Madame Vagas rose. "I think that, if signor Marlow will excuse me, I shall go to bed."

His lips twisted. "You know, my dear Elsa, that you never sleep."

"I am afraid," I said quickly, "that I have stayed too long."

"Not at all, Signore. It is very early. My husband will tell you that I invariably retire early."

"Good night and thank you, Madame."

"It has been a pleasure to meet you, Signore. Good night." She held out her hand.

Uncertain whether I was supposed to shake or kiss it, I compromised by touching it and bowing.

The next moment I felt a small piece of paper being pressed firmly into the palm of my hand. My fingers closed on it. She withdrew her hand and went without looking at me again.

The General sighed.

"I must apologise, Mr. Marlow. My wife is a little unwell at the moment. A nervous complaint. Any talk of death depresses her."

I transferred the piece of paper to my waistcoat pocket.

"I am sorry to hear that."

Ricciardo hovered in the background.

"You may leave the coffee and brandy in the next room, Ricciardo. Then go to bed."

"*Si, Eccellenza.*"

We moved into the adjoining room. A wood fire burning in the grate sent long shadows leaping over the dark hangings. One of the candles was guttering in its wax. I wanted badly to leave. I was tired. The General and his house were getting on my nerves. I was acutely conscious of the piece of paper in my pocket. It was possible that the General had seen me take it. In that case. . . .

"Brandy, Mr. Marlow?"

"Thank you."

It was obviously a note of some sort. What on earth. . . .

"A cigarette, Mr. Marlow?"

"Thank you."

"You'll find that chair comfortable."

"Thank you."

He sat down facing me so that his face was in the shadow while mine was lit by the fire. It was an old trick, but it did not help me to feel any more at my ease.

He stretched himself luxuriously. "I don't think, Mr. Marlow, that the chairs at the Hotel Parigi are quite as comfortable as this, are they?"

"No, not quite."

"And yet you contemplate moving to even less comfortable surroundings?"

"I don't care for living in hotels."

"No, of course not. Mr. Ferning had the same taste in the matter of living. But I seem to remember your saying that an apartment such as his would be too expensive."

"I shall find something less expensive."

"And less comfortable, I am afraid." His cigarette glowed. He threw back his head and blew the smoke towards the ceiling. His head dropped again. Suddenly he leaned forward.

"May I be frank, Mr. Marlow?"

Now it was coming! I was surprised to find that my heart had begun to thump against my ribs. It was stupid of me, craven if you like, but I was afraid. I had to steady my voice, to instil into it a tone of faint surprise.

"By all means, General."

"My reasons for calling upon you the other evening were not altogether social."

I emitted a non-committal "I see."

"I should like, Mr. Marlow," he went on, "to discuss some business with you."

"I am always ready to discuss business on behalf of my company, General."

"Yes, quite so." He paused. "But this is a rather more personal matter, you understand. I am no business man"—his hand fluttered contemptuously—"but I have my interests. You mentioned the matter of an apartment. Mr. Ferning, I remember, was in much the same position as yourself. It was a simple question of money. Nothing more. I was able to introduce him to some private business that provided him with an answer. I can do the same for you, Mr. Marlow."

I muttered something about its being very good of him.

"Not at all, my friend. It is a question of mutual advantage"—he seemed to like the phrase for he repeated it—"a question of mutual advantage. More, this business is in no way incompatible with the interests of your English employers. That fact is certain. Mr. Ferning was the soul of probity in such matters. He was a man with a very strict sense of honour and a very high conception of his patriotic duty."

I could not quite see where this was leading but I made no comment.

He cleared his throat. "That, however, is by the way. The simple fact is, Mr. Marlow, that I happen to be in touch with certain persons who are prepared to pay for technical assistance such as you are in a position to give them."

"Technical assistance?"

"To be more precise: technical information of a comparatively specialised nature. I should add"—he hesitated impressively—"that the opportunity I am giving you, Mr. Marlow, is one both of enriching yourself and of serving your country."

"I'm afraid that I don't understand."

"Let me explain." His voice had become soft and persuasive. "You, Mr. Marlow, are selling a special sort of machine to Italian engineering firms. You are doing so under the aegis and with the full approval of the Italian Government. These machines are designed for one single purpose, the making of shells. Very well. That is business. Good. But has it occurred to you, my friend, that these beautiful machines you are supplying, these very efficient machines, are being used to make shells which may one day burst among the bodies of your own countrymen? Have you considered the matter in that light?"

I stirred. "I have considered the point. But it is no business of mine. I am concerned with selling machine tools. I am merely the agent. I did not create the situation. The responsibility for it is not mine. There is a job to be done. If I do not do it, then someone else will."

"Quite so. The responsibility for the situation is not yours. As far as these business transactions are concerned, you are a purely impersonal agent whose task it is to make profits for the firm of Spartacus."

"I am glad you see the point."

"I do more than see the point, Mr. Marlow," he said enthusiastically. "I insist upon it. It is the very impersonality of your job that enables me to make this proposal to you. It is that very fact that places it apart from the interests of Messrs. Spartacus."

My attack of nerves had passed. I was feeling slightly irritable.

"Perhaps, General, if I knew the nature of your proposal I could judge for myself."

"I wish you to do so," he said promptly. "I wish you to do so. I wish you to judge the matter from a purely impersonal standpoint, without emotion, calmly." He drew a deep breath. "Let me put the situation to you hypothetically. Let us suppose for the moment that England was at war with Germany. England's ally would be France. Now let us suppose that you, an Englishman, were in possession of certain information about Germany which would be of very considerable value to your country's ally. What would you do? Would you decide that, as the information was of no immediate value to England, you would keep it to yourself? Or would you give the information to France who might use it against your common enemy? I think you would almost certainly give that information to France. Don't you agree?"

By now I was thoroughly on my guard. "Under those purely hypothetical circumstances," I said carefully, "I probably should."

"Then," he said gravely, "we are in perfect sympathy. That is what I should do. However," he went on blandly, "that is only a hypothetical case. Naturally, you are more interested in facts than fancies."

"Naturally."

He leaned forward so that his face came into the light. "Then let us get to facts." His voice had lost its effeminacy. It had become hard, almost peremptory. For the first time I was reminded that the word "General" was not merely a mode of address.

"Mr. Marlow, you are engaged in selling shell-production machinery to Italy. I, as I have already told you, am a Yugo-Slav. I am empowered to say that my Government would be interested in receiving from you details of all your transactions with Italian firms, and would be prepared to recognise your personal efforts in the matter with a retaining fee of at least two thousand lire a month. The details you would be asked to furnish would be of the simplest. You would, as I have explained, be expected to do nothing calculated to prejudice the interests of your employers. All we should require would be the details of the machines supplied; their nature, their production capabilities and their destination. Nothing more."

"And you are prepared," I said steadily, "to pay two thousand lire a month for just that? It seems rather a lot of money for so small a service, General Vagas."

He made an impatient gesture. "What might seem unimportant to you, Mr. Marlow, might be of great value to a military intelligence department. That is because you know nothing of such matters. It is of vital importance to the military and naval authorities of every power to know precisely the potential aggressive and defensive capabilities of every other power. That is a commonplace. It is a recognised need. Every country appoints military and naval attachés to its embassies and legations abroad. The collection of information is their official function. But consider this, Mr. Marlow. Where do these attachés obtain their information? Where else but from the very persons whose business it is to conceal it? The obtaining of accurate military intelligence concerning the resources of a possible enemy is a routine precaution essential to national security. Are we to accept what that possible enemy chooses to tell our attachés officially? Obviously that is absurd. We must make other arrangements. We must buy the information where we can. That is all. You can depend upon it, Mr. Marlow, that we only buy what we need."

I said nothing. He went on.

"Again, should there still be any doubt in your mind as to the propriety of your supplying a third party with this very harmless information, let me draw your attention to this fact. During the past nine months Messrs. Spartacus have enjoyed steadily increasing prosperity in this country. They have received more orders from Italy than ever before. Yet, until Mr. Ferning's unfortunate accident, we were in regular receipt of the information I am asking you for now. Look at it another way. If I cared to employ experienced agents for the purpose, I could secure this information quite independently. We could secure it, but it would simply be less convenient to do so by those means and more expensive. You see the idea? You would be paid, in effect, not for supplying us with a series of comparatively commonplace facts, but for saving us the trouble and expense of obtaining them elsewhere. You see, Mr. Marlow? Tell me frankly what you think."

I was silent. A log settled down in the grate. I could hear a clock ticking. So that was it. That was the proposition that Zaleshoff had wanted me to hear, the proposition that he thought might interest me.

"Well, Mr. Marlow?"

"This is a very unusual proposition, General," I said stupidly.

"Not so unusual as you might think, Mr. Marlow," he said calmly. "But let me assure you that there is nothing in it to which even the most sensitive conscience could object. It would be a simple matter of business, a confidential routine arrangement between two men of honour."

I stood up. "Yes, I quite see that. I take it, then, that you would have no objection to my referring the proposal to Mr. Pelcher, my managing director, for sanction to discuss the matter further with you?"

He fingered his lower lip. "I could scarcely counsel that course, Mr. Marlow. While any private arrangement we made together would be no concern of your company, to put the matter on an official footing would certainly embarrass your director. It would involve for him a question of honour. Rightly or wrongly, he would feel that he had an obligation of discretion to fulfil as far as his clients were concerned."

"And you don't think that I, as a representative of the Spartacus company, have a similar obligation?"

"As you pointed out yourself, Mr. Marlow, your position

is, in a sense, impersonal. You accept no responsibility for the nature of your company's activities. You do not, rightly, permit instincts of loyalty to your country to interfere with business. Why should you allow a vague sense of loyalty to your company to confuse your mind?"

"My company purchases my loyalty by paying me to represent it."

"I see. And your country does not pay you." There was no mistaking the sneer in his voice. I felt myself losing my temper.

"I'm afraid that I cannot accept your interpretation of the circumstances. I have only your word for it that any question of loyalty to my country does actually arise."

"Do you doubt my word, Mr. Marlow?"

"No, but I think you may be a trifle prejudiced."

"Your predecessor, Mr. Ferning, did not think so."

"Possibly not." I glanced at my watch. "I think, General, that I ought to be going. It is past midnight and I have to be up early. Thank you for a very pleasant evening."

He got to his feet.

"Another brandy before you go?"

"Thank you, no."

"As you please. With regard to this matter of business, Mr. Marlow." He rested his hand on my shoulder. "Don't decide too hastily. Think it over. Naturally, I don't want you to do anything that causes you the least uneasiness. But I think you will see that I am right."

The candlelight was reflected for an instant in his monocle. His hand patted my shoulder paternally. I wanted to shake it off.

"Good night, General."

"Good night, Mr. Marlow. You can always reach me by telephone here. You have my number. I shall look forward to a call from you—whatever you finally decide."

"I think I can safely tell you now that . . ."

He held up his hand. "Not now, please, Mr. Marlow. Think it over first. Wait a few days. Er—your coat will be in the hall."

It was with profound relief that I heard the door close behind me. After the hot, incense-laden atmosphere of the General's fantastic house, the cold, damp night-air was invigorating. And I had plenty to think about as I walked back to the hotel.

Several things were now explained. Ferning's apartment, for instance. Two thousand lire a month! Roughly two hundred and fifty pounds a year. It wasn't so bad for doing next to nothing. You could probably furnish a house very comfortably with two hundred and fifty pounds. And I could save a little on my ordinary salary as well. With the few pounds capital I had left after my two salary-less months, I could finance myself in England for long enough to find a good job. But, of course, it was all quite out of the question. Ferning must have been a bit of a fool to let himself become involved in that kind of game. Vagas might talk glibly about necessary intelligence, routine precautions and private business arrangements; but that was merely a polite way of putting it. The word was "espionage." And espionage was a crime. If you were caught at it you were imprisoned.

All the same, there was one thing that wasn't explained. Why had Zaleshoff been so insistent on my seeing Vagas? According to Vagas, Zaleshoff was a Soviet agent. Vagas, himself a Yugo-Slav agent, was probably in a position to know. Spying was, no doubt, like engineering. You got to know other people in the same line of business. All the same, the whole thing was rather disturbing and not very pleasant. Spies were things you sometimes read about in newspapers. The court was cleared and evidence was taken *in camera.* There was an absurd air of melodrama about the proceedings. Learned counsel adjusted their wigs and discoursed weightily on the subjects of secret documents, nameless "foreign powers," mysterious meetings and sinister third parties who had "since left the country." It all seemed unreal, part of another world, it did not touch your own everyday life at any point. Yet this world of spies and counter-spies did exist. Spies had to live somewhere. They had their work to do like anyone else. The fact that I had encountered two of them in an Italian industrial city shouldn't be particularly surprising. It certainly was not particularly melodramatic. There were no mysterious meetings, no sinister third parties, the foreign powers were not nameless, and you could scarcely call Ferning's notes a secret document. It was—I was surprised to find myself echoing Vagas' words—simply a business matter. But what had Zaleshoff to do with it? It might, I decided, be amusing to find out. It could do no harm and my curiosity was aroused. It wasn't every day that you met a spy. I ought to make the most of the opportunity. Zaleshoff obviously knew what Vagas was up to and his behaviour in the Opera House showed just as obviously that he did not wish Vagas to know that he had met me. I was, too, curious about Zaleshoff's card index system. It would be interesting to know a little more about General Vagas. Claire would be intrigued, too. I could write and tell her about it. Besides, I did, so to speak, owe Zaleshoff a cake of soap over that passport business. That wasn't quite so amusing. Well, there was probably a very simple explanation of Zaleshoff's little "prophecy"—mentally I put the words in inverted commas.

By the time I arrived at the hotel, I was, I am afraid, feeling quite jaunty about the whole affair. I was cultivating a slight man-of-the-world attitude. It was, all things considered, just as well that I did not realise just what sort of an idiot I was being and just how sinister and melodramatic reality was very soon going to prove. If I had realised those things, I should not have slept nearly as soundly as I did sleep.

It was not until I had undressed for bed and was hanging my clothes in the wardrobe that I remembered Madame Vagas' piece of paper. I retrieved it from my waistcoat pocket and unfolded it.

Scrawled across it were six words:

"Ha fatto morire il signor Ferning."

I sat down on the bed and stared at it blankly. "He killed Mr. Ferning." Who did? Presumably Vagas. Vagas killed Ferning. But that was absurd. Ferning had been run over. This was obviously a piece of spiteful nonsense. You did not have to be particularly observant to notice that there was no love lost between Vagas and his wife. And you could scarcely wonder at it. Not by any stretch of the imagination could you describe either as particularly lovable. But this! The woman was clearly unbalanced.

I got into bed. Claire, I reflected, would have been amusing on the subject of Ricciardo.

Chapter VII

DINNER WITH ZALESHOFF

ON THE Thursday morning, I telephoned down to Zaleshoff.

A woman's voice answered me in Italian.

"Pronto."

"Il signor Zaleshoff?"

"Uno momento."

A second or two later Zaleshoff came on the line.

"Qui Vittorio Saponi."

"Is it, indeed! This is Marlow."

There was a yelp of delight.

"Hal-*lo*, Mr. Marlow! How are you keeping?"

"All right, thanks."

"Did you have a good time last night?"

"Quite. And you?"

"Fine. I hope you didn't mind my high-hatting you like that."

"Not a bit. I was wondering whether you were too busy to have dinner with me this evening."

"Delighted. But look. Why not come along to our apartment and have dinner there? That dame I was with last night's my sister. She's crazy to meet you." There were sounds of altercation in the background. "Just a minute." He clapped his hand over the transmitter. There was silence for a moment. Then: "Sorry about that. We're having a show of maidenly reticence this end. Can you make it to-night?"

"Thanks, I'd like to."

"What time can you get away?"

"Not before half-past six."

"Call in for me on your way down and we'll go along together. Okay?"

"I'll be there."

At half-past six I descended to the third floor. Zaleshoff was alone in his office, hammering furiously at a portable typewriter. He waved a hand in greeting.

"Come on in and sit down, Mr. Marlow. If you don't mind, I'll just finish this before we go."

I sat down. A minute or two later he whipped the paper out of the machine, addressed an envelope, stuffed the paper inside it and sealed the flap. I watched him in silence. He had on a pair of reading spectacles. They made him look younger. The idea that he might be a Soviet agent seemed suddenly preposterous. Soviet agents were sinister figures with beards. They spoke broken English and wore large black hats. This man Zaleshoff . . . He looked up and his bright eyes met mine.

"The day's outgoing post?" I inquired facetiously.

"No. We posted that one this morning."

"I see." An idea struck me. "Do you ever look at the flaps of the letters you receive?"

He grinned. "To see if they've been steamed open? Is that what you mean, Mr. Marlow?"

"As a matter of fact, that's just what I did mean."

"Have they been steaming yours open, Mr. Marlow?"

"Yes."

"What made you notice it?"

I told him about Claire's letter.

"And now it doesn't happen any more?"

"I haven't noticed it since that letter."

He chuckled. "That must have made them mad."

"Who's 'them'?"

He was struggling into his overcoat. "The birds that do the steaming," he replied evasively. "Shall we go?"

"All right." But at the door I paused. "Aren't you forgetting something, Mr. Zaleshoff?"

"Eh?"

"There was something mentioned about a card from that card index file of yours. Reference number, V.18, I believe. Do you remember?"

He patted his breast pocket. "It's here, Mr. Marlow, next to my heart."

The Zaleshoffs' apartment was situated over a shop in a street near the Piazza San Stefano. It consisted of two rooms, a kitchen and a bathroom. The two rooms were large, and one of them was evidently used both for sleeping and for living. They had the appearance of having been furnished in a great hurry. The living-room in particular presented a very curious appearance, the furniture consisting of a deal table, a pair of packing cases thinly disguised with blue calico as occasional tables, a luxurious divan with a label still attached to one foot of it and a colossal, and obviously valuable, marqueteric bureau-cum-bookcase. The walls were distempered, rather carelessly, in white.

"It's a wonder," explained Zaleshoff, "that it doesn't look a damn sight worse. We tore the shopping list in half and went out to get the whole outfit in a couple of hours. A guy with a hare-lip sold me that bureau. It's a nice piece, but Tamara seems to think it was a waste of money. She fixed the packing cases. I sat on one yesterday and tore my pants. You'd better try the divan. I bought that, too." He raised his voice. "Tamara!" He turned to me again. "Take your things off, Mr. Marlow, and have a cigarette. You'll find some in the bookcase. Excuse me, will you, I'd better superintend the cooking."

"You're too late," said a voice.

Feeling slightly bewildered by all this, I turned round. The girl was standing in the doorway removing an apron.

"And," she added, "it's quite all right to sit on the packing cases now. I took the nails out myself."

"Oh, there you are," said Zaleshoff. "This, Mr. Marlow, is my sister, Tamara."

She smiled. I found myself smiling back at her.

"I'm glad you could come, Mr. Marlow," she said; "I was afraid that you would be annoyed with us for not speaking to you last night. Andreas has probably explained why we didn't."

"Actually," I replied, "he hasn't explained. But I'm quite sure that it was necessary."

"Andreas, you said . . ."

He flourished an arm dramatically. "Silence! We will discuss these matters after we have eaten. To your kitchen, Tamara!"

At the door she paused. "It is simply, Mr. Marlow," she explained gently, "that he was badly brought up. You must try to make allowances for these *gaucheries*." She shook her head compassionately and disappeared into the kitchen.

Zaleshoff chuckled. "Have a drink, Mr. Marlow?"

"Thanks."

"Whisky? I got a bottle in specially."

"That's very good of you."

He took some glasses out of the bookcase. "Nothing's too good for a man who can put up with Vagas for an evening."

"Oh, so you *do* know him!"

He wagged an admonitory finger. "I know *of* him. Say 'when.'"

"When!"

"I bet he warned you against me, didn't he?"

"In a sort of way."

"Ah! well, here's looking at you."

"Cheerio."

The girl entered carrying a tray with a big copper saucepan in the middle of it. "Can you eat a real paprika goulash, Mr. Marlow?"

"With enthusiasm."

"That's fine, because that's what this is."

"I should like to know," grunted Zaleshoff, "what you'd have done if he'd said it made him sick. Opened the *other* can, I suppose."

The meal proceeded amidst a running fire of amiable bickering. It was obvious that it was all a performance put on for my benefit; but it was amusing enough and I began to enjoy myself. The goulash was delicious. There was, too, something pleasantly stimulating in the company of Zaleshoff and his sister. For the first time since I had left England, I began to feel friendly towards my surroundings. At last, warmed by a stomach-full of goulash, I began a racy account of my evening with General and Madame Vagas. I made no mention, however, of the General's proposition, and Zaleshoff did not refer to our previous conversation on the subject. We might have been three very ordinary acquaintances discussing a fourth. Then, suddenly, the atmosphere changed. And it was a change for the worse.

I had been rambling on happily on the subject of Ricciardo and his incense. They were laughing. Then, quite casually, I went on to mention the note that Madame Vagas had pressed into my hand and my diagnosis of the lady's mental condition.

The effect of my statement was sensational. There was a sudden silence in the room. It was as though someone had switched off a very noisy radio.

"What did you say was in that note, Mr. Marlow?" Zaleshoff's voice was preternaturally calm. The girl's eyes were fixed on her plate.

"I've got it in my pocket if you want to see it. But why? What's the matter? You surely don't take it seriously?"

He glanced at the note in silence, then gave it back to me with a shrug.

"No, I don't take it seriously. It's the work of a spiteful woman. I wouldn't have remarked on it at all, except for one thing."

"Well?"

"That sentence happens to be very nearly true."

I goggled at him. "But Ferning was run over."

"Ferning," said Zaleshoff firmly, "was murdered."

"What on earth are you talking about?"

"Ferning."

I got up from the table. "Now look here, Zaleshoff. You've given me a good dinner, and so far I've enjoyed myself. But I tell you frankly . . ."

But he did not allow me to get any further.

"Sit down, Mr. Marlow. The time has come for you and me to have a little heart to heart talk."

"I don't . . ."

"Sit *down!*" He raised his voice.

"Yes, Mr. Marlow," said the girl; "do sit down. You'll get indigestion. Have some more whisky."

"I don't want any whisky, thank you, and I won't sit down." I was trembling with annoyance.

"Very well, then," snarled Zaleshoff, "stand up. But listen to me for a moment."

"I'm listening."

"Good. Then get this. I don't know whether you walk about in blinkers or whether you're just plain stupid. But if you don't mind my saying so, it's time the Italian representative of the Spartacus Machine Tool Company of Wolverhampton began to ask himself a few questions."

"Such as?"

"Dammit, man!" he exploded; "you've been here ten days. You've had your passport taken away from you and been ordered to report to the police every week like a paroled convict. Doesn't that seem a bit funny to you? You've had your mail tampered with, and you've had your assistant, Bellinetti, trailing you ever since you arrived. I know, because I've watched him. Doesn't that say anything to you? And what's more, you've had a proposition that stinks to high Heaven put to you by a bird who says he's a Yugo-Slav General. You've had all that, and now you're going to walk out on me." His jaw shot out like a battering-ram. "Me! the only guy who can tell you what it's all about."

We glared at one another for a moment.

"Well," I demanded, "what *is* it all about?"

He smacked his hands together. "Ah, that's better! Now, for goodness' sake have another drink."

"Very well."

"And don't say it," he added irritably, "as if I were offering you a tot of prussic acid."

"Sorry. Only," I added, "you can scarcely expect me to treat this talk of murder as if it were sewing-bee gossip."

"You mustn't take any notice of him," chimed in the girl; "he thinks that tact is something you use to nail down linoleum."

"Quiet!" roared Zaleshoff. He turned to me. "Now, Mr. Marlow," he went on in tones of sickening affability, "do you feel equal to the strain of hearing a few facts?"

"Perfectly."

"Then here's fact number one. Last night this guy Vagas put a proposition to you. It went something like this. He said that he was acting on behalf of the Yugo-Slav Government and that his people were prepared to pay you to supply them with details of the Spartacus shell-production machines as you supply them to the subsidised factories. Is that right?"

"More or less."

"He probably didn't put it as simply as that. He probably talked a lot about it being simply a matter of routine intelligence and that there wasn't the slightest risk involved. All you had to do was to let him have the dope and take your rake-off. Right?"

"Right."

"Good. That, Mr. Marlow, is exactly what he told Ferning nine months ago. Ferning . . ."

"Just a minute! Did Ferning tell you this?"

He shook his head impatiently. "I never even spoke to Ferning."

"But you said . . ."

". . . that I knew him. I did. The same as I know the President of the United States."

"Then how do you know what Vagas said?"

"It doesn't matter *how* I know," he retorted pugnaciously. "I just *do* know. Listen."

"All right."

"Vagas put the same proposition to Ferning as he put to you. It was all wrapped up in sugar in just the same way. Now, I don't know what you said to Vagas. We'll come to that later. But Ferning, the poor sucker, jumped at it. There are some guys who can never seem to learn that a something-for-nothing proposition always has a string to it somewhere. Ferning was one of them; and, unluckily for him, the string in this case happened to be more like a steel hawser. The point was that Vagas wanted a good deal more for his two thousand a month than a précis of the Spartacus correspondence files. Mind you, the story about Spartacus activities in Italy being of military interest to a foreign power was true enough as far as it went; that sort of information has to be collected somehow. But with Vagas it was only a sprat to catch a whale." He paused. "Do you realise, Mr. Marlow, just how valuable a man in your position could be to a man like Vagas?"

"I don't know what sort of man that is."

"Ho hum! I'm coming to that. What I mean is this. You spend half your time here snooping round the big Italian armament factories and you have a legitimate reason for doing so. To a foreign agent you would be a gold mine."

"Aren't you exaggerating a little?"

"Not a bit. Look at it this way. Imagine a bunch of poker players sitting round a table. You are wandering about the room smoking and wondering, let's say, what you're going to have for dinner. You've no interest in poker and still less in the players. Right. Now supposing one of the players puts a proposition to you. Supposing he says: 'Look here, Mr. Marlow, while you're just wandering about the room, supposing you take an occasional peek at these other guys' hands, tell me what you see and let me make it worth your while? It's quite easy. I'll tell you what I want to know. You just give me the dope.' You get the idea? Vagas is that player."

"Yes, but he hasn't asked me to do that."

"Wait a minute. Let's go back to the poker players. Supposing you're already taking graft from one of those birds. One day this man will say, 'Now look here, Marlow, if you don't tell me what those other boys have got in their hands I'll tell your boss that you're on my pay-roll.' What then? What are you going to do?"

"But he *can't* say that."

"Can't he? That's what he said to Ferning. A month or six weeks after Ferning started taking money from Vagas, Vagas got tough. They had a showdown. Mr. Ferning had got to make use of his entrée into the factories to supply Vagas with the vital information that he, Vagas, needed. If Mr. Ferning didn't toe the line, then General Vagas would spill the beans to Mr. Pelcher in Wolverhampton. The net result was that Ferning gave in. He still drew his two thousand a month, but he had to do a darn sight more for it."

"You mean he let himself be blackmailed? I should have called Vagas' bluff. After all, it would only have been his word against Ferning's. Pelcher's no fool."

"No, but then neither is Vagas. It wasn't just his word against Ferning's. Vagas had proof. If Pelcher hadn't believed him, all Vagas had to do was to send him the results of Ferning's first month's work. Pelcher would only have to compare Vagas' version of Spartacus dealings for the month with his own records to see that Vagas had the goods. Get me?"

"Ye-es. I see that. But what's this got to do with what you said about Ferning's being murdered?"

"Ah!" He wagged a finger at me. "That comes next. Have another whisky first?"

"Thanks. I think I need it."

"Vichy or water?" said the girl.

"Vichy, please."

We drank solemnly. Zaleshoff put his glass down with a bang.

"Have you ever heard of the Ovra, Mr. Marlow?"

"No. What is it—a vegetable?"

"The question, Mr. Marlow, was rhetorical," put in Tamara. "You needn't do anything more than shake your head. He knows perfectly well that you don't know what the Ovra is. He only puts it that way to be impressive."

Zaleshoff pounded the table with his fist. "Silence, Tamara!" He thrust his head suddenly under my nose. "You see those grey hairs, Mr. Marlow? They are the work of the loving sister you see here."

I couldn't see a sign of a grey hair, but I let the fact pass. "We'd got as far as the Ovra," I reminded him.

"Ah, yes!" He glared at us both and drank a little more from his glass. Then he went on.

"The word 'Ovra,' Mr. Marlow, is formed by the initial letters of four Italian words—*Organizzazione Vigilanza Repressione Anti-fascismo,* vigilant organisation for the repression of anti-fascism. In other words, Mr. Marlow, secret police; the Italian counterpart of the Nazi Gestapo. Its members are as nice a bunch of boys as you could wish to meet. You've heard of the Mafia, the Sicilian secret terrorist society? Well, those birds were the inventors of protection racketeering. Anyone who didn't or couldn't pay was beaten up or shot. In the province of Palermo alone they bumped off nearly two thousand in one year. Chicago was a kiddies' play-pen compared with it. But in nineteen-twenty-three, the Fascisti had an idea. They smashed the Mafia. It took them some time, but they did it. It was, they claimed, one of the blessings of Fascismo. But, like some other Fascist blessings, it was mixed. Some of the Mafia hoodlums emigrated to the United States and took their trade with them, which was very nice for the Italians but not so good for the American public. The big majority of the boys, however, were recruited by the Ovra, drafted to different parts of the country, so that they couldn't get organised again, and set to work on behalf of the Government. *That* wasn't so good for the Italian public. The Ovra's first big job was to liquidate the opposition—the Liberals and the Socialists. That was in nineteen-twenty-four. They did a swell job. The murder of the opposition leader, Matteotti, a few hours before he was due to produce documentary evidence in support of a speech indicting the Fascist Government, was an early success. But it was only a beginning. These were the holy fathers of American gangsterism and they knew their stuff. The ordinary Italian is a nice guy. He's a bit inclined to dramatise himself and his country, but he's a nice guy; he's fond of his wife and kids, he's a darned hard worker and he's as independent as they come. But you can't fight terrorism with indignation. Terrorism always wins. The Government knew that. They consolidated their position by creating the Ovra. Its liquidation of the opposition was as bloody a page of history as you'll find. Beatings, clubbings, killings—it's all in the day's work to the Ovra. The Mafiosi tradition has survived. The Ovra is all-powerful. It has become a regularly constituted secret police force. The Italian Government have even admitted its existence."

He glanced at me doubtfully. "You're probably wondering what all this has to do with Ferning, eh? Well, it has a lot to do with him for the simple reason that one of the departments the Ovra took under its wing was the department of counter-espionage. They've got a thing they call the Foreign Department which deals with nothing else. And it's efficient, darned efficient. It didn't take them long to get wise to friend Ferning."

"How did they do it?"

"Bellinetti's the answer to that one."

"Bellinetti?"

"Sure. He's an Ovra agent. Someone once estimated that at least one man in every ten in the big Italian cities works directly or indirectly for the Ovra. They conscript their agents and keep them under a sort of interlocking system. Agent A watches Agent B who watches Agent C, and so on. The man next door to you may be an Ovra agent. He thinks that you may be. What's the result? When you get together over the fence to have a chat about politics, both of you nearly bust yourselves trying to show how hard you're rooting for the Government. 'Mussolini is always right'—that's item eight in the Fascist Decalogue. You've got to have a pretty good system working to get folks to swallow that whole and keep it swallowed."

"But what about Ferning?"

"Ferning, as I've said, was marked down for action. The question was—what sort of action? Now this is only my guess, but I reckon it went something like this. Ferning was a danger. He had to be stopped. But he was also a British subject and an employee of a firm that the Government was anxious to keep on good terms with. They needed those S2 machines—as many of them as they could get. To arrest Ferning would have been too noisy. There was only one thing to do—liquidate him. They called in the murder squad."

"Do you mean to say that he was deliberately run over?"

"I do. They've done it that way before. Twice in Naples and once in Cremona. The man at Cremona had been a trade-union official once and he wouldn't lie down. He was popular with the workers, so they had to make it accidental. It works beautifully. A man's run over. Too bad! but it's happening every day. So what?"

He sat back on the divan and finished his drink. I thought for a moment, then extracted Ferning's page of notes from my wallet.

"I found this in Ferning's desk. The first two lines refer to Spartacus transactions with the Braganzetta works at Turin. I deciphered that much. Can you tell me what the rest means?"

He took the page and frowned at it for a moment. Then his face cleared.

"Yes. I can tell you what it means. As you say, the first two lines refer to three special S2 machines for anti-aircraft shell production and a standard máchine for the Braganzetta works. What comes after . . ."

"Here, wait a minute!" I put in suspiciously. "I didn't say anything about special S2 machines. How did you know?"

He looked blandly surprised. "It's obvious. You've only got to look at these notes to see it."

I thought both his manner and his explanation singularly unconvincing, but I said nothing. He went on:

"The rest refers to a forty thousand ton battleship building at Spezia and to be completed fourteen months hence. It is reported, he says, that it is to have a six-metre belt of manganese steel armour one point two metres thick. Six fifty-five centimetre naval guns with elevations of thirty degrees are being supplied, presumably by the Braganzetta works. A Genoese firm is supplying the mountings. That's probably the Grigori-Sforza works." He handed the page back to me. "It goes on to give further details."

"And you got all that just by looking at those notes?" I queried sarcastically.

He shrugged. "It's quite clear when you know what you're looking for. That is probably the draft of his last report to Vagas."

"I see." I didn't see, but it was obviously useless to argue. "Well, it's all very upsetting, but I still don't understand what this has to do with me."

"You don't!" He made a gesture of exasperation. "Tamara, he doesn't . . ."

"No, I don't," I snapped. "You know darn well I don't." His calm recital of what seemed to me to be a revolting story had both shocked and irritated me.

"It's really very simple, Mr. Marlow," said the girl soothingly. "You see, having found out that Ferning was engaged in espionage and murdered him, the Ovra was bound to regard you, Ferning's successor, with a certain amount of suspicion. You might try the same game."

"But why didn't they kill Vagas? Why kill Ferning? He was only the subordinate."

"Because," grunted Zaleshoff, "Vagas is too smart for them. He's got a new variation on the royal and ancient game of grafting and it's a honey. He doesn't confine his activities to espionage. That's where he's clever. He safeguards himself by doing a little business on the side. Quite a lot of prominent officials would lose slices of their incomes if Vagas was liquidated. They know he's a foreign agent, but as long as they can feel that they're stopping him getting hold of anything useful, they're happy. That's their mistake, because he gets the goods. He makes them think they're fooling him, when all the time he's laughing up his sleeve at *them*. The secret of it is, of course, that because their private business deals with Vagas are profitable, they *want* to think that it's harmless."

"But what about my passport?"

"There's nothing new about that. It's a good way of keeping tabs on you. They know perfectly well that it's the devil's own job to get a passport replaced even when there's every reason to suppose that it has been destroyed. There are endless formalities. When it's not definitely lost, when it's just mislaid, when there's more than a chance that it may turn up, the difficulties are multiplied. That suits them. If you wanted to leave the country, you'd have to get a Document of Identity for travelling purposes from your Consul. That would mean approaching the police for a *visa*. In other words, you can't leave the country without their say-so. They've got you pretty well taped."

"And I suppose that the letter opening was their work, too."

"Sure. They've got to keep a check on Bellinetti, too. That's their way."

I sat for a moment in silence. In my mind's eye I was trying to get the thing into its correct perspective. Vagas, Ferning, Bellinetti. Ferning, with his small anxious eyes, his protesting mouth, had been the born victim. *Inset:* the murdered man. Ferning was the sheep. Vagas and Bellinetti were the wolves —wolves which hunted in different packs. But where exactly did Zaleshoff fit in? There was nothing sheep-like about him. Was he, too, a wolf? Anyway, what did it matter? It was nothing to do with me. I wasn't going to make the same mistake as Ferning. The less I knew, the better. Ask no questions. . . .

I looked up. "Well," I said crisply, "it's very good of you to tell me all this, Mr. Zaleshoff, to warn me of some of the perils of the big city. But, as it happens, your warning is unnecessary. I have already told Vagas that I will have nothing to do with his precious proposition."

"Do you mean to say," he said slowly, "that he let you turn him down flat?"

I laughed. I was feeling very sure of myself. "Not exactly. He wouldn't take no for an answer. It was left that I should telephone my decision to him. But I had already made up my mind before I saw you this evening." I paused. "Vagas," I went on, "must be a cold-blooded devil to put me forward as the next Ovra victim."

"Vagas obviously does not know that Ferning's death wasn't an accident or he would have met you in secret. He might even have thought it a waste of time to contact you at all."

"But what about Madame Vagas? She evidently holds her husband responsible for Ferning's death. But how . . . ?"

"Exactly!" he chimed in grimly. "That's why that note startled me a bit. Madame Vagas knows more than she should."

"Well, at any rate," I said easily, "it's no concern of mine. I'd already made up my mind, and what you've told me clinches the decision."

He looked at me thoughtfully and stroked his chin. Then:

"I don't think you quite understand, Mr. Marlow," he said slowly.

"Understand what?"

He sighed. "My motives for giving you this information."

"Well, what were they?"

"I, too, have a proposition to put to you."

I laughed. "Well, let's have it. It can't be as bad as Vagas' little effort."

He coughed self-consciously. For the first time I saw signs of embarrassment in his face. "It's just this, Mr. Marlow," he began, and then stopped.

"Well?"

"I want you to telephone General Vagas and say that you have decided, after all, to accept his offer."

Chapter VIII

PROPOSITION

YOU'D BETTER have another drink," he added.

And then I began to laugh. They both surveyed me in sheepish silence.

"My dear good Zaleshoff," I spluttered at last, "you really mustn't play these lunatic jokes."

My intention had been to annoy him and I succeeded. He reddened. "It's not a joke, Marlow."

"Isn't it?" Then my own temper got the better of me. I stopped laughing. "If it isn't a joke, what the devil is it?"

He made a very obvious effort to keep calm. "If you will allow me to explain . . ."

"Explain! explain!" My voice rose. "You've done nothing else but explain. Now you let *me* do a little explaining. I'm an engineer and I'm in Milan for a specific purpose. I have a job to do and I propose to do it. I am not interested in any proposition that is not aimed at promoting the interests of my company. Is that absolutely clear? Because if it isn't clear, I must thank you for a very pleasant dinner and go."

Zaleshoff was sitting with a face like a thundercloud. As I finished, he drew a deep breath and opened his mouth to speak. But his sister forestalled him.

"Just a minute, Andreas." She turned to me. "Mr. Marlow," she said coolly, "someone once said that the English were the best hated race on the world's surface. I am beginning to understand what was meant by that. Of all the stupid, smug, short-sighted, complacent, obstinate, asinine . . ."

"Tamara!"

She flushed. "Be quiet, Andreas. I haven't finished. You, Mr. Marlow, come here knowing nothing about anything except, presumably, your business as an engineer. That I can understand. But that you should refuse even to listen to what someone has to tell you about the world outside your own tiny mind, I *cannot* understand. Haven't you a spark of vulgar curiosity in you?"

I got to my feet. "I think I had better go."

She went and stood with her back to the door. "Oh, no you don't, you're going to listen to my brother."

"Let him go, Tamara," Zaleshoff said quietly. "It doesn't matter. We'll do without him."

For a moment I stood there irresolute. I was feeling embarrassed, foolish and very slightly ashamed. After all, I had refused to listen. Besides, Zaleshoff's last sentence had touched me on the raw. "We'll do without him." It was the sort of thing you said to children to shame them into doing what they did not want to do. Unaccountably, it was having that effect on me. I have since wondered whether that had perhaps been Zaleshoff's precise intention. His was a curious, deceptive mind. He had a way of exploiting the standard emotional counters that was highly disconcerting. You could never be quite sure whether his acting was studied or not and, if it was, whether for emphasis or concealment. Now, however, I told myself that I was indeed being childish, that the best thing I could do would be to carry out my declared intention and go. But I still stood there.

The girl moved away from the door. "Well, Mr. Marlow," she said challengingly.

I sat down again with a sigh and a shrug. "I don't know what this is all about," I said shortly, "but I'll have that other drink if it's going."

Zaleshoff nodded. "Sure." Without another word, without even a hint of surprise, he got up and poured out two drinks. The girl came over to me.

"I'm very sorry," she said humbly; "that was rude of me. You must think we're very curious hosts."

I *did* think so, but I grinned. "That's all right. I'm afraid I've got rather a bad temper."

Zaleshoff handed me my glass. "It's a wonder that some good man hasn't shot her before this."

"Probably," she retorted calmly, "because most good men don't carry guns." She examined me curiously. "Why didn't you throw something at me just now, Mr. Marlow?"

"Because," said her brother sharply, "there wasn't anything handy. Now, for goodness' sake, Tamara, get on with your sewing. Are you married, Marlow?"

"No. Engaged. She's a doctor in England."

He raised his eyebrows. "I don't want to appear inquisitive, but is there any particular reason why you should have taken this job here?"

"Yes. I got caught in what is politely called a trade recession. I couldn't get a job worth having in England. My savings were nearly all gone. I was feeling desperate one day, and I accepted an offer from Spartacus."

"I see. Then I suppose you wouldn't object to Vagas' two thousand lire a month if I could give you a good enough reason for taking it?"

I hesitated. "Frankly, Zaleshoff, I don't think there's a good enough reason in existence. At this very moment I'm telling myself that I'm a damn fool to sit here listening to you when I might be catching up on some of the sleep I missed last night. But I'm curious. I can't believe that you're such a half-wit as to spend an hour putting me off Vagas' offer so thoroughly if you really wanted me to accept it."

"I wasn't putting you off. I was giving you the facts."

"The distinction is too much for me. I'm not quite crazy, you know. Do you suppose I want to share that poor devil Ferning's fate?"

"I do not suppose anything of the sort. But there's no reason why you *should* share his fate."

"That's precisely what *I'm* thinking. You, I gather, have something up your sleeve."

"No. I just want to put a situation to you."

"Fire away."

"Do you ever read newspapers?"

"As little as possible, these days. Why?"

"Have you ever heard of a little thing called the Rome-Berlin axis?"

"Who hasn't?"

"Have you ever looked at what it means on a map?"

"I can't say I've bothered to."

"You should. It's interesting. A solid, strategic unit from the Frisian Islands in the North to the toe of Italy in the South. The toe is waiting to kick Great Britain in the pants. The head is there to gobble up what's left. The Rome-Berlin axis is one of the most effective principles of European power-politics that has ever been stated. It gave Italy and Germany a free hand in Spain. It changed Austria from an independent state to a memory. It made England launch the most gigantic peace-time armament-making drive the world has ever seen.

It cocked the biggest snook yet at the League of Nations idea. It deprived France of her little Entente allies. It's frightened the rest of Europe so badly that it lives now in a permanent state of jitters. Even the United States have become uneasy. The world is slowly beginning to turn on the Rome-Berlin axis and already the strain is telling. Something's got to snap, something's going to snap; and if it's not the Rome-Berlin axis, it's going to be you and me. The statesmen of the so-called democracies, France and England, are busting themselves in their efforts to make it the axis that goes first. And they look like failing. Things are moving too quickly for them. They try to buy off Italy and fail. They try again. They can't hit out for fear of hurting themselves. They're out of their depths and they know it. They're as mixed as my metaphors. They're confused and confounded. And meanwhile we drift nearer and nearer to war. The Four Horsemen of the Apocalypse are getting ready to go; and, Marlow, if those boys ride out again across Europe, you can say good-bye to all your dreams. It'll be a war that'll make the world safe for everything except mankind. A government will be formed with King Typhus at the head of a parliament of corpse-fed rats."

He paused for a moment. "I dare say you're wondering where all this is leading. I'll tell you. It's leading to a question —this question. If someone told you that by taking a certain course you could make a very, very small, but very, very positive, contribution towards putting a kink in that axis we've been talking about, what would you say?"

"I'd say that he had a bee in his bonnet."

He grinned. "H'm, yes. *You* probably would say that. But supposing that he hadn't got a bee in his bonnet, supposing he was talking good hard sense, and supposing he could prove it. What would you do then?"

I fidgeted. "I'm not very fond of these beautifully simple parables, Zaleshoff. Vagas has a weakness for them, too. Let's get down to cases."

"Just what I was going to do." He put his hand in his pocket. "You wanted the dope; here's the first bit. It's the card from that file in my office, card number V.18. Take a look at it."

His hand came out with the card folded in two.

The picture of Vagas was obviously a photostat of a photograph taken some years before. There was more hair on top of the head and the sides were cropped. The skin of the face was tighter. He wore a high tubular stiff collar with a broad, flat tie. Below the photostat was pasted a square of type-written paper.

Johann Luitpold Vagas (I read) *born Dresden* 1889. *Heidelberg. Army* 1909. *6th Bavarian Cavalry. Berlin* 1913. *War Ministry.* 1917 *Iron Cross and Star of Leopold.* 1918 *refugee to Belgrade. Yugo-Slav citizenship* 1922. 1924 *Yugo-Slav agent for Cator & Bliss Ltd. of London. Returned Germany* 1933. *Returned Belgrade* 1934. *Rome* 1936. *Milan* 1937. *See S.22, J.15, P.207, C.64, F.326.*

I looked up. "Well, what's it all about?"

Zaleshoff frowned. "Does nothing there strike you?"

I read the card again. "Well, he appears to have been agent for a British steel firm."

"Yes, he sold guns to the Yugo-Slav Government; but that's not what I mean."

"Then what *do* you mean?"

"He was a German officer. In nineteen-eighteen when the revolution broke out he skipped to Belgrade and later took up Yugo-Slav citizenship. *But*"—he stabbed the air with his forefinger—"in nineteen-thirty-three he returned to Germany. Note the date—nineteen-thirty-three. What happened in nineteen-thirty-three in Germany?"

"Hitler came into power."

"Precisely. Germany went Nazi, so he returned."

"And left again the next year. What about it?"

"Just this. Vagas went to Germany a Yugo-Slav. He returned a German. From nineteen-thirty-four to nineteen-thirty-six Vagas was the principal German secret agent in Belgrade. It was a cinch for them. Here was a patriotic but expatriated German officer with a Yugo-Slav passport and well in with the Belgrade War Ministry by virtue of his position as an armament salesman. What more could you want? The German Secret Service have always been tight-wads, and I dare say the fact that he was drawing a fat commission from Cator & Bliss and didn't want anything except the honour of serving his country was an additional attraction. Besides, an unpaid agent is always a sounder bet than a guy who may pass on unreliable information to justify his wages."

"Yes, I see. But if he was so keen on the honour of serving the Nazis, what's he doing here now working for the Yugo-Slav Government?"

Zaleshoff lounged back luxuriously on the divan. "There now, that's fine!" He smiled seraphically. "We're getting right to the heart of the matter. What, indeed?" He leaned forward. "I'll tell you. The answer is—'nothing.' He's not working for the Yugo-Slav Government. He's working for the Nazis."

"He told me . . ."

"There's a good old-fashioned word for what he told you —'boloney.' Listen. On October the nineteenth, nineteen-thirty-six, the Italian Foreign Minister, Ciano, met the German Foreign Minister, von Neurath, in Munich. At that meeting the Rome-Berlin axis was forged. A fortnight later Mussolini hailed the Rome-Berlin axis publicly in a speech in the Piazza del Duomo just round the corner. The crowd sang 'Deutschland über alles' and the Horst Wessel song at the top of their voices. The blackshirts and brownshirts whooped it up together. Italy and Germany swore eternal friendship." He paused impressively. "A fortnight later Vagas packed his suitcases and moved into Italy."

He sipped at his whisky. "Have you ever watched a cat and a dog lie down on the same floor, Marlow? Maybe they've been brought up together, maybe they're used to one another, maybe they've got the same interest in a common owner. But they're never entirely at their ease. The cat is always watchful, the dog self-conscious. They can never quite forget that there is such a thing as a cat-and-dog fight. There's an undercurrent of mutual suspicion between them that they can never quite forget. So it was with the Nazis and the Fascisti. They'd come to an agreement over Austria. They'd agreed on parallel action in Spain. They'd agreed to boycott Geneva. They'd agreed to present a united front to the Western powers. But Johann Luitpold Vagas was sent into Italy. The dog was keeping one eye open, just in case."

"Don't the Italians know he's really a German agent?"

"They certainly do not. How should they know? He wouldn't be the first German officer to take service with another country. I only found out by accident. After all, the guy has got a Yugo-Slav passport, and that beautiful fiction about his being a Yugo-Slav agent has been handled very cleverly. No, if they ever arrest Vagas, it'll be for espionage on behalf of Yugo-Slavia. And that suits the German Foreign Ministry. It would be embarrassing for all concerned if an important German spy were to be caught on Italian soil."

"But what does Vagas do?"

Zaleshoff emitted an exasperated sigh. "What does he do? Listen, Marlow, if an Englishman came to you to-morrow and swore black and blue that Spartacus were going bankrupt next month, what would you do? You might believe or disbelieve him, but you'd write to a friend in England and ask him to check up on the situation for you. That's Vagas' job—checking up. If the Italians tell their Nazi boy friends that they're building *two* hundred and fifty new-type bombing planes this year, Uncle Vagas gets busy and checks up to make sure that it isn't *five* hundred and fifty. Dictators who can't even trust their own subordinates out of their sight aren't likely to trust each other very far. And, the way things are going at the moment, that mutual distrust is deepening. It's the one weak spot in the Rome-Berlin axis, and it's because of that weak spot that I'm sitting here talking to you."

"I was wondering why it was," I murmured.

"Then now you know." He projected his jaw at me aggressively. "The point is that things are not what they were between Italy and Germany. Austria is gone. The Reichswehr is on the Brenner Pass. Mussolini is scared of that fact, and because he's scared he's dangerous—to Germany. The Nazis are on their guard. Vagas is working overtime."

"I still don't see what this has to do with me."

The girl looked up from her sewing. "My brother's very fond of the sound of his own voice."

"So fond," snarled Zaleshoff, "that I'm going to tell him a little story." He turned to me again. "When I was at school in Chicago, Marlow, there were two big boys named Joe and Ted who used to bully us little kids. It went on for months. We got pretty sick of it. We tried ambushing them and they beat up a whole lot of us. Then one day we had an idea. There was one kid who used to follow Joe about like a shadow. His name was Augustus, if you can imagine that. We used to call him 'Augie.' He was a snivelling little rat, this Augie. He'd been bullied by Joe, and to protect himself he'd taken to cleaning Joe's boots and running errands for him. Joe let him. Then Augie took to working off his private hates by getting Joe to beat up the other kids for him. Joe was only too ready to oblige. Augie became a kind of protégé of Joe's. Wherever Joe and Ted went he used to tag along behind. It used to make us mad until we got our idea. One day two of us waited for Augie near the city dump at the end of the street. We said we'd got something funny to tell him. We said that we heard Ted say that Joe was nothing but a yellow rat who wouldn't dare to let out a squeak if he, Ted, challenged him. Then we beat up Augie a little and waited for results. We didn't have to wait long. Augie ran straightaway to spill the beans to Joe. After school that day Joe and Ted got together. Naturally, Ted denied that he'd said anything about Joe. Joe said that Ted must be too yellow to repeat it to his face. Then they began. Joe finished up in hospital with three stitches in his scalp where Ted had hit him with a brick. Ted had a beating from Joe's father. What do you think of that?" he concluded triumphantly, and stared hard at me.

I was wilfully dense. "Very nice. But what's the moral?"

He looked slightly crestfallen. "Don't you see?" He drew a deep breath. "I'll put it plainer. Supposing Vagas obtained information concerning Italy's activities that surprised him very much, information that she wouldn't like the Nazis to have. Vagas would tell the Nazis and then, you see . . ."

"Yes, I see. It would put that kink that you were talking about in the Rome-Berlin axis. But there's just one thing you seem to forget. The Nazis are not as simple as Joe. They'd find out in five minutes that it was just ballyhoo."

He tapped my knee triumphantly. "But, my good friend, if it wasn't just ballyhoo, if it were true . . ."

"True!"

He grinned. "The cat and the dog!"

"Well, what is this precious information?" I did not really believe that he had any.

"Do you remember that, some time ago, Mussolini made one of his blood-and-thunder speeches on the subject of Italian defence. I know he's always making them about something, but this one was a little more specific than usual. It was a speech aimed at making you British shiver in your shoes. He referred in particular to the power of the Italian air force, and made a special point of six secret Italian aerodromes that had been built for war use. Naturally, the German General Staff was interested. Shortly afterwards, the German and the Italian Staffs had conversations and drew up fresh plans for common action in the event of French support for Czechoslovakia. Those secret aerodromes were mentioned. The Italian General Staff was obliging. It gave the Germans full particulars. The aerodromes were near the French and Swiss frontiers. The Germans went away satisfied. *But*"—he wagged his finger slowly—"the fact of the matter is that at least three of those secret aerodromes are in the Trentino near what used to be the Austrian frontier, and the Germans don't know it!"

"Very interesting."

"Now," he went on persuasively, "the question is how to get that information to Vagas in such a way as to leave no doubt about its being accepted as true. That's where . . ."

"I know," I interjected; "that's where I come in."

"Exactly and . . ."

"There's nothing doing, Zaleshoff."

"But just . . ."

"Absolutely nothing doing," I repeated firmly. "I'm . . ."

"Yes, yes," he put in testily; "you're an engineer and you're here on business, and you're not going to get yourself into the sort of spot Ferning got into. I know. But wait a minute." He became eager. "There's no question of your getting into a spot. The only thing is to avoid any actual meeting with Vagas. As long as the Ovra don't see that you're in touch

with him you're all right. You can telephone him and arrange to communicate through the poste restante with assumed names. He won't mind that. It'll please him. If he
thinks you're scared but dead set on the money, he'll also
think that you'll be easier to deal with when it comes to
putting the screw on. As for Spartacus, you needn't give
Vagas the real dope, you can cook up anything. He won't
bother to check it. Then if he *should* turn nasty over anything and write to Pelcher, you'll be quite O.K. All you have
to do is to send Vagas three letters. The first'll be a cooked
Spartacus report on the past month's activities. He'll want
that. When he's got it he'll increase his demands. Right. Your
next report in a month's time will contain some additional
dope, among it an item about the delivery of three special
hydraulic lifts for aircraft. The third report will give news
of consignments of ammunition bound for the same places.
Just enough for him to be able to piece the story together
for himself. For doing just that, Marlow, you get six thousand
lire from Vagas *and*"—he looked me in the eyes—"another
six thousand from me."

I looked from one to the other. The girl, her head bent
over the hem of the blouse she was making, was apparently
unaware that we were there; but I saw that the needle had
stopped moving and that her fingers were poised delicately
like those of a woman in a Dutch painting. Zaleshoff had
suddenly busied himself with the lighting of a cigarette.

I cleared my throat loudly. "I think, Zaleshoff," I said
evenly, "that the time has come for you to explain just what
personal interest you have in this business. Where do you
come in? In other words, what's your game?"

He looked with well-simulated surprise. "My game? I have
no game." An expression of disarming sincerity, of rugged
candour, appeared suddenly on his face. "Put me down, Marlow, as a simple American with a little more money than
I need"—he repeated this—"more money than I need. That's
the plain truth of it, I guess. I'm a simple American who hates
war. But I want to do something more than hate." His voice
vibrated with evangelical feeling. "I want to help make the
peace we all want in a more practical way than just by talking. The world is in a bad way, Marlow. What it needs is
good management. I'm a business man, Marlow, a pretty successful one, though I say it myself. This little old world
wants running on business lines. I'm a doer, Marlow, not a
thinker. Thinking's not going to get us any place. We need
the co-operation of practical men. That's why I'm appealing
to you, Marlow. You're a practical man. We men of goodwill have just got to get together, roll up our sleeves and ge'

something done, eh?" He beamed at me, a benevolent Babbitt with a parcel of real-estate to unload.

It was nauseating, it was grotesque. I stared at him, speechless. At last I got to my feet.

"Well, well. I'm afraid it's rather late. I shall have to be going." I went across the room and picked up my overcoat. They watched me in silence. Zaleshoff's beam had eased into a scowl. I put my overcoat on and went towards the door. "Thanks again," I said, "for a very good dinner."

"Just a minute." It was Zaleshoff, a very hard-voiced Zaleshoff.

"What is it?"

"I'm waiting for an answer from you."

I turned round. "Yes, of course. I was forgetting." I put my hand into my overcoat pocket and drew out a small parcel that was in it. I had purchased this parcel that afternoon. Now I planked it down on the table.

"What's that?" demanded Zaleshoff suspiciously.

I opened the door.

"It's the cake of soap I owe you," I said carefully. "Luckily, I was able to get one in the shape of a lemon." I nodded genially. "Good night to you both."

Not a muscle of Zaleshoff's face moved. He just stood there looking at me, a curious expression in his eyes. The girl shrugged and returned to her sewing. I went.

The entrance to Zaleshoff's place was in a short alleyway at the side of the shop. It was very dark in the alleyway. The man standing on the far side of the street did not see me immediately; but as I stepped into the light I saw him turn away quickly and stare into a shop window.

I turned in the direction of the Parigi. A little way down I stopped and lighted a cigarette. Out of the corner of my eye I could see that he was following me. It was not, however, Bellinetti. This man was taller. I did not look back again but walked straight on to the hotel. If what Zaleshoff had said were true, the best possible thing I could do was to behave as naturally as possible. I had nothing to hide and did not intend to have anything to hide. If the secret police wished to waste their time following me, that was their lookout.

All the same, it was an uncomfortable feeling. I felt myself walking a little stiffly and self-consciously. I began to think of the story Zaleshoff had told me about Ferning's death. In my mind's eye I saw him walking along a street as I was now walking. He must have heard the car coming before it hit him: and in that final second those anxious eyes, that flat, plump jowl must have been distorted with terror. I thought of his bald head. It must have bobbed absurdly as he went down. But it was all, I told myself, a product of Zaleshoff's imagination. Such things didn't happen. Then a stray car swinging out of a side street in front of me made me jump badly. I felt myself break out into a sweat. It was all I could do to prevent myself from running. I was heartily thankful when I reached the hotel.

The clerk beckoned to me from his desk.

"There is a letter for you, Signore. And a gentleman is waiting to see you. He was told that you might be late, but he wished to wait. He was shown into the writing-room where it is warm."

I took the letter. "Who is it?"

"I was not on duty when he arrived, Signore. He left no name."

"All right, thanks."

I went into the writing-room.

Sitting comfortably near a radiator and reading a paper was Vagas.

Chapter IX

O.V.R.A.

AS I CAME into the room, he put his paper down and got to his feet. He was in evening clothes.

"Good evening, Mr. Marlow."

"Good evening, General." I did not feel particularly cordial, and could not have sounded so, for he coughed apologetically.

"I hope you will forgive this intrusion. I was particularly anxious to see you."

"By all means." I made an effort to sound enthusiastic. "May I offer you a drink?"

"Thank you, no. Perhaps one of your English cigarettes . . . thank you. Shall we sit down? I shall not detain you long."

"I beg your pardon. Yes, please sit down."

"Thank you." He sat down and glanced round the room distastefully. "I should find this a very depressing atmosphere, Mr. Marlow. This Utrecht green, these faded reminders of an effete imperialism. Buonaparte always seems to me a slightly pathetic figure; a parvenu with a talent for making fools of wiser men: a man with a taste for the grandiose and the soul of an accountant. Don't you agree with me?"

"Most of my time here I spend in bed." It was perhaps a little too pointed, but he nodded calmly enough.

"Yes, of course. You must be a very busy man. I will explain the reason for this somewhat unconventional visit. Last night . . ." He stopped. "By the way, I hope you weren't too bored."

"Not in the least. It was a most pleasant evening."

"I'm so glad. My wife found you charming."

"Please convey my respects to Madame Vagas."

"Thank you. However," he went on, "there is one matter on which I should like to say more."

"Yes?" I thought I knew what was coming; but I was wrong.

"The matter of Commendatore Bernabò. I am most anxious that you should meet him again, Mr. Marlow. I had occasion to see him to-day and happened to learn from him some very interesting news. Interesting," he added, with a meaning look, "from your point of view."

"Indeed?"

"Yes. I learned," he went on impressively, "that the Government is considering heavy purchases of shell-production plant from a German firm. It is plant of a type your firm has been supplying."

He obviously expected me to make some comment on this, but I waited. He drew at his cigarette and expelled the smoke slowly. Then he went on again.

"With you in mind, Mr. Marlow, I had a little talk with the Commendatore on the subject. I am afraid that the German firm is very well entrenched. Naturally, for political reasons Italy is disposed to buy from Germany rather than from other countries. But the German firm has also procured friends by, shall we say, unethical means." He stared at his cigarette. "Now I don't know what your attitude towards these regrettable practices is, Mr. Marlow, but if your company does allocate an appropriation for—how shall I put it?—for entertainment and such things, I cannot help feeling that here is a case in which a comparatively small expenditure would be richly rewarded. Naturally, the matter is now somewhat urgent, but the Commendatore was agreeable that I should mention the matter to you. Of course, if you would prefer to take no action, there is no commitment on either side."

He waved a graceful hand. My nose caught a faint waft of perfume.

"You mean," I said bluntly, "that if the Commendatore

gets a decent rake-off he is prepared to switch this contract my way?"

He smiled thinly. "That is a crude way of putting it, Mr. Marlow, but it is reasonably correct."

"I see. May I ask which German firm is concerned?"

He told me. I recognised the name as that of my principal competitors.

"And what is the value of the contract, General?"

"About eight hundred and fifty thousand lire if your prices are the same as the German."

I thought quickly. That was just over eight thousand pounds—nearly forty S2 machines. It did sound like an Ordnance Department contract, and the fact that the German firm had tendered . . .

"And how much should I earmark for the Commendatore?"

"Two per cent. of the gross value of the contract."

"That seems reasonable enough. But what about the Germans?"

He smiled. "They are very confident, Mr. Marlow. So confident that they are not prepared to offer more than one and a half per cent. for the privilege of handling the contract."

"May I ask, General, the extent of your interest in the transaction?"

He raised a protesting hand. "Please, Mr. Marlow, please! There is no question of my participating financially. It is purely a friendly affair as far as I am concerned. I know you, I know the Commendatore. I am delighted to be of assistance to you and the Spartacus company."

He exuded disinterested goodwill. I felt a little embarrassed.

"You must allow me to recognise your efforts in some way, General."

"My dear Mr. Marlow, I shouldn't dream of it. It is just a small affair between friends. I was able to help Mr. Ferning in similar ways from time to time. Besides, the business is not concluded yet. Naturally, you will have to arrange matters personally with the Commendatore. In the ordinary way he is a little inaccessible and difficult. But the fact that you are a friend of mine will, I think you will find, smooth over the embarrassing preliminaries. Incidentally, he prefers to conduct his private dealings in cash. I mention that because . . ."

"Quite so."

He smiled and stood up. "I can see, Mr. Marlow, that you have a certain amount of experience in these affairs. I suggest that you call on the Commendatore in the morning."

"I shall do so. And thank you again, General. I hope you will let me repay you in some way for your help."

"It is nothing. As I say, I was able to give Mr. Ferning some help of a similar nature from time to time." He hesitated. Then, as if he had just remembered something: "But if you *should* wish to recognise this very trifling service . . ." He paused.

"Yes, General?" But I had already perceived the trap into which I had fallen.

"Please give your very sympathetic consideration to the proposal that I put to you last night."

"I am afraid, General . . ."

"One moment, Mr. Marlow. In addition to the very valuable goodwill of the Commendatore, goodwill valuable, of course, only to the Spartacus company, I can increase my offer for your personal collaboration with me to three thousand lire a month."

"Then the goodwill of the Commendatore towards my employers is contingent on what you call my personal collaboration. Is that it, General?"

He looked shocked. "Dear me, no. It is just that these things must be arranged on a basis of mutual confidence and friendly co-operation. Think it over, Mr. Marlow. In any case, go and see the Commendatore. The matter of this contract is, as I have said, urgent, but the Commendatore has promised me that he will take no final steps without seeing me again. A day or two either way can make little difference, and in a few days"—he paused meaningly—"much can happen." He extended his hand. "Good night, Mr. Marlow, and once again my apologies for troubling you at such a late hour."

"A pleasure, General."

He went gracefully. I sat down and smoked a cigarette. Zaleshoff was right in one thing at least. Vagas was no fool. It had all been done so skilfully. The sprat had been offered with generous abandon. It had not been until I, poor fish, had risen to it and swallowed that the hook and line had been disclosed.

Again, my objection to his proposal on the grounds of the loyalty I owed to my employers had been neatly met by providing me with a ready-made sop to my conscience. Part of the bribe would benefit Spartacus. The complete pill was sugared with an increase in my "personal interest."

I was left in a quandary. Should I go and see the Commendatore and begin negotiations in the hope of carrying them through without Vagas' goodwill or should I forget the whole thing? I had an idea that to take the first course would be a pure waste of time. Vagas would scarcely have given me so much information if I could use it on my own account. Yet eight hundred thousand lire contracts were not everyday affairs. I ought, in any case, to make an effort to secure this one on my own. It was all very trying.

I went up to my room, opening the letter the clerk had given me. It was, to my surprise, from Mr. Pelcher.

Dear Mr. Marlow (I read),

You must pardon my writing to your private address; but as this letter concerns your confidential memorandum to me on the subject of Bellinetti, I deemed it advisable to do so.

Let me say at once that I am in perfect agreement with you in principle. Bellinetti's work certainly leaves much to be desired. I did not do more than hint at this when you were in Wolverhampton, as I was anxious not to prejudice you against him before you had had an opportunity of judging for yourself. It was possible that you might have got on well with the man. That you have not done so does not, to be frank, surprise me. Which makes it all the more painful for me to have to tell you that I cannot under any circumstances agree to his dismissal.

I feel that this calls for some amplification.

Bellinetti was engaged by me, when I was in Milan shortly after Ferning joined the company, at the request of a man with whom we had done a certain amount of business—a petty government official. We needed an assistant for Ferning and so we took him on. A few weeks later I received a report from Ferning couched in almost the same terms as yours. I replied agreeing immediately to his suggestion. Ferning gave Bellinetti notice.

I will not go into details here; but four days later pressure was put on us to reinstate Bellinetti. You may judge of the nature of the pressure and of the quarters from which it came when I tell you that I wired Ferning to re-engage Bellinetti forthwith. You must accept my assurance that had I failed to do so our interest in Italy would have suffered seriously. Bellinetti has, evidently, friends at court!

Well, that was another addition to Zaleshoff's score. Bellinetti was an Ovra spy. Mr. Pelcher's statement was a circumstantial confirmation of the fact. I read on.

As a consequence, I feel that I must ask you to do the best you can at the moment. I would like to be able to tell you to engage additional assistance in any case. I am afraid, however, that the turnover being handled through the Milan office does not warrant the expenditure. I heartily approve of your actions with regard to the girl engaged by Bellinetti (without permission I may add) and to the increased wages for the boy; but we must go cautiously. Bellinetti's salary is not, as you know, insignificant, while your own is also chargeable to the Milan office.

While we are on the subject of turnover (this, I thought, was a rather skilful juxtaposition of ideas) *I should like to remind you of our conversation when you were in Wolverhampton concerning the works extension. This, I am glad to say, has been completed since you left, and we should be in production shortly. The great thing now is to get it busy and keep it busy. I want you to make every effort to make fresh contacts at your end. Our German competitors are, I know, doing quite well in Italy, which means that there is the business to be had. I suggest in this connection that you draw freely on your "special appropriation." When in Milan do as Rome does!* (I could see him beaming happily over this jest.) *I do not want the money wasted, naturally; but Spartacus has a name for generosity which you will do well to maintain. I look forward to your news with interest.*

The rest was kind regards, best wishes and a huge signature.

My first reaction was one of irritation. How on earth could I be expected to make new contacts? I had not yet had time to make sure of the old ones. And then another thought put that aspect of the business out of my head. It had been Fitch who had explained to me the details of what he referred to with mournful jocularity as the "corruption fund." Mr. Pelcher had used the word "appropriation." So had Vagas. Ferning had possibly told him about it. It was also possible that Ferning's successes on behalf of Spartacus had had something to do with Vagas. Vagas had hinted as much himself. In that case my solitary efforts were not going to prove very productive by comparison. It would end by my being in the absurd position of having to explain to Mr. Pelcher that Ferning had only been able to get business by doing a little espionage on the side. The fact that I should be totally unable to produce any proof that this preposterous assertion were true would make it look like a very silly and rather churlish excuse. Mr. Pelcher would probably say, *"De mortuis nil nisi bonum."*

And there was another disquieting thought. What Vagas had given Vagas could probably take away; and if he had been responsible for Ferning's securing valuable contracts, my failure to fall in with his wishes might even lead to a loss of existing turnover. Mr. Pelcher would not like that at all. Neither should I. Even if I were able to secure new business to make up for the loss, my commission arrangement only held good for turnover over and above the original figure.

I shrugged. It was, after all, mere supposition and too early yet to start complaining. What I had to do was to make the best of things as they were and do my best to get new business. It would, I reflected on a sudden wave of optimism, be nice to be able to present Mr. Pelcher with the Commendatore's eight hundred thousand lire order. I should certainly see the Commendatore in the morning.

I undressed, got into bed and closed my eyes.

It had been a tiring day—another tiring day—and I hadn't written to Claire since Tuesday. That was something I must do without fail to-morrow—write to Claire. I had a lot to tell her. The question was whether it was wise to put it in a letter. Probably not. But still . . .

My feet began to get warm. The warmth stole up my legs to my body. Vagas could say what he liked about the Parigi, but the beds were comfortable. I felt drowsy. I ought to see about my passport again in the morning. What a lot there was to do! Rome-Berlin axis. What an odd idea that of Zaleshoff's! A world turning on an axis not its own. You would get a sort of cam action. Did people ever use eccentric spheres for anything? Probably not. There was no point in such a thing. It was useless. A pity that. There ought to be some use for a spherical cam. Perhaps I could find a use for it, some way of transmitting power with lower losses. The Marlow Spherical Cam Action. Patents Applied For in All Countries and the U.S. Absurd!

And then, as I drew nearer to sleep, two sentences of Zaleshoff's began to recur in my mind. *Vagas is working over-time.* I eased my pillow until it was wedged under my shoulder. *As long as the Ovra don't see that you're in touch with him, you're all right.* I began to regulate their rhythm to my breathing. Then, as my mind slid gently below the surface of consciousness, I forgot both the sentences.

I was to be reminded of the second before many hours had passed.

On my way to the Commendatore's office at the Ordnance Department the following morning, I called at the Consulate for news of my passport.

There was no news. The fact did not surprise me. It was obvious that the Consulate was doing its best to get satisfaction, but there wasn't much to be said to the police authorities' blank assurances that the passport had been mislaid. The Consul couldn't very well express disbelief and insist upon searching the *Amministrazione* with his own hands. I was again assured that if I wished to leave the country I could be furnished with a Document of Identity to take me across the frontiers. I expressed my thanks politely and went my way. There was nothing else I could do.

From the fuss attending my application to see him, I concluded that the Commendatore was even more important a person than Vagas' references to him had seemed to me to imply. Lips were pursed doubtfully. Had I an appointment with the Commendatore? No? Ah, then, it was difficult. It would be best if I wrote for an appointment. I persisted. Eventually, on the understanding that I knew the Commendatore personally and that, although I had no definite appointment with him, he was expecting me, I was allowed to fill in a form stating my name and business. I put down my name, hesitated, then wrote across the space left for the description of my business: "The subject of your conversation with General Vagas." I sat down prepared for a long wait, but two minutes later I was ushered by a uniformed secretary through a pair of tall double doors into the Commendatore's office.

In his carpeted office, behind his expensive desk and without his wife, Commendatore Bernabò looked considerably more impressive than I had thought at first. He was dressed in a dark suit with a flower in the buttonhole. He frowned, fingered the flower, then motioned me to a chair. We disposed of the usual courtesies. He twirled his moustache a trifle impatiently and became businesslike.

"What can I do for you, Signore?"

This, I decided, was mere fencing. Obviously he had understood my message.

"General Vagas was, I believe, good enough to intimate to you, Commendatore, that my company might be of assistance to you."

"And so?"

"And so I should very much like to be given the opportunity of tendering for the machinery you need. I don't think I need enlarge on the reputation of the Spartacus S2 machine. Your government has already displayed its confidence in that connection."

He nodded, but said nothing. It was heavy going, but I went on.

"Naturally, Commendatore, I appreciate that you have a

personal responsibility in seeing that the best material is secured." I placed a slight emphasis on the word "personal." I wanted to get the conversation on a more confidential footing.

"Naturally it must be of the best."

I tried a more direct method of attack.

"I am prepared to offer personal guarantees to you, Commendatore, concerning the quality of the Spartacus machine."

He pulled at his moustaches thoughtfully. Then his eyes met mine for a second. "And when would these guarantees be forthcoming, Signore?"

This was distinctly better.

"On the signing of the contract, Commendatore."

He raised his eyebrows. "Not before?"

"A provisional guarantee might be arranged, Commendatore, as evidence of our confidence in the matter. The figure two was mentioned by General Vagas. If we were perhaps to say one per cent. in cash as a provisional guarantee and the remainder . . . ?"

He held up his hand. "I understand perfectly, Signore. I am agreeable to that course. You may submit your tender. Good morning." He stood up and extended his hand.

"Thank you, Commendatore. Perhaps you would be so good as to arrange for me to have specifications in order that we may submit our estimate."

He looked puzzled. "Specifications, Signore? I do not understand you. They were given to General Vagas for transmission to you. Have you not received them?"

I shook my head. I was beginning to understand.

"No doubt General Vagas will let you have them, Signore."

"I may not be seeing the General. Perhaps your secretary could furnish me with another set, Commendatore."

"Unfortunately," he replied blandly, "there are no more available. I recommend your making an effort to see the General." He sat down again. "And now, Signore, if you will excuse me . . ."

I went. So that was that. Without Vagas' approval I was not to be allowed even to quote.

I returned to my office in a bitter temper. I found that I was again being followed by the tall man who had seen me to the hotel the night before. The sight of Bellinetti sitting with Serafina at a *caffè* near the Via San Giulio when he should have been at his work did nothing to improve the situation. And there was a telephone message for me. One of the machines supplied to a firm in Cremona had broken down. The spare parts would not fit. If I could make it convenient to go to Cremona and advise their engineers concerning repairs and subsequent readjustments they would be very glad. The matter was urgent.

Cursing heartily, I told Umberto to telephone back and say that I would go to Cremona the next day. Then I sat down at my desk. There were mountains of work to be done. If I were to spend the next day at Cremona I should have to work late. I attacked the first mountain.

It was after nine o'clock and my eyes and back were aching when at last I switched off the lights and locked up. The stairs were, as usual, in darkness; but there was a slit of light under the door of the Agenzia Saponi. Zaleshoff was, I felt, the last person I wanted to talk to at the moment. I went past on tip-toe.

In the street I stood for a moment trying to make up my mind where to eat. I had not yet written to Claire. If I had a quick meal somewhere I could, perhaps, write the letter at the Parigi and catch the last post. I looked round for the man who had been following me earlier in the day, but I could not see him. He was probably, I decided, somewhere in the shadows waiting for me to move. I remember that it occurred to me that it must be very dull for him. Then I made up my mind and started to walk in the direction of the station.

It was in a small street off the Via San Giulio and not much more than a hundred yards from the office that it happened.

I was walking fairly quickly, for I was both hungry and thirsty. I had a cigarette in my mouth. It was as I tossed the end away that I noticed the car turning the corner behind me. For a moment its glaring headlights picked me out. My shadow, long, distorted and grotesque, lay along the pavement and a foot or two up the side of a long, dark, steel-shuttered building that was, I think, some sort of warehouse. Then the shadow twisted as the car accelerated. It passed me—a big, black American limousine—still going slowly.

Suddenly, a few yards ahead of me, it swung across the road to the kerb and stopped. As it did so, the doors opened and four men got out and stood across the pavement facing me.

I walked on towards them.

Probably the best thing I could have done would have been to turn round and run; but I did not do so. It had occurred to me that it was rather an odd place for them to have stopped, for there was no doorway for several yards on either side of the car and on the opposite of the road was a long hoarding. But the thought was no more than one of casual curiosity.

It was only when I was a foot or two from them that I realised that something was wrong. They made no effort to give me room to pass. My heart thumped suddenly against my ribs. I hesitated, then made to squeeze past between the shutters and the end man.

He moved over slightly, blocking my path.

I stopped and muttered an "excuse me." Then I saw that the two near the car had moved round to form a semi-circle with myself as the centre. Involuntarily I backed against the shutter.

They were dressed in dark clothes with soft hats pulled down over their foreheads. In the darkness their faces were no more than white shapes.

"*Come vi chiamate?*"

The question came suddenly from one of them. I could not tell which. It was the only thing that was said. But for that they might have been mutes. I said my name and added that I was English.

One of them, the man nearest the car, turned his head and nodded to the others. They moved forward, closing in on me. It was done in complete silence. I looked round wildly. We were alone in the street. Then I lost my head. There was a gap between a pair of them. I dived for it frantically; but, even as I did so, I knew that it was useless. I felt two hands grip the lapels of my overcoat. The next moment I was flung back violently against the shutter. I started forward again to speak. "I . . ." I began. Then a fist hit me in the stomach.

My chin dropped forward. I began to retch. Another blow landed on my mouth, I felt a ring on the man's finger crush the skin against the bone. Then I hit the ground. They began to kick me.

As I fell I had rolled over, in an instinctive effort at self-protection, so that my back was against the shutter. The blow in the stomach had brought my knees up under my chin. Now my hands went to my face. The kicks rained on my arms and legs. Then a heel was driven into my ribs. An excruciating pain shot through my body. As I strove to force air into my lungs I gasped and grunted. A red mist was swimming in front of my eyes. Dimly I was conscious of the shocks of the blows, but they no longer seemed to hurt me. It was as though I were under the partial influence of an anaesthetic.

I do not remember when they stopped. I have a faint recollection of hearing the car start, but the blood was thumping in my head and it was as though my senses were blanketed with cotton-wool. It seemed an age that I lay there, my knees still drawn up, my hands still over my face. Then, gradually, very gradually, I began to get my breath back and with it came the pain, sickening waves of it that made me want to cry out.

At last I got slowly to my feet and stood for a time motionless, leaning against the shutter. My flesh felt liquid. I was conscious only of my bones and my joints, of the skeleton which was my body's structure. I could feel every inch of it. I knew that I could not stand there indefinitely; and yet I had not the courage to move. In the distance I heard the sound of a train chuffing slowly out of the station. Then the chuffing ceased and there was the faint *clink-clink* of trucks being shunted.

For some reason, the sound seemed to rouse me. I must do something. The silent, deserted street was suddenly terrifying. I decided to get back to my office. There I could rest for a bit and it was near.

My legs had begun to tremble violently and it was all I could do to keep my feet, but I began to make my way back. When I reached the entrance to the office building I was staggering, but I managed to get my key out and unlock the door before I finally fell down. I lay there for a minute or two trying to keep my senses. After a bit, however, I got a hold on the rail and began to drag myself up the stairs.

By the time I had got to the second floor I was nearly done. My head was aching violently and I wanted badly to be sick. I made an effort and began to climb again. Then I saw the light under Zaleshoff's door and remembered that Zaleshoff had some brandy.

I crawled up the last few stairs and got to the door. I steadied myself against the door-post. I could hear Zaleshoff talking to somebody. I knocked once. Then, as my head began to swim, I closed my eyes. It seemed hours before I opened them again, but they couldn't have been shut for more than a few seconds for, when I did open them, there was Zaleshoff standing holding the door open and staring at me blankly.

"What, for Pete's sake, is the matter?"

"If you don't mind," I said carefully, "I should like a drink of your brandy." But almost before I had finished the sentence I felt my knees sagging. The next moment I sprawled forward at his feet.

The girl, Tamara, was there with him. Between them they got me to a chair. The cotton-wool was in my ears again but I could hear their voices.

"Is he drunk?" This from the girl.

"No—beaten up. Go and get the cognac."

She got the brandy. I felt it burning its way down my

throat and into my stomach. With my eyes still closed, I grinned at him. "Sorry to be such a nuisance."

"Shut your trap and drink some more of this. You can talk in a minute." I felt him examining my legs. "Tamara, go and get some hot water from the *portinaia*. Then get a taxi and get some tincture of arnica from a chemist."

She went. I drank some more brandy and my head began to clear. I opened my eyes. Zaleshoff was frowning at me.

"How many were there of them?"

"Four."

"Could you recognise them?"

"No." I told him what had happened.

He looked puzzled. "I don't understand it." Suddenly he leaned forward, took a piece of paper from the side pocket of my overcoat and held it up to me.

"Is this yours? It was sticking out of your pocket."

"What is it?"

He opened it. It was a sheet about ten inches by eight inches. He glanced at it, then held it up for me to see. Scrawled across it in Italian was a single sentence:

NEXT TIME YOU WILL BE HURT

I stared at it, and as I stared I could feel my brain getting colder and colder and a slow sick rage rising in my chest.

"Have you seen Vagas to-day?" demanded Zaleshoff.

"He was waiting to see me at my hotel when I got back last night."

"Were you followed?"

"Yes."

"Vagas must have been seen leaving. They're thinking . . ." He broke off. "Why did he come?"

"To increase his offer."

He struck the palm of his hand with his fist. "They must be pressing him from Berlin. If only . . ."

"If only what?"

"Never mind. You've had enough for one night. Remember what I told you about the Ovra?"

"Yes, I remember." But I wasn't listening to what he was saying. I was busy with my own thoughts. I was making a decision.

The girl came in with the hot water. Between them they undressed me and he began to bathe the abrasions on my legs and arms. The process was painful. When it was finished he stuck a cigarette between my thickening lips and lighted it for me.

"Are you going to the police about this?"

"It would be rather a waste of time, wouldn't it?"

"What about your Consul?"

"He can't do more than badger the authorities, and as I've no description of the men to give, I can't reasonably expect him to do anything."

"I guess not." Behind the smoke of his own cigarette he surveyed me speculatively. "What *are* you going to do?"

My lips tightened. "I'll show you. Give me the telephone, will you?"

He glanced at me quickly but said nothing. He put the telephone at my elbow.

"Now give me Vagas' number."

"Nord 45-65." He might have been telling me the time. I dialled the number. I had just got through to Vagas when Tamara returned.

"This is Marlow here, General . . . yes, very well. I saw the Commendatore this morning . . . charming. What I telephoned you about was to tell you that I have reconsidered the suggestion you made to me the other night . . . yes . . . yes, I think so. Naturally these things have to be carefully considered . . . quite. Now I suggest that this business would be handled more discreetly through the poste restante . . ."

When at last I put the telephone down they were both staring at me as though I had gone mad; as, indeed, I had.

"You'd better understand here and now, Zaleshoff," I said grimly, "that I'm not taking any money from you over this business. I'm doing it to satisfy my own private sense of the fitness of things. And now, if you've quite finished staring, I'd like someone to get busy with that tincture of arnica. Then, if your sister doesn't mind, I'd like something to eat."

"Yes, surely!" For the second time, I saw Zaleshoff disconcerted. Then, as he began to dab the arnica on my legs, he chuckled.

"Tamara."

"Yes, Andreas."

"Wasn't Spartacus the slave who rebelled?"

Chapter X

CORRISPONDENZA

FROM "N. Marinetti" to "J. L. Venezetti," Poste Restante, Wagon-Lits-Cook, Milano.

MILANO,

Dear Sir, *April 9.*
Further to our telephone conversation of yesterday, I enclose details of the past three months' transactions and trust that this meets with your approval.

Yours faithfully,
N. Marinetti.

From "J. L. Venezetti" to "N. Marinetti," Poste Restante, American Express, Milano.

MILANO,
April 11.

Dear Sir,
Thank you for your letter and enclosure. I had expected only the details for the current month. The remaining material is, however, of value. I therefore enclose five thousand-lire notes instead of three as arranged in consideration of the extra material supplied. I also enclose the specifications and form of tender handed to me by Commendatore B. and trust that this business will go well. I look forward to your further communications.

Yours faithfully,
J. L. Venezetti.

From "N. Marinetti" to "J. L. Venezetti," Poste Restante, Wagon-Lits-Cook, Milano.

MILANO,
April 12.

Dear Sir,
Your letter and enclosures safely received. I shall be writing to you again in three weeks' time. With thanks.

Yours faithfully,
N. Marinetti.

From myself to Claire.

HOTEL PARIGI,
April 11.

Darling,
I'm afraid that I'm turning out a very bad correspondent, after all. It's at least a week since I wrote to you, and to make it worse I had your letter this morning. It made me feel very guilty. But the fact is, my sweet, that I had a bit of an accident a day or so ago. Nothing serious. A few bruises only. But I had to spend a day in bed; and with the way things are at the office that has meant that I've had the devil's

own job catching up with the work that has accumulated. I've also had to waste to-day going to Cremona to see some people about a complaint—an additional complication. All of which is by way of being not only an apologia, but also a delicate preamble to what I really have to say.

Do you remember, darling, that when we discussed my taking this job originally, we decided that it should be a sort of stop-gap, something to tide over an awkward period? It was, we told each other, only for a little while, a few months at most, just until things got better in England.

Although it's only a few weeks back that we said it all, it seems like years ago to me; and, just as if it were, indeed, years ago, I can look at the whole thing without too much prejudice. I can't help wondering, my sweet, just how much we thought we were deceiving ourselves. Although neither of us said as much, I fancy that we were both afraid of facing the simple truth that, barring miracles, there was not a ghost of a chance of my being able to come home in anything like the near future—without going back to the point at which I started when Barnton Heath closed down on me.

So what? Simply this, darling. I have decided to come and take my chance again. I fancy that it was a little unwise of me to take on this job at all; but that is beside the point. You will probably be thinking that this decision is merely the result of a natural home-sickness and love-sickness plus the usual misery of a brand-new job. I wish it were; but I'm afraid it isn't. I don't think I'm a particularly chicken-hearted sort of person and I've had enough experience to know that the depression that is liable to develop over a new job in strange surroundings and away from old friends is transitory. But this, as I say, is different. It may be that I'm not cut out to be a business man, that I should have stayed in works where I belong; but even if that is true (and I think it is) it doesn't account for everything. If I were the smartest business man in Europe, I fancy that I should still be making the same decision.

You must be wondering what on earth all this rambling is about, why, after the optimistic note of my second letter (I'd just sacked Serafina and was feeling very competent), I've changed my tune so suddenly. I'll try to be a little more explicit, darling, but you'll have to take my word for a lot. The truth is that there are things about this job which I didn't know of when I took it, things that Pelcher and Fitch didn't and still don't know, things that, in the few days that I have been here, have landed me in about as absurd a position as you could imagine. I don't think that I have acted with any less gumption or with any more spirit than any other man in my place would have acted. Nevertheless, the situation is intolerable. I have made my decision in cold blood, and after weighing everything very carefully, I have no conscience about Spartacus. I am in the process of securing a contract for them which will more than repay them for any inconvenience I may cause them.

I have decided to send in my resignation at the end of next month. Why wait? Well, there are some things I have to attend to here which I anticipate will take me some few weeks to dispose of. To be as frank as I dare, my love, I have committed myself to doing something rather foolish, something that, in the ordinary way, I should not have dreamed of doing; but something that in this madhouse we call Europe seems to contain for me at the moment the elements of a crude poetic justice. I must finish what I have begun. Curiously enough, I think your father would sympathise. Do you remember what he was saying that night, so long ago, when we ate at a Chinese restaurant, saw a film afterwards, and then went home? He was waiting for us with a whisky decanter and all the discretion in the world.

I feel sure that all this mystery will irritate you exceedingly. Believe me, I don't want to be mysterious. If you were here, I should dearly love to tell you all about it. To have to write this incoherent balderdash pleases me not at all. But I knew that you would be making arrangements to spend your holiday here and thought I had better break the news now. You don't know, dear, how much I am looking forward to being with you again. All my love, sweet, and don't be too cross with me.

Nicky.

I'm glad to hear that the work is going so well. You professional people don't know how well off you are. Or do you?

From myself to Alfred Pelcher, Esq.

Via San Giulio, 14, Milano,
April 16.

Dear Mr. Pelcher,
    Thank you very much indeed for your letter on the subject of Bellinetti. I quite understand the circumstances and have endeavoured to reorganise the work of the office to suit them.

I have delayed replying to your letter until now as I have been hoping to have something of special interest to report to you. Events have now made that possible, and I am very pleased to be able to tell you that I have secured, in direct competition with our German rivals, an order from the Ordnance Department here for thirty-eight S2 machines of the standard type with minor modifications.

The price at which the order has been secured is 843,000 lire, and although two per cent. of that amount will be offset by an allocation from the special appropriation, the price per machine will still, I think you will find, be higher than any we have been able to obtain previously. Officially, this fact will be accounted for by the modifications. Actually, these modifications are purely nominal in character. Delivery is required within six months.

I am, however, sending full details through to Mr. Fitch in the ordinary way. I thought I would take this opportunity of giving you the news.

Yours sincerely,
Nicholas Marlow.

From Claire to myself.

LONDON,
April 14.

Nicky darling,

I read your letter in the bus this morning and I'm dashing off this reply in the hospital's time, so it's going to be shorter than I should like it to be.

Let me say at once, my dear, that never did it occur to me that this Spartacus job was anything more than a postponement of the evil day. But I thought, and still do think, that you were wise to take it. I think that the Barnton Heath mess was a bigger shock to you than you realised yourself. You both under- and over-estimated yourself and started off on the wrong foot to retrieve the situation. I fancy that I may have had something to do with that. I was too anxious to keep your spirits up. You should have begun by worrying yourself sick and ended by not caring a damn. In fact, you began by worrying a little and ended by worrying far too much. Father uttered a mild truth on the subject. "Your young man," he said. That's the way he always refers to you. "Your young man ought to get a Government job. He's a technician pure and simple and out of his element in an acquisitive society." It makes you sound a little flimsy, my pet, but it's not so wide of the mark. Incidentally, it's one of the reasons why I approve of you.

But that has very little to do with your letter. To be honest with you, darling, I'm a little worried. Not, I hasten to say, by your decision about Spartacus. I have enormous faith in

*your judgment and good sense. If you feel that you would be
better out of Spartacus, then get out of it with all speed. But
as for the rest of it; I'm not going to pretend that I even
begin to understand what you're driving at. Mysterious is a
mild word for it. I can quite easily remember what father
talked about when we arrived home after we had agreed to
make honest folk of one another. Easily, because your re-
plies to the poor dear were so stupid that he asked me at
breakfast next morning whether we proposed to get married
before or after you had been psychoanalysed. I can't, I'm
afraid, see what possible connection there could be between
the Rome-Berlin axis and machine tools, but I'm quite prepared to make allowances for a little mystery. I seem to
remember doing a little research for you into the surface
tension of gum. You probably have that in mind.*

*No! what worries me, Nicky, is what you decided to omit
from your letter. With you, my love, I never attempt to read
between the lines. But I do sometimes read under the
lines. You have a habit of crossing out words you don't like
and writing over them the words you do like. Your crossing
out is very inefficient on the whole and usually, by holding
the paper up to the light, I can read the rejected words. So
that when I read you have committed yourself to doing something "foolish" and find that the word has been put in to
replace a scratched out "dangerous," you can understand how
I feel.*

*It is true that "dangerous" might have been the wrong
word, but it couldn't have been so hopelessly wide of the
mark or you wouldn't have put it down at all. Besides, taken
in conjunction with the rest of your letter (what, by the way,
was that "bit of an accident" you were so airy about?)
it seems to me that it may very well have been the right word,
but that you were anxious not to alarm me.*

*I don't want to be silly and hysterical about it, but what-
ever it is you're doing, Nicky, do take care. Not that I'm such
a fool as to think you won't take care. It seems to me that
feminine exhortations of that sort must always be rather irritating. But do take care. And, since you have decided to
leave, come back to me as quickly as possible. Must you wait
for so long before resigning? I suppose you'll have to give a
month's notice, and that means that you won't be home until
the end of June. Quite apart from the fact that it's very
lonely here without you, I am consumed with curiosity.
Write to me again very soon.*

My love to you, darling, and bless you.

Claire.

I had an idea that most poetic justice was pretty crude.

From Alfred Pelcher, Esq., to myself.

WOLVERHAMPTON,
April 19.

Dear Mr. Marlow,
Congratulations! It's a fine piece of news and, as you say, the price is quite the best we have been able to get so far. Mr. Fitch, who asks me to add his felicitations to mine, tells me that, according to the specifications you have forwarded to him, the total cost of modifications will add about thirty shillings to the works cost of each machine. Your own personal estimate probably told you that. It is, I must say, a most "ingenious" arrangement.
Mr. Fitch will be writing to you concerning the way in which the financial details are to be handled and other matters, but I thought that I should like to send you this personal word of congratulations. It is a splendid start. Now we must see if we cannot "repeat the dose." What do you say?
Yours sincerely,
Alfred Pelcher.

From Maggiore Generale J. L. Vagas to myself.

CORSO DI PORTA NUOVA,
MILANO,
April 20.

My dear Mr. Marlow,
I am anxious to have a chat with you on a matter of some importance. I should be pleased if you could spare time to dine with me at my house to-morrow. Shall we say at eight o'clock? Perhaps you would be good enough to telephone me if you are unable to come.
With kindest regards,
Yours sincerely,
J. L. Vagas.

From myself to Maggiore Generale J. L. Vagas. By hand.

HOTEL PARIGI,
MILANO,
April 21.

My dear General,
I am afraid that I cannot dine with you to-morrow.

May I remind you of our conversation on the subject of future communications between us?

Yours very truly,
Nicholas Marlow.

From "J. L. Venezetti" to "N. Marinetti," Poste Restante, American Express, Milano.

MILANO,
April 21.

Dear Sir,

I should not have requested an interview unless the matter were of vital importance. It is imperative that I see you at once. Will you please let me know by return of post when and where I can meet you. I leave the time and the place to your selection.

Yours faithfully,
J. L. Venezetti.

From "N. Marinetti" to "J. L. Venezetti," Poste Restante, Wagon-Lits-Cook, Milano.

MILANO,
April 22.

Dear Sir,

I shall be driving a dark-blue Fiat limousine at about 35 km. per hour along the Milan-Varese autostrada at about 10.45 on Sunday night. I shall stop only for a car drawn up at the side of the road facing Varese and about 25 km. from Milan and showing two rear lights close together.

Yours faithfully,
N. Marinetti.

Chapter XI

BLOOD AND THUNDER

IT WAS Zaleshoff who had made the arrangements for the meeting between Vagas and myself. I had received his proposals with some amusement.

"Blood and thunder," I had commented.

He had frowned. "I don't know about the thunder, but if the Ovra gets on to the fact that you're meeting Vagas, it'll be your blood all right."

"Where's the Fiat coming from?"

"I'll fix that."

"But why on Sunday?"

"Because there'll be a procession here on Sunday afternoon."

"What's that got to do with it?"

"You've been under surveillance practically ever since you came here and since that beating up they gave you, you've had two of the guys on your tail. Did you know that?"

"Yes, I've seen them. They hang about opposite the office all day."

"Before you can meet Vagas you'll have to get rid of them. This procession'll make it easy."

"How?"

"You'll see. You write that letter."

I had written it.

Waiting to be blackmailed is an odd experience. I could not help wondering how Vagas would set about it. What line would he take? He had, hitherto, been all amiability. There was even a sort of oily charm about him. Would he shed his amiability or would the charm intensify, a velvet glove to enclose the mailed fist? I amused myself by speculating.

There was about those days I spent in Milan a curious air of the fantastic. That I had regretted the mood of bitter resentment that had led me into agreeing to carry out Zaleshoff's plan, goes without saying. Yet, such is the mind's ability to adapt itself to an idea, the thought that I might back out of the whole business occurred to me only as a sort of protest, an unexecutable threat. And I had decided to resign from Spartacus. That was the important thing. It was, perhaps, that decision more than anything else that determined my attitude. I was shortly to leave Milan. The fact lent a disarming air of impermanence to the situation. In two months or so I should be home and then I really could get down to the business of getting a good job. What happened between now and then seemed of secondary importance. I no longer identified myself with Spartacus. As I had told Claire, I had no conscience about the company. I had, with Vagas' assistance, secured a valuable order for them. That was that. All I had to do until the time came for me to leave was to see that their interests were adequately protected. If the opportunity presented itself I would secure still more business for them. That was all. In point of fact, it was no less than I should have done if I had been remaining with them. But my attitude was different, it was qualified. I had a sense of being independent, of being to some extent on holiday. This business of Zaleshoff's was, I felt, almost in the nature of a game. That I did not know the rules of it was, no doubt, just as well for my peace of mind.

Since the night I had spent in his office, I had seen Zaleshoff practically every day. At first his mood had been one of lip-smacking anticipation. Everything, he assured me repeatedly, was prepared. It was only a question of waiting for Vagas to begin to turn the screw. Then, as the month wore on without any sign of life from Vagas, his jubilation gave way to gloomy forebodings. He became irritable. Several times I was tempted to abandon the whole thing and twice threatened to do so. On both occasions he offered exasperated apologies. My admiration for his sister's forbearance increased daily. Yet, to a certain extent, I could understand his anxiety.

"I'm beginning to think," he declared gloomily on one occasion, "that it was a mistake to cook those Spartacus figures."

"You know darn well I wouldn't have given him the correct ones."

"Very likely. But he's probably gone to the trouble to check the first lot and found that they're phoneys. He probably thinks you put one over on him to get that Ordnance Department contract and has written you off as a bad investment."

"How could he check them?"

"How should I know? But it's the only thing that can have happened. How else can you explain this silence? He's got all the stuff he wants to blackmail you with. Why doesn't he get on with it?"

"Perhaps he's waiting until I send in this month's figures, sort of lulling me into a sense of false security."

"Maybe. I hope you're right. This waiting is getting on my nerves."

That much was obvious. The reason for it puzzled me. I myself was conscious of a sense of anti-climax, almost of disappointment; but I was intrigued by his attitude. Why should the situation get on his nerves to so absurd an extent? For me it was no more than a somewhat sinister game. For him it looked like a matter of life and death importance. A great many of the things which Vagas had told me were, no doubt, lies. But, in one thing, at least, he had, I felt, told me something approaching the truth.

Over our coffee one evening I worked round to the subject. It was fairly easy to do. His despair had been more than usually extravagant. I awaited an opening. Then:

"I admit that it's all very irritating. But, for the life of me, Zaleshoff, I cannot see why you should take it so much to heart."

"No?"

"No."

"You don't think that the peace of Europe is something that a guy can get anxious about?" His tone was almost offensively sarcastic.

"Oh yes. The peace of Europe, to be sure! But if we could get down to Mother Earth for a minute. . . ."

"Mother Earth!" His voice rose angrily. "Mother Earth! Say, listen, Marlow. It pains me to have to tell you this because, dumb cluck that you are, it would be just as well if you didn't know it: but you, Heaven protect us, happen to be of some importance at the moment. Say, have you ever had a suitcase to unlock and a bunch of odd keys in your hand? There's just one key that fits. None of the others matters a curse. They're keys but they're not *the* key. Well, it's like that now. And you're *the* key."

I was a little irritated by his manner. "What about leaving out the metaphors and trying plain English?"

"Sure! In plain English, the Germans are doing their damnedest to drive a wedge in the Anglo-Italian Mediterranean accord. They're out to preserve the Axis. Without it they can't make another move in Eastern Europe. And they've got to make that move. You know what old man Aristotle said. The tyrant who impoverishes the citizens is obliged to make war in order to keep his subjects occupied and impose on them permanent need of a chief. Italy's sitting pretty now. She can play off Germany against France and England. But that's only because she's got a stake in both camps. The Axis is just as vital to her as it is to Germany. If once she gets into a position where she has to become a dependency of the City of London, she's done. They'll finance her heavy industries, choke her with credits until the lira is so sick it can't stand. Then they'll tie a ribbon round Mussolini and give him to the Germans as a Christmas present. Italy's strength in the south is the Axis in the north. It's only mutual distrust that is going to counteract the identity of interests between Germany and Italy. For some crack-brained reason you, Marlow, are in a position to turn their suspicions into downright distrust. And you ask me why I'm anxious!"

"And I still do ask you why *you* are anxious."

He knitted his brow, a man driven to exasperation but restraining himself with an effort. "Do I have to go over all that again?"

"I think," put in the girl, "that what Mr. Marlow is getting at is what the heck it's got to do with you."

He drew a deep breath. "I'm an American citizen," he began impressively, "and . . ."

"I know," I put in furiously; "you're an American citizen and you think that us men of goodwill ought to get together and co-operate to save the peace of Europe. I know. I've heard it all before. But it still doesn't answer my question. Vagas warned me against you. You knew that he might, didn't you? And you thought you'd take the sting out of that warning by letting me see that you'd expected it. But what you don't know is that he told me that you and your sister were Soviet Government agents. What have you got to say to that?"

He looked at me. His jaw dropped. Then he looked at the girl. Her expression was utterly non-committal. He looked back at me again. I nearly permitted myself a grin of triumph. Fortunately for my dignity I did not do so for, suddenly, he began to roar with laughter and slap his knee. "Soviet agents!" he bellowed hysterically; "that's too good! Oh my!"

I waited stolidly until he had finished. Then:

"You still," I said dryly, "haven't answered my question."

He became suddenly serious. "One moment, Marlow. Before you jump to any rash conclusions, think. What would I, a respectable American, want with . . ."

Disgustedly, I waved him into silence. "All right, all right! let it go."

"And . . ."

"Let it go. But"—I wagged a finger at them—"don't blame me if I draw my own conclusions, will you?"

"Why should we blame you, Mr. Marlow?" said the girl pleasantly.

For some reason the question embarrassed me. I let the subject drop. Privately, however, I registered a decision to bring it up again: but the opportunity of doing so did not present itself immediately. Three days later, to Zaleshoff's noisily expressed delight, I received Vagas' letter.

At half-past two on the Sunday afternoon, I left the Hotel Parigi, followed, as usual, by two drab-looking men, and met Zaleshoff at a *caffè* near the Castello. Tamara was not with him. He ordered a coffee for me and looked at his watch.

"We've got about ten minutes to go before we need start."

"Start what?"

"To lose those two shadows of yours."

"But I'm not meeting Vagas until nearly eleven to-night."

"Maybe not, but we start the good work this afternoon."

"Look here, Zaleshoff," I protested irritably, "isn't it about time you told me what this is all about?"

"I was just going to. Listen. You've got to get rid of those two guys somehow, and they're not going to fall for anything elementary like walking into an hotel with two exits. I've watched them on the job. They know their stuff. Besides, if you try to put one over on them they'll know you're up to something, and that'd be nearly as bad as their knowing what it is you're up to. We don't want that. You've got to give them the slip by accident—at least so that it looks like an accident. That's where the procession comes in."

"What procession?"

"Fascist Youth Movements—the *Balilla* and *Avanguardisti* —military boy scouts. They're marching up from the Centrale station, about ten thousand of them, with bands and a detachment of Blackshirts. They're all coming in from Cremona, Brescia, Verona and a few more places by special trains. Then they're going to march to the Piazza Duomo to listen to one of the Fascist bosses telling them what a fine thing war is and be reviewed. Then they're going to sing the *Giovinezza* and march back again. It's when they're marching back that you do the trick."

"What trick? Don't tell me that I've got to dress up as an Italian Boy Scout and fall in with the procession, because I won't do it."

"This is serious."

"Sorry."

He leaned forward solemnly. "Have you ever wanted to cross a road when a big procession was going by?"

"Yes."

"Did you get across?"

"No."

"Exactly! Well, now then, listen."

For five minutes he talked steadily. When he had finished I looked at him doubtfully.

"It might work," I admitted.

"It will work. It's just a question of good timing."

"Supposing they won't let me through?"

"With Tamara doing her stuff, they will."

"All right, I'll try it."

"Good. Finish your coffee and let's go. Are those two guys in the black velour Homburgs the ones?"

"They are."

"Then we'll all go and have a nice look at the procession."

It was a fine afternoon. The air was cold but the sky was clear and blue and the sun cast strong black shadows on the dusty roadways. The pavements were crowded. It seemed as if every family in Milan were out. The men and women wore black, the small girls white, the boys and youths wore *Balilla* and *Avanguardisti* uniforms. Men selling flags and favours with portraits of Mussolini in the centre were doing a roaring trade. Corsetted young air-force men strutted about in threes and fours eyeing groups of giggling factory girls. Empty wall spaces had been decorated with stencil daubs depicting Mussolini's head in semi-silhouette. The *caffès* near the route of the procession were packed with weary-looking men and women, the parents and relations of the participants in the procession, who had arrived, so Zaleshoff informed me, by special trains in the early hours of the morning. Many of the women carried squalling babies.

With some difficulty we established ourselves on the steps of an apartment house in the Corso Vittorio Emanuele. The pavement in front of us was a solid mass of spectators. Beyond them, lining the route at intervals of three yards, stood armed Blackshirt militiamen, facing alternately inwards and outwards. Jammed against the wall a few yards away were the two plain-clothes detectives, pale, impassive middle-aged men, obviously of the regular police.

At last there was a faint burst of cheering in the distance. The noise of the crowd, except for a baby crying on the opposite side of the road, subsided into an expectant murmuring. Ten minutes later, amidst a roar of hand-clapping, *vivas* and cheering, and to the accompaniment of a dazzling display of flag-waving, the procession, led by a big military band and a drum-major with huge, curling moustaches, came into view. The *Avanguardisti* came first, taking themselves very seriously. They carried dummy rifles, as did the *Balilla*, the younger boys, who followed them. The ranks were flanked by Blackshirt standard bearers. There were also detachments of Sons of the Wolf, the Italian equivalent of Wolf Cubs, and of the two girls' organisations, the *Piccole Italiane* and the *Giovani Italiane*. There were many bands. It was all very impressive and took over forty minutes to march into the square.

As the tail end of the procession passed, the crowd swarmed past the militiamen and across the road and surged forward towards the square.

"Come on," muttered Zaleshoff.

We plunged into the crowd and were carried by it towards the square. Over my shoulder, I saw the detectives elbowing their way after me.

When we reached the street that runs towards the Scala we extricated ourselves from the crowd and walked slowly towards the Via Margheritta. The plain-clothes men allowed the distance between us to increase and followed, looking in shop windows as they went along and making pantomime gestures of relief at escaping from the crowd.

Zaleshoff grinned. "They must think you're pretty dumb."

"Why?"

"They think you still don't know you're being followed."

"I've taken care not to let them think otherwise. Besides, it's a different couple every day. I've got used to it."

"Well, it makes it all the easier for us. You're clear now as to what you've got to do?"

"Perfectly."

We had reached the end of the street. The Via Margheritta, which was part of the return route of the procession, was lined with Blackshirts in preparation for the crowds that would presently begin to stream away from the Piazza. Already, the edges of the pavements were lined with people, mostly women and children, prepared to sacrifice the sight of the ceremony in the square to secure the best possible view of the returning procession.

Zaleshoff made as if to turn in the direction of the Via Alessandro Manzoni, away from the square. I stopped and indicated the waiting people. For a moment or two we put up a show of arguing, then Zaleshoff glanced at his watch, shook hands with me and walked away towards the Scala. I appeared to hesitate, then make up my mind. There was a space on the kerb behind a Blackshirt. I took up my position there and settled down to wait. Out of the corner of my eye I was able to see that the plain-clothes men had established themselves against a newspaper kiosk some yards away. So far, things were going according to plan. The impression we had created was perfectly natural. Zaleshoff obviously had an appointment to keep. I was intent on seeing the procession again. The detectives, I was glad to see, were looking abjectly bored.

The Piazza Duomo was not more than a hundred yards from where I stood. Fifty yards away a cordon of police with fur-edged, three-cornered hats and swords had been drawn across the entrance. Beyond them was the crowd that would presently be split into two parts, one of which would be forced along the pavement behind me. From the square came the sound of sentences being bellowed from loudspeakers, sentences punctuated with cheering, cheering that, from where I stood, was like the harsh roar of the sea receding over shingle.

The Balila and the Avanguardisti of to-day will be the natural heirs of Fascismo. Cheers. *Italy deserves to be the biggest and strongest nation in the world.* Louder cheers. *Italy will become the biggest and strongest nation in the world—Il Duce has willed it.* A roar. *Youthful conscripts of the Fascist revolution receive the rifle as the youth of ancient Rome received the toga of virility—it is one of the most beautiful celebrations of the party and most significant*

—war is, for a true son of Fascismo, the consummation of his love for his country. Was it my fancy or was the applause that greeted this a shade less vociferous? *Youth be strong!*

The loudspeakers bellowed on. At last it was over. The massed bands struck up the *Giovinezza*. The huge crowd sang it.

> *Youth, youth, thou lovely thing,*
> *Time of springtime's blossoming,*
> *Fascismo bears the promise*
> *Of Liberty to the People.*

The cordon of police was beginning to push forward into the crowd to clear the road for the procession. It was nearly time! I looked across the road. According to plan, Tamara should have been in her place by now. It was possible that she had been hemmed in by the crowd somewhere. I was beginning to get anxious when I saw her.

The crowd on the opposite pavement had already begun to thicken. Tamara was jammed between a large fat man clutching a very small flag and a middle-aged woman in mourning. I saw that she had seen me, for she was very carefully looking in the direction of the square. My heart beating a little more quickly than usual, I waited.

The police had succeeded in splitting the crowd and I could now see into the square to where the leading band was getting into position for the march to the station. I looked over my shoulder. The crowd behind me was now ten deep. My two shadowers were well hemmed in against the kiosk. One of them cast a casual glance in my direction. I managed to avoid his eye just in time and turned my attention to the militiaman behind whom I was standing. As far as I could make out, he was about twenty-one years of age, but I could not see enough of his face to enable me to form any opinion as to his kindness of heart. I would have to chance that.

Eventually the band struck up and began to move forward slowly. Now was the time, I began to rehearse feverishly the one simple sentence I had to say. The crowd began to cheer. The first detachment of *Avanguardisti* wheeled out and formed up behind the band. The drum-major threw out his chest, his legs stiffened into the Roman goose-step, he tossed his baton into the air, caught it neatly and twirled it. The band stepped out.

They were now not more than fifty yards away. Thirty yards. I waited frantically for Tamara's signal. But it did not come. Then I remembered my part and began to wave excitedly to her. Twenty-five yards. The applause of the crowd was swelling up, sweeping along the street like a tide over sand-flats. I was nearly sick with apprehension. Another second and it would be too late; Zaleshoff's fine plan would have failed. He would have to think of something else. The noise of the band and the cheering became deafening. Then I saw her waving to me. It was the signal.

I started forward into the roadway and gripped the militia-man's arm. He was getting ready to come to attention and half-turned in an effort to shake me off. I hung on.

"My wife, Signore!" I shouted in his ear. "We were sep-arated in the crowd and she is opposite—can I get across?"

As I said it, I released his arm and started forward. I heard him shout something after me but what it was I do not know. On top of his anxiety to come to attention at the right mo-ment, my question had disconcerted him enough to prevent his making an effort to stop me. Now it was too late. I was half-way across the road.

It could not have taken me more than eight seconds or so to cross. It seemed like eight minutes. I felt, and probably was for that short space of time, the most conspicuous object in Milan.

In the middle I stumbled and for one ghastly instant I saw the procession advancing head-on towards me. Then the faces and the fluttering flags on the opposite kerb came nearer and I saw Tamara again flapping her handkerchief at me. The militiaman in front of her frowned at me, but he was now standing stiffly at attention and made no movement. The fat man waved his flag in my face. The woman in mourning mouthed angrily at me but the noise drowned what she said. Then the girl caught my arm and started to draw me after her through the crowd. The fat man, divining that the move-ment would give him more room, made way. A moment or two later we were behind the crowd. I drew a deep breath.

"Phew! Thank Heavens that's over!"

She was choking with laughter.

"What is it?" I demanded irritably.

"Their faces! You didn't see their faces!"

"Whose faces?"

"Your two shadowers. They tried to push through the crowd after you. The crowd thought they were trying to get to the front to see the procession better and got mad. Someone knocked one of their hats off. It was lovely."

"I thought you were never going to signal."

"I know you did. But I had to leave it to the last moment." She indicated a side turning. "We go down here."

Two streets away, in the Via Oriani, we came upon a large

Fiat limousine standing with its engine running. Inside it was Zaleshoff. As we came up, he got out.

"All right?" he asked the girl.

"All right. Couldn't be better. They won't be able to get to this side for another three-quarters of an hour at least."

"Good." He nodded to me. "Nice work. Hop in."

I got in the back and he followed me. The girl got into the driving-seat.

Reaction had set in. For some reason I had begun to shake from head to foot.

Zaleshoff offered me a cigarette. I took it.

"Well," I said acidly, "what do we do from now until half-past ten to-night? Hide?"

He lit his own cigarette and stretched himself luxuriously on the cushions. "Now," he said comfortably, "we're going to enjoy ourselves. Step on it, Tamara."

We drove out along the *autostrada* to Como, went for a trip on a lake steamer and had dinner at a restaurant overlooking the lake. I enjoyed myself enormously. The sun had only just gone down by the time we had finished our dinner and for a time we sat out on the terrace drinking our coffee and smoking.

The stars were almost dazzlingly bright. At one end of the terrace there was a clump of cypresses looking like thick black fingers against the blue-black sky. There was a smell of pine resin in the air. I had forgotten about my companions and was thinking of Claire, wishing that she had been there, when Zaleshoff spoke.

"What are you going to do when you get back to England?"

I came out of my trance and looked towards him. I could see his shadow and that of the girl and two cigarette tips glowing.

"How did you know I was going back to England?"

I sensed rather than saw his shrug. "I guessed from your manner. There's been an atmosphere of suspended animation about it." He paused. "This business has kind of taken the heart out of the Spartacus job, hasn't it?"

"This business and other things." I felt suddenly that I wanted to talk to someone about it; but all I did was to ask a question. "Do you know a man named Commendatore Bernabò?"

"The guy you bribed to get that machinery order?"

I jumped. That was something about which I had *not* gone into details with Zaleshoff.

"Yes, that's the man. But I didn't tell you *that* either."

"These things get around. Bribery's an old Italian custom."

"There are a lot of old Italian customs I don't like."

He chuckled. "For a business man, you're a bit fussy, aren't you?"

"I'm not a business man. I'm an engineer."

"Ah yes. I was forgetting. My apologies."

"Besides, I still have a bruise or two on my body." I hesitated. "I suppose I shall have to get another job."

"Making shells instead of selling the machinery for making them?"

"There *are* other things for an engineer to make."

"Sure!" He paused again. "I thought you told me that you only took the job because you couldn't get anything better."

"I read in a trade paper yesterday that there's a shortage of skilled engineers at the moment."

I heard him blow smoke out of his mouth. "Yes, I read that article too."

"*You* read it?"

"I read a lot of things. That article was, if I remember, based on the statement made by the managing director of an armament firm, wasn't it?"

To my annoyance, I felt myself blushing. I was glad that it was dark.

"What of it?" I said indifferently. "Someone's got to do the job."

He laughed, but without good humour. "The stock reply according to the gospel of King Profit. Industry has no other end or purpose than the satisfaction of the business man engaged in it. Demand is sacred. It may be a demand for high explosives to slaughter civilians with or one for chemical fertilisers, it may be for shells or it may be for saucepans, it may be for jute machinery for an Indian sweat-shop or it may be for prams, it's all one. There's no difference. Your business man has no other responsibility but to make profits for himself and his shareholders."

"All that's nothing to do with me."

"Of course it isn't," he rejoined sarcastically, "you're only the guy that makes it possible. But you also may be the guy that gets squashed to a paste when those shells and high explosives start going off—you and your wife and kids."

"I haven't got a wife and kids," I said sullenly.

"So what?"

"Damn it, Zaleshoff, I've got to eat. If there's a shortage of skilled engineers and I'm a skilled engineer, what do you expect me to do? Get up on a soap box?"

"In a year's time, my dear Marlow, the same trade paper will be telling you that there are too many skilled engineers.

Too many or too few—too much or too little—empty stomachs or overfed ones—the old, old story. When are you English going to do something about it?"

"Are you speaking as an American or a Russian?"

"What difference does it make? Isn't it common-sense to replace an old, bad system with a better one?"

"You mean Socialism?"

I must have said it derisively for he laughed and did not answer.

"The moon's rising," said Tamara suddenly. I looked. A curved sliver of yellow light was visible above the trees.

"Picture postcard," commented Zaleshoff; "but good picture postcard." He got up. "It's time we went."

We paid the bill and in silence began to walk back to where we had left the Fiat. The way lay down a lighted road. We were about half-way down it when, without thinking, I looked over my shoulder.

"No," murmured Zaleshoff, "they're not there. We left them behind in Milan."

"I wasn't . . ." I began. Then I stopped. He was right. I had got used to the idea of being followed. Things, I reflected bitterly, had come to a pretty pass. I had a sudden nostalgia for home, for London. I would go home next week, get away out of this miserable atmosphere of double-dealing, of intrigue, of violence. It would be fine to see Claire. The night I got back we would go to the Chinese place to eat. You didn't get a moon or stars like this in London, but there you weren't followed by Italian detectives in Homburg hats. The Boy Scouts didn't march as well as the *Balilla*, but there were no loudspeakers to bawl stuff at them about the beauties of war.

And then, for no particular reason, I found myself thinking of something Hallett had once said. It had been after lunch and we had been looking at some newspaper photographs of a Nazi mass demonstration. I had made some comment about the efficiency of German propaganda methods. He had laughed. "It's efficient because it's got to be. The British governing class never has that particular worry. In England, people read their newspapers and kid *themselves*." But then, as I was always reminding myself when I thought of things Hallett had said, the man was a Socialist. And Zaleshoff I believed to be a Communist, a Bolshevik agent. It was time that I pulled myself together and behaved like a reasonable being. It was sheer lunacy to go through with this plan of Zaleshoff's. I had had one very forcible warning. Next time I should no doubt be dealt with in the same way as Ferning had been dealt with. I made up my mind.

"By the way," I said, as I got into the car, "I've decided to call this business off this evening." As I said it I felt ashamed. But there was, I told myself, no other way.

Zaleshoff had been about to follow me into the car. He stopped. The girl turned her head and giggled.

"A bad joke, Mr. Marlow; but then I always said the English sense of humour was distinctly . . ."

"Just a minute, Tamara." Zaleshoff's voice was quiet enough, but the words were like drips of ice-cold water. "You *are* joking, aren't you, Marlow?"

"No." It was all I could manage.

"A bad joke, indeed!" he said slowly. He got in the car and sat down heavily beside me. "May one inquire the reason for this sudden decision?"

I found my tongue. "Put yourself in my position, Zaleshoff. I've got everything to lose by doing this and nothing to gain. I . . ."

"Just a minute, Marlow. Listen to me. I give you my solemn word that in doing this you are not only helping your own country considerably but also millions of other Europeans. The other day you asked me what the devil this had to do with me. That I cannot explain to you for reasons that you, I fancy, may have a shrewd notion about. You must take my word for it that I am on the side of the angels. And by angels I don't mean British and French statesmen and bankers and industrialists. I mean the people of those countries and of my own, the people who can resist the forces that have beaten the people of Italy and Germany to their knees. That's all."

I hesitated. I hesitated miserably. At last: "It's no use, Zaleshoff," I muttered, "it just isn't worth my while to do it."

"It isn't worth your while?" he echoed. Then he laughed. "I thought you said you *weren't* a big business man, Mister Marlow!"

Towards eleven o'clock I drove slowly along the *autostrada* away from Milan. I had left Zaleshoff and the girl at a *caffè* a mile back; but Zaleshoff's final instructions were still churning round inside my head. "Fight him tooth and nail. Be as angry as you like. But for goodness' sake don't forget to give in."

The April sky was now clouded over. It was warm enough inside the car, but I found myself shivering a little. I found that my foot kept easing gradually off the accelerator. Then I saw ahead two red lights close together.

Although I had been expecting to see them, they made me start. I slowed down and switched on the headlights. It was a large car, well into the side under some bushes over-hanging the road from the embankment above. I switched off the headlights, drew up a few yards behind it and waited. Then I saw General Vagas get out and walk back towards me.

Chapter XII

BLACKMAIL

THE MANNER of the General's greeting was that of a man ruefully amused at the antics of a rather troublesome child.

"Good evening, Mr. Marlow."

"Good evening, General. You wanted to see me?"

"Yes, I did. But this"—he waved his hand expressively at our surroundings and broke off—"I hope your taste for the melodramatic is satisfied?"

"I do not like melodrama any more than you do, General," I retorted. "I was anxious only to be discreet."

In the reflected light from the lamp on the instrument board I saw his thick lips twist humorously.

"A very desirable anxiety, Mr. Marlow. You must forgive me if I find the result a trifle exaggerated."

"You wanted to see me?" I repeated.

"Yes." But he was evidently determined to take his time. "I understand that you secured the Commendatore's contract."

"I did. I trust that you were satisfied with my efforts to return the compliment?"

"Quite." He hesitated, "But it was on that subject that I wanted to speak to you."

"Yes?"

He peered inside the car.

"Ah, leather seats! I think that my car is a little more comfortable than yours. Supposing we go and sit in it."

"I find this one quite comfortable."

He sighed. "I don't seem to sense that atmosphere of mutual confidence and respect that I am most anxious should surround our relations, Mr. Marlow. However"—he opened the door—"I hope that you will not mind if I get in and sit beside you. The night air in the country is cold and my chest is delicate." He coughed gently to emphasise the point.

"By all means, get in."

"Thank you." He got in, shut the door and sniffed the

air. "A cigar, Mr. Marlow, and a very bad one. Really, I cannot congratulate you on your choice of tobacco."

Inwardly I twitched with annoyance. The smell of the atrocious weed Zaleshoff had smoked on the way back from Como still clung to the upholstery. I muttered an apology. "I have some English cigarettes, if you would prefer one."

"I would. Thank you." He took one, lit it at the match I held out to him and inhaled deeply. He blew the smoke out slowly and gently. I waited in silence.

"Mr. Marlow," he said suddenly, "something a little unfortunate has happened."

"Indeed?"

"Yes. Something that, quite frankly, I feel almost ashamed to tell you."

"Oh?"

His manner became that of a man who had decided on a policy of complete candour. "I will put all my cards on the table, Mr. Marlow. You may remember that when we originally discussed this arrangement at my house, a figure of two thousand lire a month was mentioned."

"Naturally I remember."

"Subsequently, I mentioned another figure, three thousand lire a month, which was the figure finally agreed upon."

I uttered a non-committal "Yes." I was puzzled. This was nothing like any of the gambits I had anticipated.

He tapped my knee. "What I did not tell you at the time, Mr. Marlow, was this. That it was entirely upon my own responsibility that I increased the figure from two to three thousand lire."

I said, "I see." But I didn't see. I was extremely confused. I began to wonder if Zaleshoff had perhaps made a mistake or taken too much for granted in supposing that Vagas' object in seeking this meeting was blackmail. After a pause, he went on.

"You will understand my feelings in the matter, Mr. Marlow. I was anxious to secure your collaboration. It seemed to me that, in acting as I did, I was representing my country's interests to the best of my ability." There was the reproachful tone of the upright man unjustly accused in his voice as he continued. "Judge then of my chagrin, Mr. Marlow, I might almost say of my disgust"—he lingered over the word—"when I was advised several days ago that my principals in Belgrade could not agree to the arrangement I had made."

"Yes, of course." Now, I thought that I understood. Zaleshoff *had* been wrong. This was nothing more nor less than an attempt to go back on a bargain.

He sighed heavily. "I don't think I need tell you, Mr. Marlow, that I was annoyed. I got into touch immediately with Belgrade and protested vigorously. I put it to them as an affair of honour. But to no purpose. They were adamant." He became confidential. "Between ourselves, Mr. Marlow, I have very little patience with these permanent officials who sit in Government offices. They are invariably intransigent, narrow in outlook and absurdly parsimonious. I am only a simple soldier, a simple soldier anxious to do his duty as he sees it, but I can assure you, Mr. Marlow, that there are times when I feel my loyalty sorely tried."

His voice was vibrant with insincerity. The air of manly protest was vitiated somewhat by the wafts of Chypre liberated from his person by the emphatic movements of his arms. He seemed to be expecting me to make some comment, but I waited in grim silence.

"Mr. Marlow," he continued heavily, "I have been instructed by my principals in Belgrade to make certain proposals to you. Needless to say, I disagree entirely with the spirit of them. But you will realise that I have to obey orders. The proposals concern the arrangement whereby you are employed as an agent of the Yugo-Slav Government."

I jumped. The phrase was a new one. "Employed as an agent of the Yugo-Slav Government." Substitute "German" for "Yugo-Slav" and you had the situation in a nutshell. I didn't like the sound of it a bit. And from his silence, I gathered that he was allowing the phrase to sink in.

"I suppose," I said coldly, "that you wish me to agree to accepting a revision of the terms of our arrangement on the basis of the figure originally mentioned." I shrugged. "Well, if you wish to go back on the bargain, there is, I suppose, nothing I can do about it. But I must say that I cannot see how you can expect me under the circumstances to feel this mutual confidence on which you place so much emphasis. That, General, is all I have to say. If you wish me to do so, I will return three thousand lire out of the five thousand you gave me. Or I can regard it as payment in advance."

I was feeling relieved, but I was also feeling slightly disappointed. Zaleshoff had obviously placed far too much faith in his own deductions. The fact that Vagas had adopted one set of tactics as far as Ferning had been concerned was no guarantee that he would adopt the same tactics with me. Perhaps, I flattered myself, he had judged me to be a little too strong-minded. Well, in any case, the sooner this interview was over and I could get to bed, the better. But I was to receive an unpleasant shock.

The General coughed. "I am afraid, Mr. Marlow," he said

gently, "that the situation is not quite as simple as that. Inflexible they may be, but I can assure you that my principals are not in the habit of going back on a bargain, a financial arrangement, even though they cannot altogether agree to the terms of it. No, their proposals are of a different nature."

"I don't see . . ."

"One moment, Mr. Marlow!" The same peremptory, military quality that I had remarked before had crept into his voice again. "As a salaried agent of my Government, you are naturally bound, as I am, to take and obey instructions. The proposal is that, as you are receiving a salary in excess of that specified for the work you are doing, you should regularise the position by carrying out certain additional duties."

"That was not part of the bargain," I snapped.

"A bargain is a bargain, Mr. Marlow, only as long as it is useful to both parties to it."

This was German *Real Politik* with a vengeance.

"What do you mean by additional duties?" I demanded.

"Your business," he said coldly, "takes you into a number of important Italian heavy engineering works. You are required to incorporate in your future reports not only details of Spartacus activities but also details of the activities of the factories you visit. It will not be difficult. You have probably a retentive memory and you are a trained engineer. We wish to know principally what is being made and its destination. Any other particulars that your intelligence tells you are relevant will also be welcomed. Information you can pick up in conversation with works managers and technicians will be particularly valuable. You should have no difficulty in fulfilling our requirements. That is all."

For a moment I said nothing. I felt that I had nothing to say. I stared ahead. Two cars roared down the *autostrada* towards and past us. The sound of their engines died away. I wondered if their occupants had noticed us. But what was there to notice about two men sitting smoking in a car drawn up by the side of the road? Nothing. I felt that there ought to be something, some external evidence of the fantastic nature of what was being said within. When at last I spoke it was to utter one of the feeblest remarks of which I have ever been guilty.

"But that," I said, "would make me a spy."

His reply was delivered in tones of infinite contempt.

"My dear Mr. Marlow," he said deliberately, "you already *are* a spy." He paused. Then: "I shall expect your first report within the next two weeks."

He made as if to get out of the car. Suddenly, I came to my senses. My anger was very nearly genuine.

"Are you mad, General?"

With his hand on the door latch, he looked round. "I would remind you that you are addressing a superior, Mr. Marlow!"

"Superior be damned!" I snarled. "As you were good enough to remind me just now, signor Vagas, a bargain is a bargain only as long as it is useful to both parties to it. Excellent! What I am going to do, signor Vagas, is to go straight back to my hotel now, put your five thousand lire in an envelope and post it back to you to-night. As for your precious report, you can ask Mussolini for it. You're just as likely to get it from him as you are from me. And you can tell your principals that they have my permission to take running jumps at themselves."

"I'm afraid you're being a little foolish, Mr. Marlow." His voice was as dangerous a sound as I have heard. It very nearly reduced me to silence, but not quite.

"Foolish?" I repeated ironically. "Listen to me. If you're not out of this car in thirty seconds, you'll go out on your neck."

He adjusted his monocle carefully. "I think I ought to tell you, Mr. Marlow, that I have a revolver in my pocket which I shall not hesitate to use if necessary." I did my best to look slightly cowed. It was not difficult. When he went on his tone was conciliatory. "Now listen to me for a moment, Mr. Marlow. I can, to a certain extent, appreciate your annoyance, but I can assure you that I am only carrying out my instructions."

I contrived to let this fiction appear to mollify me somewhat.

"That may be. I cannot believe that you would for one moment imagine that I might agree to this—this preposterous suggestion."

"It is not a suggestion," he returned quietly, "it is an order." And then, as I opened my mouth to speak: "Please listen to me before you say any more. You seem to think that the maintenance of friendly relations between us is no longer of personal interest to you. Allow me to correct that impression."

"If you think that a few dirty lire . . ."

He held up his hand. "Please! What I was about to say had nothing to do with your salary. But it *is* of interest to you to preserve this association. For one very good reason. My principals in Belgrade have intimated that they *might* see fit, should you prove obstinate in this matter, to send a letter to

Mr. Pelcher in England with photostat copies of your enclosures to me of three weeks ago. I cannot help thinking that that would prove a little embarrassing for you."

I drew a deep breath. "So that's it! Blackmail, eh!"

"Not at all," he returned easily, "merely a reminder of the mutual confidence that must exist between business associates. There is no question of our asking anything more from you than you are able to give us without trouble or risk to yourself. In return, we keep our part of the bargain by paying you three thousand lire a month. It is all quite simple and reasonable."

I was silent for a moment. When at last I spoke it was with the obvious intention of salving what was left of my dignity.

"Very well," I said, "I see that I have no choice but to agree. But let me tell you this, General. If I did not believe that you were acting on instructions you had no part in, not even a revolver would prevent me expressing myself very forcibly."

He smiled; not, I thought, without a hint of triumph.

"My dear fellow, we are all of us at the mercy of blockheads. We can only accept the inevitable with the best possible grace. There are no bad feelings between us, I hope."

"Oh no. No bad feelings."

"Then let us shake hands on it."

We shook hands. He opened the door and got out.

"My wife asked me to give you her kind regards, Mr. Marlow."

"Please thank her."

"By all means. I shall look forward to your report within the next fifteen days. You understand, I think, what is required."

"Yes, I understand."

"Then, *a rivederci.*"

"Good night."

He went, leaving a faint odour of Chypre behind him. I watched him turn his car round and drive off in the direction of Milan. After a while, I followed him slowly. I ought, I knew, to be feeling pleased with myself. But I was not: for, such are the frailties of human logic, I felt that, had my report to Vagas been genuine and had I had no ulterior motives whatever, my behaviour that evening would have been precisely the same.

Some ten minutes later I pulled up outside the *caffè* at which I had left Zaleshoff and Tamara.

The table before which they were sitting was littered with empty coffee cups. He watched me steadily as I walked towards them and sat down in the vacant chair. Then:

"O.K.?"

"O.K.," I said, "but I think I'd like a brandy with my coffee. It's been a tiring day."

The two plain-clothes men, looking tired and very cold, were sitting in the *caffè* opposite the Parigi when at last I got back. They had the self-contained air of men who have been quarrelling.

A fortnight later "N. Marinetti" posted his second report to "J. L. Venezetti."

The part that referred to Spartacus, I had supplied. The rest was Zaleshoff's. It had taken him some time to compose. Most of it consisted of nondescript facts about the work in progress in the factories of three big customers. According to Zaleshoff, who supplied them, these facts had been known to every intelligence department in Europe for the past three months. They would, he declared, supply a stodgy but confidence-promoting background to the really important items. Just how he had come into possession of them I did not trouble to inquire. To do so would, I knew, have been a waste of time.

The important items were singularly unimpressive. There were two of them. One referred in the vaguest terms to three special hydraulic aircraft lifts and to the fact that they had been designed at the request of a municipal authority in the Trentino. The other was a bald statement to the effect that the same municipal authority had retained a well-known Italian civil engineer, named Bochini, as a consultant, and that this engineer was no longer working for the Italian Air Ministry. I had looked at the report a little despondently.

"It looks pretty feeble to me, Zaleshoff."

He had chuckled. "Don't you worry. It's dynamite. You see what happens when he gets it. He'll react all right."

Vagas *did* react. Two days after I had despatched the report I collected his letter from the poste restante. In addition to the three thousand lire there was a letter:

Dear Sir,
Your report received. I enclose 3,000 lire as arranged. There are two points mentioned in your report about which I should like further details as soon as possible. The points in question are those relating to the hydraulic lifts and to the retention of the engineer Bochini. The details I require are as follows:

1. What arrangements have been made for paying for these lifts? Is it the Italian Government who is paying? What form of credit facilities have been extended by the manufac-

turers? You might approach the subject by saying that you have heard on good authority that the municipality in question is in financial difficulties.

2. Who designed the lifts? On what date are they being delivered?

3. Has Bochini had anything to do with the order for the lifts?

I realise that to secure this information quickly you will have to re-visit Torino. Please do so as soon as you possibly can. I am prepared to pay a bonus of 5,000 lire over and above the present arrangement for this information.

Yours faithfully,

J. L. Venezetti.

Zaleshoff crowed when I showed it to him.

"What did I tell you?" he demanded triumphantly.

"I don't understand it."

"It's perfectly simple. For purposes of secrecy the Italian Air Ministry have issued their orders for the equipment for these three aerodromes through this municipality. Officially, the municipality will take delivery. Actually it will be the Air Ministry. This guy Bochini is their head man on the subject of underground aerodrome construction. Vagas got the idea immediately. I knew he would. But it's too important a thing for him to make mistakes about. He wants confirmation."

"But how am I going to get this information?"

"You needn't worry. I've got it already. We'll wait a couple of weeks before we deliver, just to make it look all right. Then we'll be sitting pretty."

Four days previously my spirits had been raised considerably by the discovery that I was no longer under surveillance, that the plain-clothes men had been withdrawn. Now, Zaleshoff's enthusiasm completed the cure. That night the three of us ate at a more expensive place than usual. I ordered a bottle of Asti Spumante. We drank to the confusion of Vagas, and Zaleshoff and I took it in turns to dance with Tamara. Looking back on that evening now, I can still recapture the feeling I had of sitting in the sun after a particularly unpleasant storm has passed. We were very gay. But now our gaiety seems more than a little pathetic. I have, these days, a mistrust of celebrations that amounts to a superstition. I can never quite forget the grim spectre of anti-climax that lurks in the ante-room.

The following day I replied to Vagas' letter, assured him that I would do my best to obtain the information he wanted, and settled down to the work of the office.

Thanks chiefly to Umberto's efforts, the work had begun

to assume more reasonable proportions. Bellinetti, I was almost relieved to find, was spending less and less time at his desk and more and more in the *caffè*. His manner towards me was jauntily cordial. I imagine that he thought that the new broom had worn down and that the dust was settling once again into the old corners. I did not bother to disillusion him. Things were going smoothly. Fitch, in one of his weekly memoranda, had made a jocular reference to the growing efficiency of the Milan office. I almost regretted my decision to resign at the end of the month—almost, but not quite.

That week I wrote to Claire and received a reply from her. I also wrote to Hallett asking him to let me know if he heard of a job going that might suit me. I was, I said with perfect truth, anxious to return to England. With memories of the envelope steaming episode, I asked him to address his reply care of Claire.

I paid my weekly ceremonial visits to the Consulate for news of my passport and to the *Amministrazione* to have my permit date-stamped. The officials at the Consulate were, as always, charming and sympathetic. The policeman on the door at the *Amministrazione* greeted me by name. We exchanged opinions on the subject of the weather. The evenings I spent at the cinema or with Zaleshoff and Tamara. When it was warm, which it was on most days now, we walked in the new Park. That Saturday I watched with Zaleshoff a highly acrimonious football match between a Milan team and a team from Verona. The latter won, and the referee was manhandled and seriously injured by the crowd. Three days later I went to Rome.

The summons from Rome I received late on the Tuesday afternoon. There had been a fire at the works of one of our customers just outside the city. The fire had spread from the stores to a machine shop containing a battery of S2 machines. The fire had been put out, but five of the machines had been damaged. The machines had been busy on a Government contract with a penalty clause not covered by insurance. I was wanted immediately to advise as to the speed with which the necessary spare parts could be obtained from England and the possibility of increasing the output of the undamaged machines and to place a valuation on the damage done.

Bellinetti was, as usual, out of the office. I told Umberto where I was going, and went back to the Parigi. There, I packed a suitcase with the things I might require for a night in a hotel, snatched an early dinner and caught a night train to Rome.

I spent the following day amidst the ruins of the burnt-out shop. The damage was more extensive than I had anticipated, and the unhappy signatories of the contract with the penalty clause had lost their heads. Eventually, I sent a long telegram to Fitch, and was able to get one back from him with reassuring news concerning the delivery of the spare parts. The works manager kissed me on both cheeks. It was, however, very late when eventually I got away, and I was dog-tired. I decided to spend the night in Rome and travel back to Milan the following day.

It was towards half-past six the following evening when my train drew into the *Centrale* at Milan. It had been full for most of the way. Now it began to empty. The corridor was jammed with luggage and people. I was standing outside my compartment waiting impatiently for the way to clear when I saw Zaleshoff.

The platform was crowded with people meeting the train. He was standing on the outskirts of the crowd, scanning the alighting passengers anxiously. I leaned out of the window and waved. Then he saw me.

He made no effort to wave back. I saw him glance quickly up and down the platform and then edge his way through the crowd towards the window through which I was leaning. A second or two later he was standing below me. I was about to ask him who he had been waiting to meet when he looked up. Something in his face alarmed me.

"What's the matter?"

"Get back into your compartment and stay there."

There was extraordinary urgency in his voice. His eyes had dropped. He was looking down the platform.

"What the . . . ?"

"Do as I tell you."

"But this train goes on to Venice."

"That doesn't matter a damn. Get back inside and keep out of sight. Open your suitcase and be looking inside it. I'm coming aboard in a minute. I'll join you when we've left the station."

He had not raised his voice, but his tone was so vehement that I obeyed him. Utterly bewildered, I returned to the compartment and opened my suitcase. Out of the corner of my eye I saw him, a moment or two later, plant his back against the glass door of the compartment. He remained there motionless until the train began to move. Then he took out his handkerchief and wiped his forehead. He did not turn round until the train had left the station. Then he slid the door open, stepped inside the compartment, shut the door behind him and pulled the blinds down.

Then he turned to me. He grinned.

"I've met every train from Rome to-day," he said. "I think they were beginning to take an interest in me."

"What on earth is this all about?" I demanded.

"Sit down and I'll tell you."

"What's happened?"

He took out his cigarettes and sat down facing me.

"The fat's in the fire," he announced calmly.

"What does *that* mean?" I was worried and beginning to get irritated.

"Yesterday afternoon, Vagas skipped it by air to Belgrade. He could only have got away by the skin of his teeth because your friend Commendatore Bernabò was arrested at seven o'clock. They were waiting for him when he got home. And there's a warrant out for your arrest. About eight o'clock last night they raided your offices. It was the Ovra all right, not the regular police. They went through the place with a fine comb. They've been at it all day to-day. Bellinetti's been enjoying himself no end, I guess. The only trouble was that they didn't know where you were. But they're watching all three stations. You wouldn't have got out of the *Centrale* without being arrested."

"But what's it all about?"

"The actual charge is one of bribing Government officials. That means Bernabò, of course. But the real trouble is that they've found out about your reports to Vagas."

I swallowed hard. I felt suddenly very, very frightened. "But who . . . ?" I began.

He laughed shortly and not pleasantly.

"That's easy. The one person we didn't reckon on taking a hand—your girl friend, Madame Vagas."

Chapter XIII

"YOU HAVE NO CHOICE"

THE TRAIN gathered speed. Zaleshoff went on talking. I listened to him in stunned silence.

"This is the way I see it," he said: "Madame Vagas had it in for her ever-loving husband. That note she slipped you the night you went to the Opera proves that. You remember what she said? 'He killed Ferning.' It was obvious that she knew a lot. I've an idea she knew more than Vagas knew. And there's only one way she could have found out about

Ferning's being bumped off. My guess is that the Ovra, knowing that she fancied Vagas about as much as a dose of poison, got at her and persuaded her to keep tabs on him. She agreed, with reservations. She didn't tell them, then, that he was actually a German agent. She must be a bit crazy. You could see the way her mind worked in that note. She knew that Vagas hadn't actually killed Ferning with his own hands. But she saw that he was, in a sort of way, morally responsible. Her hatred twisted that moral responsibility into a direct one. She must," he added reflectively, "have hated him plenty."

In my mind's eye I saw the baroque hangings of that house in the Corso di Porta Nuova, the obscene wall paintings, Ricciardo, pale and dainty in his blood-red satin knee breeches, gliding across the hall. There had been a smell of incense in the air. I remembered that sudden deadly passage of hatred between the husband and the wife. "Any talk of death depresses her." For a moment I thought that I understood Madame Vagas, saw through and round her mind, and found her horribly sane; then the moment passed. I looked up at Zaleshoff.

"Vagas got away, you said?"

"Yes, he got away. I don't even know if they've issued a warrant for him. Maybe not. What happened probably was that his wife, having spilled all the beans to the Ovra, couldn't resist telling him that she had done so. When he knew that they knew he was a German agent, he knew that it was time he went. His pensioners have saved his bacon before, but he couldn't rely on their being able to repeat the process. You can't buy your way through all the time. Sooner or later you come up against folks who haven't had their cut. Then you're done. Vagas took it on the lam like any other sensible guy in his position would have done. He was darn lucky to have the chance, and he knew it."

"What did you mean by saying that they'd found out about my reports? Madame Vagas may have known nothing about them."

"Ah, I was coming to that. Tamara and I were in our office last night when they raided your place. Bellinetti was with them, sort of official guide, but your lad had gone home. I knew you were away, as I'd called you up at the Parigi about some dinner the evening before, and they'd told me. Well, I, as a respectable citizen wondering what the devil all the fuss was about, marched up and threatened them with the law. They were a dirty lot of thugs. They shot me out straightaway, of course; but I discovered two things. One was that Bellinetti didn't know where you were, which was odd. The other thing was that they had found out about the poste restante business. As I barged in I heard one of them telling the others to look for any correspondence from a man named Venezetti. That clinched it. Nobody but Vagas' wife could have known about that."

I remembered something. "Vagas told her that he was meeting me that night on the *autostrada*. She sent her kind regards."

"Oh, did she! Well, now you've got them. Vagas must have been crazy to trust her. But his own self-esteem would place her above suspicion."

"Why should she start off by warning me and then do this?"

"She probably thought that having ignored her warning you had only yourself to blame. And then Vagas must have done something that sent her completely nuts."

"You may be right. But what I can't understand is why Bellinetti didn't know where I was. I told Umberto. Incidentally, how did *you* know I'd gone to Rome. I tried to telephone you before I went, but there was no reply."

He grinned. "Ah, that's the rest of the story. I told you that they began again on your office this morning. Well, Tamara and I were downstairs pretty early. We hadn't a ghost of a notion what had happened to you. I don't mind telling you we were damnably worried. You might have gone straight back to the Parigi and been arrested. I went along to try and find out, but the place was alive with Ovra agents, and if I'd started asking after you there might have been some trouble. We decided that the best thing was to stay at the end of the telephone in case you'd found out what had happened and called us up. Then, towards ten o'clock there was a scratch at the door, and your lad—Umberto, is it?—slipped in with his knees knocking together and frightened out of his wits, wanting to know if I was a friend of yours. I told him yes. He said that he'd been questioned upstairs, and then told to go home until he was sent for again. He'd come to me because he was worried about you. He seems to like you, that kid. They'd asked him where you were, and they hadn't asked any too gently, because he had a cut lip and a hand-mark on his cheek that looked pretty nasty. But he hadn't told them. He'd said he didn't know. It appears that he knew who and what they were, and was afraid for you."

"His father was murdered by them," I said shortly.

"Ah! Well, it was a bit of luck for you that you told Umberto. He'd forgotten to tell Bellinetti, who'd been out most of the previous day. But he told me, and so I left Tamara at the telephone and camped out at the station."

I was silent for a moment. My thoughts were far from pleasant.

"Well," I said at last, "what do we do now?"

Zaleshoff was looking out of the window. "The first thing we do," he said slowly, "is to get out of this train. I don't think it stops before Brescia, but there'll be a ticket collector along before then and neither of us has a ticket. Besides . . ." he broke off and added: "How much money have you got?"

I examined my wallet.

"About four hundred odd lire, nearly five hundred."

"Is that all? What about Vagas' three thousand?"

"I paid most of it into the bank."

"What have you got in that suitcase?"

"Pyjamas, a change of underclothing, a dirty shirt, toothbrush and shaving things."

"Put the toothbrush and shaving things in your pocket, your underclothing too if you want it, then give me the suitcase."

"But look here, Zaleshoff . . ."

"We'll talk later," he said impatiently; "we'll be slowing down soon for Treviglio."

I did as I was told. He took the suitcase and examined it carefully.

"No initials, no name and address anywhere on it?"

"No."

"Good. Let's go."

He led the way into the corridor.

"Now," he said, "I'm going to walk along the corridors to the last coach before the van. You follow me, but not too closely. Someone may wonder what the hell I'm doing carrying a suitcase about when we're nowhere near a stop and *you* don't want to get involved in any arguments."

He disappeared towards the rear of the train. I began to follow slowly. Suddenly he reappeared, walking quickly towards me. He was frowning.

"Go back and get into the lavatory at the other end of the coach. There's a ticket collector coming along. Don't lock yourself in or he'll wait for you to come out. Give him ten minutes to pass, then join me at the back of the train."

He turned and disappeared with the suitcase into a lavatory. I followed suit at the other end of the corridor. I waited there nervously for five minutes. Then I heard the ticket collector slide open the door of the compartment next to the lavatory and ask to see the occupants' tickets. There was a long pause, then the door slid to again. The man paused as he drew level with the lavatory door, evidently to glance at the indicator on the lock, then passed on. A few minutes later I joined Zaleshoff at the end of the train. I was feeling guilty.

"I don't see why," I said bitterly, "we couldn't have bought tickets from him."

"You'll see why, to-morrow," he said cryptically.

Then I noticed that he no longer had the suitcase.

"Threw it out of the window when we were going through that tunnel," he explained.

"I don't see where this is getting us, Zaleshoff," I said. "Frankly, I'm worried, damned worried. I think the best thing I can do is to get off at Brescia and telephone the Consulate in Milan. If there is, as you say, a warrant out for my arrest, I'm not going to gain anything by playing the fool like this. The sooner I get in touch with the Consulate, the better."

"Do you *want* to go to jail?"

"Of course not. But there's surely no question of jail. There may be a fine, possibly a heavy one, and I shall probably be given twenty-four hours in which to leave the country. All very unpleasant, no doubt, but that's the worst of it. Good gracious, man, I'm a British subject, known to the Consulate, and fairly respectable, I . . ."

"The British authorities," he interrupted, "would, in the ordinary way, see you through anything from petty larceny to murder. But a charge of espionage puts the thing in a different category. They'll drop you like a hot cake as soon as they know about it."

"But you yourself said that the charge was bribery."

"Until they catch you. Then you'll get the whole packet."

"Well," I said disgustedly, "even if you are right, I still don't see any alternative for me."

"The only place you'll be safe is out of the country, and that's where we're going."

"You seem to forget," I said witheringly, "that I have no passport."

"I hadn't forgotten."

"Well then!"

"I said we'd talk later. . . ."

"And in the meantime, I suppose . . ."

"In the meantime," he interjected, "you get wise to yourself and do as I tell you."

I shrugged. "Well, I suppose it doesn't make much difference."

"It makes a lot of difference. Have a cigarette. It'll steady your nerves."

"My nerves," I snapped, "are perfectly all right."

He nodded calmly. "That's good. You're going to need

them in a minute. We're going to drop off this train when it slows down for the curve at Treviglio."

I did not answer. Things were moving too quickly for me. Twenty minutes before, I had been a comparatively composed Englishman returning from doing what I was conscious of being a sound piece of work. I had been looking forward to a quiet dinner, a couple of hours in a cinema and an early bed with a new book to read. Now I was a fugitive from the Italian secret police, hiding in lavatories, cheating ticket collectors and contemplating leaving a train in an unconventional and illegal manner. It had all happened far too suddenly. I couldn't adjust my mind to these new and fantastic circumstances. I found myself wondering seriously whether perhaps by pinching myself I might wake up to find that I was, after all, still in bed in Rome. But no: there was Zaleshoff smoking and gazing intently out of the window and in my pocket there was a safety-razor, a leaking tube of shaving cream and a pair of American underpants. I looked down on to the track by the side of the train. It looked a long way away and dangerous. The train was going too fast for me to see whether the track was of small or large stones. It was a long, even, grey-brown smear. It seemed to me that the train had begun to make a curious thumping noise. I tried to separate the noise, identify it, and realised that it was the sound of the blood pumping in my head. I knew suddenly that I was scared, scared stiff.

Zaleshoff touched me on the arm.

"We're beginning to slow down. We'll give it another minute, then we'll get outside on the steps, ready. Don't forget to let yourself go limply if you can't keep your feet when you land."

I nodded, speechless, and looked down again.

To me it seemed as if the train were going as fast as ever. It was running along the top of a steep embankment between ploughed fields. I looked again at the ground streaming past. Then I saw Zaleshoff put his hand on the latch of the door. It was madness, I told myself, madness! We should both break our legs or our arms or we should get flung under the wheels of the luggage van behind us and mangled to death. Suddenly there was a grating noise below us.

"They're braking," said Zaleshoff, "come on. You'd better go first."

He opened the door and the roar of the steel coach seemed suddenly to be lost in the blustering wind.

"Down with you," said Zaleshoff. "Make it snappy, now."

I looked down. There were four steps down, then the track. I clutched the rail and went down three steps. The wind tore at my hat. With my free hand I jammed it down over my ears. Then I swung myself round facing the direction we were going. I could see the engine now as it began to round the curve. The smoke was flying in a long cone from the funnel. Below me the ground seemed to be going at a sickening speed. I felt suddenly giddy and retreated a step. I looked up. I had to shout against the wind.

"It's no good, Zaleshoff, I . . ."

But he misunderstood me. "We'll talk later," he bellowed. "Get on with it."

He got down on to the step above me. I could feel his knees pressing against my shoulder-blades. I moved down to the bottom step. Now I could see the wheels as they ran screaming over the rails of the curve. I watched them, fascinated. They reminded me irresistibly of bacon-slicing machines. As a boy I had seen a man cut off half his thumb with one of those machines. Grease was oozing out of one of the axle-boxes. Something poked me sharply in the back. It was Zaleshoff's toe.

"Go on!" he yelled.

I straightened my back, flexed my legs and swung one foot forward slightly. Then I hesitated again. No, I couldn't do it. We were going too fast. If the train would slow down a little more . . . but it seemed to be gathering speed now. Then Zaleshoff's toe jabbed me again. I drew a deep breath, clenched my teeth and jumped.

The next moment the ground was flailing the soles of my shoes with astounding force. I felt myself pitching forward on my face and put out my arms to save myself. My legs strove madly to reach the speed of the rest of my body. But not for long. A bare second later I had tripped. Just in time I remembered Zaleshoff's advice and let myself go limp. I saw the ground sliding past sideways. Then I hit the edge of the embankment.

The impact nearly stunned me, and before I could stop myself I was tumbling down the side of the embankment. I came to rest at the bottom of it against the concrete stanchion of a barbed-wire fence. For several moments I stayed there, winded. Then, very gingerly, I got to my feet and began to dust myself down. Zaleshoff came scrambling diagonally down the embankment from the point at which he had finished up twenty yards or so away.

"Are you all right?"

I was still short of breath, but I managed a rather quavering affirmative.

"Through the fence," he panted urgently, as he came up, "we can clean up as we go."

"What's the matter?"

"The guard saw us," he said curtly; "that means that he'll report the fact at Brescia. We daren't go into Treviglio."

"Well, where *are* we going?"

"We'll see when we get there. Come on."

We wormed our way through the fence and set off in silence to skirt the ploughed field. The sun was beginning to go down behind the trees on the horizon when we eventually got on to a road. We turned right, away from Treviglio. Twenty minutes later we walked into a small village. Next to the post office there was a *caffè-ristorante*.

"This'll do," said Zaleshoff.

We went inside and sat down.

"Well," I said, "what now?" I was feeling tired and shaken.

"We eat and we share a decent bottle of wine if they've got one. Then we get down to business."

The place was small and not too clean. There was a zinc-topped bar and four marble-topped tables covered with white paper napkins. The wall behind the bar consisted of shelves packed tight with bottles. On the other walls were Cinzano posters, a lithograph of Mussolini and a poster advertising Capri. The proprietor was a phlegmatic middle-aged man with a long, greying moustache and amazingly grimy hands. He did not seem in the least surprised by our presence, a fact which I found curious until it came out in the course of our brief conversation with him that he assumed that we were something to do with a mineral water factory close by. We did not correct this impression.

We ate spaghetti and a great deal of bread and drank a tolerable Barbera. By the time the coffee arrived I was feeling very much better. Zaleshoff summoned the proprietor and ordered a bottle of cognac.

"We can't drink all that," I protested.

"We're not going to drink any of it now. But we shall be glad of it later."

I did not understand him, but I nodded.

"What about sleeping? Do you think this man can put us up? You know, you might just as well have chucked the case overboard just before we jumped off ourselves. We should have had at least one pair of pyjamas between us."

He dropped three lumps of sugar into his coffee one by one. "We aren't going to need pyjamas. To-night we're walking."

"Walking? Where?"

"Listen. By the morning this district will be thick with police in and out of uniform. We wouldn't be able to move a yard. If we put up for the night anywhere they'll want to see your passport. You haven't got one."

"I've got my permit."

He snorted. "And a fat lot of good that'll do you. Don't you realise that the particulars on that permit, including your name, go straight to the police?"

"Dammit, we've got to sleep *somewhere!*" I cried.

"Maybe we can have a nap somewhere to-morrow."

"Thanks very much," I said sarcastically. Then I became serious. "Look here, Zaleshoff, it's very decent of you to try to help me like this, but I do think that my original idea was better."

He sighed. "I've told you once. Your Consulate won't lift a finger to help you. If they did, they might compromise themselves. If you were innocent and the victim of an obvious frame-up, they might do something. But you're not innocent—at least, technically you're not. You're as guilty as hell, and they can rake up the evidence to prove it."

"But supposing there's no question of a charge of espionage?"

"Do you think," he said patiently, "that they'd bother to issue a warrant for your arrest just for bribery? Don't make me laugh! If they started anything like that, the prisons would be overflowing in a week and most of the top men would be in them. Look here: we know that they've got on to that poste restante set-up of yours with Vagas. There's very little doubt that Madame Vagas gave them the whole works. That means that they've got hold of the report I wrote. Do you remember that you didn't think much of it? Well, I told you it was dynamite and dynamite it is. You saw how Vagas reacted to it. Well, believe me, that would be nothing to the way the contra-espionage department of the *Organizzazione Vigilanza Repressione Anti-fascismo* would react when *they* saw it. I'm not a good gambler, but I would not mind betting heavy money that at this very moment there's enough sweating going on among the big boys in Milan and Rome to float that new battle-cruiser of theirs. And they let Vagas slip through their fingers. They must be kicking themselves good and plenty. But they're not going to make the same mistake twice. They're going to get you or bust themselves trying."

"I don't see why I should be so important."

"No? The first thing they'd do, they've certainly done it by now, is to descend in a cloud on the Turin factory where those aircraft lifts are being made, to discover just how the leakage of information took place and how much you found out."

"But I haven't even been there."

"Just so. You haven't been there. You must have got the information from somewhere else. And the rest of the information in that report was stale before you arrived in the country, so you couldn't have got that by yourself either. In other words, they're going to tumble like a sack of potatoes to what's being put across them. That's why you've got to get out of the country, and pretty damn quick."

For a bit I said nothing. I was impressed; very much so. I could feel something cold gripping at my insides. "Pretty damn quick." There was a horrible urgency about those three ugly little words. I saw, suddenly, the naked realities of the mess I was in. My mind involuntarily turned away from them. Heavens, what a mess! If only . . .

I began to regret, to try and rearrange things in a more pleasing pattern. Finally I began to argue with Zaleshoff in an effort to get him somehow to modify his conclusions. I wanted him to minimise the danger. It was a plain case of funk, and it deceived him not at all.

"It's no use," he said at last. "I'm not going to call black pale-grey just because you'd like it better that way. You're in a spot. I think I can get you out of it. I'll do all I can to do so because I reckon I did a good deal to get you into it. But you'll have to do as I say. It isn't going to be easy. If we have to lose a night or two's sleep it'll be just too bad, but you'll have to put up with it. If that's all we lose before we're through, I reckon we shall have done swell."

I did not like the sound of that at all.

"Well, anyway," I said with feeble heartiness, "the worst that can come of it is a nice stay in prison."

It was as much a question as a statement. I was afraid, as soon as I had said it, that he would answer the question, and he did.

"Prison? Yes—maybe."

"What do you mean by 'maybe'?"

"They have a formula for these things hereabouts. It's called 'shot while attempting to evade arrest.' "

"And if you don't attempt to evade arrest?"

"Then," he said calmly, "they make you kneel down. Then they put a bullet through the back of your neck and call it 'shot while escaping.' "

I laughed, not very convincingly, but I laughed. I decided that he was trying to frighten me.

"Newspaper talk!" I said.

He shrugged. "My friend, when you're above the law, when you *are* the law, the phrase about ends justifying means has a real meaning. Put yourself in their place. If you felt that the state which you worshipped above your God was endangered by the life of one insignificant man, would you hesitate to have him shot? I can tell you that you wouldn't. That's the danger of Fascism, of state-worship. It supposes an absolute, an egocentric unit. The idea of the state is not rooted in the masses, it is not of the people. It is an abstract, a God-idea, a psychic dung-hill raised to shore up an economic system that is no longer safe. When you're on the top of that sort of dung-hill, it doesn't matter whether the ends are in reality good or bad. The fact that they are your ends *makes* them good—for you."

But I was scarcely listening to him. I was trying to sort out the confusion of my thoughts. Claire! what would she have done? But Claire was not there. In any case, she would have been too wise to have involved herself in such an affair. I tried to strike out along a new line, but eventually I found that it turned back on itself. I was thinking in circles. In desperation I turned again to Zaleshoff.

He was busily crushing a lump of sugar in the bottom of his coffee cup.

"Tell me what you propose."

He looked at me quickly. Then he put the spoon down, put his hand in his pocket and drew out a small map of Northern Italy. He spread it on the table in front of me. With his pencil he indicated a point north-east of Treviglio.

"We're just about here. Now we could make for Como and the Swiss frontier. But if we did that we'd be doing precisely what they'll expect us to do. Even if we got as far as Como, the lake patrols would get us. I propose that we make for the Yugo-Slav frontier between Fusine and Kranjska. We can go most of the way by night trains, so that we can sleep. In the daytime we can double on our tracks across country and pick up the railway at another point. Now, that's going to cost money. Trains here are expensive unless you have the tourist discount, and we can't very well claim that. I've got a bit more than you, but it only makes about fifteen hundred lire between us. That's not enough. Before we leave here I shall telephone Tamara and tell her to get some money to Udine. Then we'll make cross-country for the railway where it runs south of Lake Garda at Desenzano. What do you think about it?"

There was a pause.

"Well," I said grimly, "if you really want to know, I

think it's one of the most remarkable pieces of understatement I've ever listened to. It sounds like a Sunday-school treat. Auntie Alice will distribute the buns at Udine."

His brows knitted. He opened his mouth and drew breath to speak.

"But," I went on firmly, "we'll leave that side of it out for the moment. What I want to know is why on earth you should choose the Yugo-Slav frontier. What about the French? What about the German?"

He shrugged. "That's precisely what *they'll* say."

"I see. The French, Swiss and German frontiers are going to be stiff with guards, but the Yugo-Slav frontier's going to be like the Sahara Desert. Is that right?"

He frowned. "I didn't say that."

"No," I retorted angrily, "but you wish you could. I suppose the fact that we're going to make for the Yugo-Slav frontier wouldn't have anything to do with the fact that Vagas is in Belgrade would it? or with the fact that, as I haven't got a passport, I could not get into Yugo-Slavia from France or Switzerland or Germany without swearing affidavits and heaven knows what else in London first?"

He reddened. "There's no need to get hot under the collar about it."

I spluttered furiously. "Hot under the collar! Dammit, Zaleshoff, there are limits. . . ."

He leaned forward eagerly.

"Wait a minute! Don't forget that you've got close on two hundred and fifty dollars to collect from Vagas. It would look perfectly natural for you to make for Belgrade to collect them. For all he knows, you may be flat broke. You will be, anyway, by the time you get to Belgrade. Besides, what difference does it make? If they catch you, you won't get much change out of them by explaining that you'd decided, after all, not to cause them any more trouble. You started a good job of work. Why not finish it?"

I regarded him sullenly. "I made a fool of myself once. I see no reason why I should do so again."

He stared at the tablecloth. "You realise, don't you," he said slowly, "that without me to help you, you'll be sunk? You haven't got enough money. You'll be caught inside forty-eight hours. You *do* realise that?"

"I'm not going to wait to be caught."

He still stared at the tablecloth.

"Nothing will induce you to change your mind?"

"Nothing," I said decidedly.

But I was wrong.

The proprietor was out of the room, but in the corner of the bar a radio had been quietly churning out an Argentine tango. Suddenly the music stopped. There was a faint hiss from the loudspeaker. Then the announcer started speaking:

"We interrupt this programme at the request of the Ministry of the Interior to request that all persons keep watch for a foreigner who has escaped from the jurisdiction of the Milan police. He is wanted in connection with grave charges of importance to every loyal Italian. A reward of ten thousand lire, ten thousand lire, will be paid to anyone giving information as to his movements. He is believed to be in the vicinity of Treviglio. He may attempt to pass himself off as an Englishman named Nicholas Marlow. Here is a description of the man. . . ."

Zaleshoff walked over to the instrument and twisted the dial to another station. He returned to the table but did not sit down.

"That's not a bad price, Marlow, not at all a bad price! They're doing you proud."

I did not answer.

He sighed. "Well, I suppose you'll be wanting the local police post. I wish you joy of it."

Except for the radio, there was silence in the room. I was conscious that he had walked across the room and was examining the Capri poster.

"If you're going to telephone your sister before we leave," I said slowly, "you'd better do it now, hadn't you?"

I was staring at my empty plate. When I felt his hand on my shoulder, I jumped.

"Nice work, pal!"

I shrugged. "I have no choice."

"No," he said softly, "you have no choice."

Chapter XIV

CROSS-COUNTRY

ZALESHOFF WAS not gone long.

"There'll be five thousand lire for us at Udine when we get there," he said when he got back.

"But what about your sister?"

"She's got some things to clear up, then she's leaving for Belgrade to keep a line on Vagas. She'll meet us there."

"You've got everything planned beautifully, haven't you?" I said, not without bitterness.

"Naturally. It's better that way."

He paid the bill and we set out.

For a quarter of a mile or so we retraced our steps; then we struck out in a north-easterly direction.

It was a cold night and cloudy. I was wearing a thin over-coat and I had no scarf; but the pace that Zaleshoff set soon made up for those deficiencies.

To begin with we exchanged a few desultory remarks. Soon we fell silent. Our footsteps grated in unison on the flinty road. My mind seemed with my fingers to have gone numb. I felt emotionally exhausted. All that I was conscious of for a time was a dim, unreasoning resentment of Zaleshoff. He was responsible. But for him, I should be sleeping comfortably in my room at the Parigi. I thought, absurdly, of a favourite shirt I had left among my things there. I should never see *that* again. I tried to remember where in London I had bought it. Perhaps they wouldn't have any more shirts like that. Zaleshoff's fault. Useless to tell myself that Zaleshoff had done no more than make suggestions, that what I was paying for now was the fit of bravado, of temper which had led me that night in Zaleshoff's office to telephone Vagas. Zaleshoff was the villain of the piece.

Out of the corners of my eyes I glanced at him. I could see him in dim outline, his hands in his pockets, his shoulders hunched, plodding along beside me. I wondered if he was conscious of my dislike, of my mistrust of him. He probably was. He did not miss very much.

And then I had a sudden revulsion of feeling. It was not true to say that I disliked him; you could not dislike him. I felt suddenly that I wanted to put out my hand and touch his arm and shake it to show that I bore him no ill-will. I wondered idly, unemotionally, if, had Vagas already received my second report, or had Zaleshoff been able to transmit it to him in any other way but through me, I should have been helped in this way. Probably not. I should have been left negligently to my fate. Zaleshoff was a Soviet agent—I had come without effort to take that fact for granted—and he had his work to do, he had the business of his extraordinary government to attend to. I supposed that, strictly speaking, I, too, was a servant of that government. Oddly enough, I found that idea no worse than curious. Vagas' suggestion

that I was a servant of *his* government I had found highly
distasteful. Perhaps that was because I liked Zaleshoff and
disliked Vagas, or because one had paid me and the other had
merely offered to do so. Still, it was odd. After all, I had no
particular feelings about either of their countries. I knew
neither of them. When I thought of Germany I thought of
parades, of swastika banners flapping from tall poles, of loudspeakers, of stout field marshals and goose-stepping men with
steel helmets, of concentration camps. When I thought of
Russia I thought of dark, stupid Romanoffs, of the Winter
Palace, of Cossacks, of crowds streaming in terror, of cano-
pied priests swinging censers, of Lenin and Stalin, of grain
rippling in the breeze, of the Lubianka prison. Yes, it was
odd. I found suddenly that we were slowing down. Then
Zaleshoff cleared his throat and muttered that we turned
right. We passed the fork in the road and increased our speed
again. The moon shone for a moment through a thin patch
in the drifting clouds, then disappeared again. In the darkness
the silence walked with us like a ghost.

In the east the sky became pale and smoky. The trees and
a line of pylons sprang out in silhouette against it like scenery
against a dimly lighted cyclorama. The sky yellowed. The
silhouettes changed slowly into three dimensional figures. A
slight breeze sprang up.

I peered at my watch. It was half-past five. We had been
walking without a break for over six hours. I had on only
thin "pavement" shoes, and the roads had been rough. My
feet were sore and swollen. My eyes were smarting and I felt
weak at the knees. Zaleshoff saw me glance at my watch.

"What time is it?"

I told him. It was the first thing either of us had said for
several hours.

"What about a shot of cognac and a cigarette apiece?"

"I could do with both."

In the half light I could see that we were walking along a
narrow road between fields lying fallow. It looked very much
the same sort of country as that we had landed in from
the train. We sat on a pile of flints by the side of the road.
Zaleshoff produced the brandy and we drank some of it out
of the bottle. We lit cigarettes.

"Where are we?" I said.

"I don't know. There was a signpost a kilometre or so
back, but it was too dark to read it. How are you feeling?"

"Not too bad. And you?"

"Tired. We must have done about thirty-five kilometres
or so. It's not bad for a start. There should be a village or
something a little way ahead. We'll push on for a bit. Then

you can hide up somewhere while I go and forage for something to eat. We've got to eat."

"Yes and we've got to sleep."

"We'll think about that too."

We finished our cigarettes and set off again. The cognac had done me good, but my feet were worse for the rest and I felt myself developing a limp. Somewhere, not very far away, a cock was beginning to crow.

We walked on for another hour and a half. Then we came to a stretch of road bounded by a wood of young birch trees. Zaleshoff slowed down.

"I think it wouldn't be a bad idea if you stopped here. I think we must be pretty close to a village now and there may not be such good cover as this farther on. You'd better take the brandy. You may get cold and, anyway, I don't want to take it with me. I may be gone some time. But don't move away and don't show yourself near the road. There'll be farm labourers about soon now. Have you got plenty of cigarettes?"

"Yes."

"All right then. I'll see you later."

He tramped off down the road. I watched him out of sight round the bend, then threaded my way through the trees to a spot sheltered by some bushes about twenty-five yards from the road. I sat down thankfully on the ground and prepared to wait.

Zaleshoff was gone nearly two hours. The sun had risen and was glancing through the trees, but it was still cold. Soon I gave up sitting on the ground in favour of a sort of sentry-go pacing between two trees. Fifty times I looked at my watch and fifty times I found that the hands seemed not to have moved. Once, a man passed along the road whistling. My heart was in my mouth until he had passed. I resumed my pacing. After a bit I drank some more of the cognac. My stomach was empty and the spirit made me feel sick. I began to wonder if Zaleshoff had perhaps been arrested until I remembered that there was no reason why he should be. Then I made up my mind that he had regretted his offer to get me out of the country and made for the nearest railway station and a train back to Milan. That, too, was absurd. He was probably, I decided, having a good breakfast of hot, crisp rolls with a great deal of ice-cold butter and scalding coffee. I suddenly became ravenously hungry. I could almost smell the hot yeastiness of those rolls. The swine! The least he could have done would have been to get me a bite to eat. Then I began to think of Claire. I ought somehow to let her know what was happening. Pelcher, too. Perhaps I could send them telegrams. No, that would be awkward. The Italian authorities might trace the telegrams back to the sending office and thus find out where we were. I must be careful, discreet. I could send them a letter each. That would be all right. Zaleshoff could not object to that. Better perhaps, though, not to tell him. But I had not got any notepaper or envelopes. I should have to tell him. As I paced up and down my mind wandered on. But of all the many reasons I had to feel sorry for myself, the one that made the others seem trifling was the lack of those hot rolls. It was, no doubt, just as well that it was so.

I was disturbed in these reflections by the snapping of a twig. I started violently. Then Zaleshoff hailed me softly. I pushed my way through the screen of bushes that hid me and found him struggling with a number of paper parcels.

"Oh there you are!" he said.

"You made me jump. Where have you been all this time?"

"I'll tell you in a minute. Help me with this stuff."

"What is it?"

"You'll see."

He handed me two heavy parcels and we pushed our way through to the clearing behind the bushes. There he sat down with a sigh of relief. I saw that his face was drawn and tired. He looked up at me and smiled wearily.

"First," he said, "I've got you some breakfast."

From his overcoat pocket he drew a large bag of buttered rolls. As I took the parcel from him I felt that they were still warm from the bakery. I tore the bag open and started to eat ravenously. Hot rolls! You couldn't help liking Zaleshoff!

From his other pocket he got out a bottle of milk. I extended the bag to him. He shook his head.

"No, thanks. I ate while I was waiting for the shops to open. Thank goodness, we're in the country. They opened early. I'd have brought you some coffee, but it would have been cold by the time I'd got it here."

"What's the name of the place?" I said with my mouth full.

"Remini. It's small and a good half-hour's walk from here. I . . ." He broke off suddenly. "Would you like to see what I've got in the other parcels?"

I nodded, and he opened the two heavy parcels and displayed the contents. I goggled at them.

"Boots?"

"Yes, a pair for each of us and some thick woollen socks. I noticed you had a bit of a limp this morning and when we stopped along the road I measured your foot against mine. We take the same size."

I regarded the huge, hob-nailed soles and heavy uppers with some misgiving. He interpreted my look correctly.

"We've got a whole lot of walking to do and they'll be less tiring than blisters."

"I suppose so. What's in the other parcel?"

"A muffler for one thing. You need one. And a hat."

"But I've got a hat."

"Not like this one. Have a look."

I had a look and what I saw did not please me. It was a very cheap Italian soft hat, black, with a high crown and flat brim.

"What on earth is this for?"

He grinned. "To make you look less conspicuous. That hat of yours is very natty but it shrieks English to high Heaven. There's nothing like a new hat for making you look different."

I tried on the hat. To my surprise it fitted me.

He nodded. "I had a look at your size in hats last night."

I felt it gingerly. "I can't help feeling," I said crossly, "that I shall look a damn sight more conspicuous in a low comedy affair like this than in my own hat."

"That's only because you're not used to it. Here, give it to me."

I gave it to him with pleasure. The next moment he was wringing it between his hands like a dish-cloth. He then proceeded to clean his shoes with it. Having done that he rubbed it vigorously on the ground until it was filthy. Then he shook the leaves off, punched it into shape again, dinted the top and handed it back to me.

"That's a bit more like it should be. No, don't dust it any more. Stick it on and give me your own."

I obeyed him. He surveyed me critically.

"Yes, much better. It's a good thing you're dark. That unshaven chin goes swell with the hat."

I lit a cigarette and yawned. The food had made me sleepy. My eyelids felt very heavy.

"Well," I said, "I feel like a sleep. What about it? Shall we stay here or try to find somewhere else?"

He did not answer immediately and I looked up from my cigarette. He was looking at me steadily.

"There'll be no sleep for us to-day," he said slowly. "We've got to get on."

"But . . ."

"I didn't tell you before because I thought I'd let you eat your breakfast in peace, but we're in a pretty tough spot here."

My heart sank. "What do you mean?"

"There are patrols out on all the roads."

"How do you know?"

"I ran slap into one just outside the village. Police and a couple of Blackshirt militiamen. We're still in the Treviglio area, you see. I had to show my passport and permit, and they were suspicious. I made up a story on the spur of the moment about having started out early from Treviglio to get to a business appointment in Venice and having the car break down. It wasn't very good, but it was the best thing I could think of to explain what I was doing along this road at this time and in these clothes. They let me by but they took a note of my name and the number of my passport. They also told me where the nearest garage was. I couldn't very well go back along the road with all those parcels—that *would* have wanted a bit of explaining—so I had to make a detour through the fields. If they remember me and it occurs to them to check up with the garage man they'll be beating the bushes before long. And there's another thing." He pulled a folded newspaper out of his inside pocket. "Take a look at this. It's this morning's."

I took the paper and scanned the front page. It was an early edition of a Milan sheet. It did not take me long to see what he wanted me to see. There, in the middle of the page, were two squared-up half-tones, each about three inches deep. Both were pictures of me.

Above them were the words, "ATTENTI, L. 10,000," in heavy black capitals. Below, also in bold type, was the message, slightly altered, that had been given over the radio the previous night. I examined the pictures carefully. One had obviously been taken from the prints I had supplied for my permit. It had been a "flat" photograph with hard, sharp lighting. The result was a reproduction that, in spite of the poor paper, was almost as clear as the original. It was easily recognisable as a picture of me. The other was less clear but it interested me very much for it had obviously been made from a photoprint of the photograph on my "lost" passport. I could see faintly where the black impressions of the British Foreign Office stamps had been painted out. I looked up.

"Well," said Zaleshoff; "now you know why I didn't want the ticket collector to see your face yesterday. The other papers have got those pictures too."

"Yes, I see." I paused. Again I felt fear gripping at my stomach. "What the devil are we to do? If they're patrolling the roads and everybody's got these pictures, there's nothing we *can* do. You know, I think . . ."

He interrupted me.

"Sure, I know! You think the best thing you can do is to give yourself up. Don't, for Heaven's sake, let's waste our strength talking all that over again." He got out the map. "We're not done yet. All the roads are patrolled but they can't patrol the fields as well. Now Reminini isn't marked on this map—it's too small—but according to my reckoning it's just about here"—he jabbed the paper with his finger— "and that means that we're only about thirty kilometres south of the railway line from Bergamo to Brescia. If you'll look at the map you'll see that all the major roads run almost due north in this area. In other words, if we go north cross-country we ought to be able to reach the railway to-day without much risk of running into a patrol."

"But in daylight …"

"I told you. The only roads we'll have to worry about are those we cross and they'll be secondary roads. As for the rest, all we've got to do is keep our eyes open."

I pounced bitterly on the last phrase. "Dammit, Zaleshoff, I can hardly keep my eyes open now. I'm all in. And so are you by the look of it. We shall never do it. It's no use your sticking your jaw out like that. It just isn't reasonable to think that we can do it. Anyway, supposing we *do* get to the railway; what then?"

"We can jump a goods train that'll take us to Udine."

"Supposing there isn't one?"

"There will be. It's the main goods line from Turin. We may have to hide out until it's dark, that's all. And as for feeling tired, you'll find that if you sprint a bit the tiredness'll wear off."

"Sprint!" I could hardly believe my ears.

"Yes, sprint. Come on, change your shoes for the boots and let's get going. It's not healthy here."

I had not the strength to argue any more. I took off my shoes, pulled the coarse woollen socks over my own and then put on the boots. They were very stiff and felt like diving-boots look. My hat and shoes and the bottle and wrappings we buried under the leaves.

We walked through the trees to the fields on the opposite side of the wood to the road: then Zaleshoff produced a small toy compass he had bought in the village. After some trouble with the compass needle which, until we found that the glass was touching it, seemed willing to indicate north in any direction, we marked as our objective a group of trees on the brow of a slope about a kilometre away and set off.

For a minute or two we walked. Then, suddenly, Zaleshoff broke into a sharp trot.

"Race you to the end of the path," he called back to me.

I detest at the best of times people wanting to race me to the ends of paths. I flung an emphatic negative after him, but he seemed not to hear. Feeling murderous, I picked up my heels and pounded after him. At length we slowed down, panting, to a walk.

"Feeling better?"

I had to admit that I was. The morning breeze had cleared away the remnants of the clouds. There was a suggestion of haze in the middle distance that presaged heat. We could hear a tractor working somewhere nearby, but we saw nothing on legs but cows. For a time we stepped out briskly. Then, as the sun became hotter, I felt my exhaustion returning.

"What about a rest?" I said after a while.

He shook his head. "We'd better keep going. Do you want some cognac?"

"No, thanks."

We plodded on. It was open farming country with few trees and no shade. Swarms of flies, awakened by the heat, began to worry us. By midday I was feeling horribly thirsty and had a bad headache. For most of the time we seemed to be miles away from any sort of habitation. According to Zaleshoff we should have been near a secondary road running from east to west, but there was no sign of it ahead. The new boots had "drawn" my feet and become intolerably heavy. My legs began to feel shaky. The situation was not improved by our having to waste twenty minutes cowering in a dry ditch out of sight of a labourer who stopped to eat his lunch by the side of a cart track we had to cross. When at last we were able to push on, my feet and ankles had swollen. Our pace became slower. I found myself straggling behind Zaleshoff.

He waited for me to catch up with him.

"If I don't have a drink of water soon," I declared, "I shall pass out. As for these damn flies . . ."

He nodded. "I guess I feel that way too. But we should make the road almost any time now. Can you keep going a bit longer?"

"I suppose so."

But it was two o'clock before we reached the road. It might have been an oasis in a desert instead of a dry strip of dusty flints. Zaleshoff uttered a husky exclamation of satisfaction.

"I knew we weren't far away. Now you get among those bushes and lie low while I see what I can find in the shape of a drink. Don't move away."

The exhortation was unnecessary. Nothing but the direst

necessity could have induced me to move. Through the pumping of the blood in my head I heard Zaleshoff's footsteps crunch slowly away into the distance.

Looking back now on those days with Zaleshoff one thing makes me marvel above all else—my complete and unquestioning belief in Zaleshoff's superior powers of endurance. It was always Zaleshoff who coaxed me into making a further effort when no further effort seemed possible. It was always Zaleshoff who, when we were both at the end of our strength, would walk another kilometre or more to get food and drink for us both. That it was safer for Zaleshoff to do so was beside the point; and, in any case, it soon became as dangerous for Zaleshoff as it would have been for me. My acceptance of the situation was based on the tacit assumption that Zaleshoff would naturally be in better shape than me. It is only now that I realise that Zaleshoff's was not physical superiority, but moral. I remember now, with a pang of mingled conscience and affection, the grey look of his face when he was tired, his habit of drawing the back of his hand across his eyes and one little incident that happened later. He had stopped suddenly to lean against a tree. With weary irritation I had asked him what the matter was. His eyes were shut. I remember now seeing the muscles of his face tighten suddenly. Then he looked angry and said that he had a stone down the inside of one of his boots. That had been all. He had pretended to extricate the stone and we had walked on. No, you could not dislike Zaleshoff.

I was nearly asleep when he got back. He shook me. I looked up and saw his face near mine. The sweat was trickling down in rivers through the dust and grime on his unshaven cheeks.

"Something to drink and eat," he said.

He had bought some bread and sausage and a bottle of water mixed with a little wine from a woman in a cottage about a quarter of a mile away. Her husband had been at work in the fields. He had seen nobody else but the driver of a passing lorry.

"I'd have preferred plain water myself," he added; "but she said it was safer with a little wine in it. I didn't argue the toss about it. We don't want to add stomach trouble to the rest of it."

I was feeling too tired to eat much. When we had finished, we put what was left in our pockets, together with the now half-empty bottle, smoked one cigarette each and set off again.

The afternoon was worse, if anything, than the morning. It was the first really hot day I had known in Italy. We marched with our overcoats and jackets slung over our shoulders. The flies pestered us almost beyond endurance. Twice we had to make wide semicircular detours over rough ground to avoid being seen by labourers. We crossed another secondary road. Towards four o'clock Zaleshoff called a halt.

"If we go on like this," he panted, "we shall kill ourselves. We can't be so very far from the railway now. For God's sake let's have a drink and wait for the sun to cool off a bit."

For an hour we rested in the shade of a tree, talking inanities to prevent ourselves going to sleep. When we got to our feet again the sun had started to dip down towards the trees on the western horizon. The flies seemed less attentive. Zaleshoff suggested singing as we went to keep a good marching rhythm. At first I was inclined to regard the proposal as a piece of very shallow heartiness, but to my surprise I found that the dingy humming that we managed to produce cheered me considerably. My legs seemed to be moving automatically as though they did not belong to me. All I could feel of them was the aching thigh muscles and the burning soles of my feet. We began to descend a long gentle gradient.

It was about half-past six that we heard the train whistle. Zaleshoff gasped out an exclamation. "You heard it, Marlow? You heard it?"

"It sounded a darn long way away."

"Electric train whistles always do. Another couple of kilometres and we'll have done it."

Twenty minutes later we crossed our third road. It was a little wider than the others and we had to wait for a private car and a van to pass before we broke cover and crossed.

The way now was more difficult. Before, we had been traversing open country partly under cultivation, with only an occasional hedge or low stone wall to mark property boundaries. Towards the railway the properties were smaller and sometimes fenced with wire. We passed at no great distance a fair-sized factory with two tall metal chimneys. Then, as we breasted a low slope, Zaleshoff pointed to what looked like a thin strip of grey cloud right down on the horizon ahead of us and said that it was the hills above Bergamo. Not long after we saw the railway line.

It emerged from a cutting about a quarter of a mile away below us. For some reason, the sight of it depressed me. We had arrived; but the worst lay ahead of us. The curving rails looked extraordinarily inhospitable.

"Well, what now?" I said helplessly.

"Now, we wait until it's dark."

We found a hollow screened by grass and piles of brown stones near the cutting and finished the remains of the food we had with us. We washed it down with some cognac. My eyes burned and stung and were half-closed, but I felt suddenly very wide awake.

"We'd better put our coats and scarves on," said Zaleshoff: "it'll be cold soon."

We lay there in silence watching the sun grow and redden as it sank into the streaky blue-black clouds that seemed waiting to receive it. The light faded. When it was nearly dark we left our hiding-place, moved down near to the line and began to walk in a direction parallel to it away from the cutting. By the time we saw the lights of a station it was quite dark.

We approached the station slowly. It was very small. In common with most small Italian country stations there were no platforms, only the white stuccoed station buildings, the neat wood fences, and the clipped hedges. Beyond it was a level crossing and a signal cabin. An electric floodlight suspended from a tall concrete standard cast a circular pool of light in front of the station house. Standing talking in the light were two men. One was a station official. The other was a Fascist militiaman with a rifle slung across his back.

"What's the one with the rifle doing there?" I whispered stupidly.

"What do *you* think?" retorted Zaleshoff. "The siding's over the other side. We'll go back and cross the line a bit lower down."

We groped our way back along the wire fence that bounded the track, then dived under it and scuttled across the rails. On the far side we remained on the track side of the fence and began slowly to work our way back towards the station.

The track level was only about a couple of feet above that of the surrounding land and we had practically to crawl along on our hands and knees to keep under cover. Then the fence curved away to the left and I saw ahead the bulky outlines of tarpaulined goods trucks. A moment or two later we were able to stand upright with the trucks between us and the station house.

There were about twenty trucks in the siding and all appeared to be loaded. We walked alongside them until we reached the buffers at the end. Then Zaleshoff stopped.

"This looks like us," he whispered. "All loaded and ready to go. Probably parked here last night. Come on."

He led the way back a little, then stopped again.

"Lend me your matches," he muttered.

I passed them to him in silence. He struck one and, shielding the flame with cupped hands, held it up against the side of the truck beside which we were standing. Then I saw that there was a metal frame there and that in the metal frame was a card. There was a lot of writing on the card, but as Zaleshoff blew out the match almost immediately I saw only one thing:

TORINO A VENEZIA—DIRETTORE PROV. MAR.

"Director of naval supplies, Venice," murmured Zaleshoff. "It won't get us to Udine because it'll be side-tracked again before then, but it'll get us on our way."

He reached up to one of the ropes securing the tarpaulin and untied it. Then he grasped an iron staple, clambered up the toe-holes in the side of the truck and turned back the free corner of the tarpaulin. I followed him. A moment later I slid under the tarpaulin. My boots struck something hard and slippery.

"What on earth is it?" I whispered.

I heard him chuckle in the blackness. "An egg box. Get down on your knees and feel. It's something you ought to know something about, I guess."

I got down on my knees. Then I understood why he had chuckled. The truck was loaded with big naval gun shells held upright by a sort of framework of wood. I could feel their cold, smooth surfaces each tapering to the ring bolts that had been screwed in for lifting purposes where the fuse would one day go. There was a smell of grease and machine oil.

As I wedged myself along the framework between two of the rows I heard Zaleshoff pulling the tarpaulin back into place.

"Now you can have your nap," he said.

I closed my eyes.

It seemed to me no more than a few minutes after that the jolt of the truck half woke me. Actually I must have been asleep some time. As the truck began to rumble on its way I drifted off once more into sleep.

The next thing I remember is a strong light shining in my eyes blinding me, of fingers gripping my arm hard and shaking me, and of a voice bawling at me in Italian.

Chapter XV

HAMMER AND SICKLE

NORMALLY I am a heavy sleeper and do not wake easily; the wakening is a long, slow journey back to consciousness; a journey through a country of fantastic confusions and strange images. But on that morning I awoke quickly. Even as I screwed up my eyes against the first blinding flash of the foreman's torch, I had remembered where I was and why I was there. A dream of fear changed suddenly into the reality.

The man shaking my arm was Zaleshoff. Then I felt a blow on my legs. With my eyes still closed I heard him speak quickly and angrily.

"Leave him alone. We'll get down all right."

I felt the glare leave my eyes and opened them again. It was still dark and there was a single bright star winking in a dark-blue sky. The head and shoulders of a man in uniform showed over the side of the truck.

"Be quick about it!" he snapped.

I scrambled to my feet. Zaleshoff already had one leg slung over the side of the truck.

"Where are we?" I whispered.

"Brescia. Speak Italian," he muttered.

I clambered out after him. In the gloom I could see four men standing waiting for us. Three were in workmen's overalls; the fourth, the uniformed man with the torch, was a foreman. As our feet touched the ground the four of them closed in on us and seized our arms.

The foreman flashed the torch over us. "To the weighbridge office," he said abruptly; "they can be kept there until I consult with the yard manager and the police. Keep a firm hold of them. Come on, march!"

He jerked my arm and we began to walk across a network of lines and points towards a massive, dark building.

We appeared to be in a big goods yard. Beyond the building ahead there was a haze of light coming from a row of floodlights which the building concealed. I could hear a diesel-motored engine shunting a long line of trucks and the receding *clink-clink* of the buffers. In the distance was the reflected glare in the sky of street lighting. It was cold and my body, still warm from sleep, shivered. One of the men holding Zaleshoff said something and the other laughed. Then we walked on in silence.

The dark building turned out to be an engine shed. About fifty yards beyond it a gang of men with a travelling crane working below the floodlights was loading motor-car chassis on to long two-bogie trucks. We turned away to the left along a narrow concrete path. The path curved round a signal cabin. Then we crossed another track and approached a small building with a large window in one side through which I could see a naked electric lamp suspended above a sort of counter. The foreman pushed the door open and we were led inside.

It was really little more than a hut. A youth was seated on a high stool before the counter, which I now saw was the recording part of the weighbridge on the adjacent track; and as we came in he slipped off his stool and stood goggling at us.

I could see the foreman's face now. He was a dark, grey-faced man with a little spiky moustache. He looked intelligent and bad-tempered. He frowned at the youth.

"Have you finished checking the cement loadings?"

"Yes, Signore."

"Then you can go and work at your own table. This is no business of yours."

"Yes, Signore." The youth gave us a frightened look and went.

"Now then!" The foreman relaxed his grip on my arm and motioned to the men holding Zaleshoff to release him. Then he pointed to the opposite wall of the office. "Stand over there, both of you."

We obeyed. His lips tightened. He surveyed us grimly.

"Who are you?" he snapped suddenly; and then, without giving us a chance to reply to this: "What were you doing in that truck? Don't you know that it is forbidden to ride on goods trains? You are cheating the State. You will be put in prison."

There did not seem anything to be said to this. Obviously, the moment the police saw me the game would be up. It was, I thought, remarkable that I had not already been identified with the picture in the paper. Perhaps the hat accounted for it. But it was only a matter of time. I wished they would hurry up. Perhaps it would be best if I told them myself.

"Well," snapped the foreman, "what have you got to say for yourselves?"

Then, to my surprise, Zaleshoff stepped forward a little. "We were doing no harm, Signore," he whined, "we were trying to get to Padova. We had heard that there was work there and we had no money. Do not give us up to the police, Signore."

It was abject; but Zaleshoff, with his filthy face and heavy growth of beard, was a villainous-looking object and anything but pitiable. I was not surprised when the foreman scowled.

"Enough. I know my duty. Where do you come from?"

"Torino, Signore. We were only trying to get work."

"Show me your identity card."

Zaleshoff hesitated. Then: "It is lost, Signore," he said quickly; "I had it, but it was stolen from me. It . . ."

It was a hopeless exhibition of shiftiness. The foreman cut him short with a gesture and turned to me.

"Show me your identity card."

"I have none, Signore, I . . ."

He laughed angrily. "Do you also come from Torino?"

I thought quickly. Now was the time to give myself up. Zaleshoff must have known what was passing through my mind for he coughed warningly. I hesitated.

"Answer!" snapped the foreman.

"No, Signore. From Palermo."

My Italian was not nearly as good as Zaleshoff's and I thought that I had better give an answer that would explain away my accent.

"I see." His lips tightened. "One from Torino and one from Palermo. Both without identity cards. This is clearly a matter for the police."

"But . . ." whined Zaleshoff.

"Silence!" The workmen had been watching the scene with blank faces. Now he turned to two of them. "You two stay here and see that they don't try to escape while I consult with the yard manager and the police." He turned to the third man. "Go back and see if they have done any damage inside the truck. If it is all in order refasten the tarpaulin properly. Those trucks will go on to Verona to-day."

A moment later the door closed and we were left with our two gaolers.

For a moment or two we exchanged stares.

They were brawny fellows with red, grease-smeared faces. They were wearing filthy light-blue overalls and berets. One of them was about my own age; the other looked about ten years older. He carried a long wheel-tapper's hammer. The younger man was, judging by the state of his hands, a greaser. They both looked very determined. It seemed obvious to me that if we tried any rough stuff we should accomplish nothing and probably get badly knocked about.

I glanced at Zaleshoff and caught his eye. His face was quite impassive, but he raised his eyebrows and shrugged slightly. I took it that he had resigned himself to the inevitable.

But I was wrong.

Four men standing in silence in a small room staring solemnly at one another produces after a while an atmosphere of extreme nervous tension. The desire to break the silence or establish some sort of communication with the other three becomes overpowering. The man with the hammer was the first to give way. His face puckered suddenly into a sheepish grin.

Zaleshoff promptly grinned back at him.

"Do you mind if we sit down, comrades?" he said.

The grin faded from the workman's face as suddenly as it appeared. I saw him cast a quick apprehensive glance at his companion. The younger man was frowning. I realised that it was the word "comrades" that had been the trouble. It was, I thought, very tactless of Zaleshoff.

The wheel-tapper nodded slowly. "Yes, you can sit down," he said.

There were some packing-cases in one corner of the office. We moved over and sat on them. Zaleshoff began to hum softly.

I stared wretchedly at the bare wood floor. So this was the end of our plan for getting out of the country! We might, I reflected bitterly, have saved ourselves those twenty-four hours of walking. I had, I told myself, always known that it was hopeless, that Zaleshoff had only been postponing the evil moment; yet, now that it had come, I was conscious of being disappointed. It must, I decided, have been that I had expected something different. I had expected to be recognised. In my mind's eye I rehearsed the scene as it should have been played. I imagined the sudden gleam that should have lighted my captor's eyes when he realised that he had earned himself ten thousand lire. Then there would be the formalities at the police station and the armed guard back to Milan. I pictured the pained courtesy of the young man at the Consulate. "Naturally, Mr. Marlow (or would he omit the Mister?), we shall do all we can, but . . ." Or perhaps it would not get as far as that. "Shot while escaping"—that had been the phrase Zaleshoff had used. "They make you kneel down. Then they put a bullet through the back of your neck." That was horrible. You knelt down as if you were going to pray. There was something helpless and pitiful about a man kneeling. I yawned. I kept yawning. It was absurd. I was not tired, I was not bored—my God, no! I was scared, scared stiff, in the bluest of funks, and I was yawning. It was grotesque. I shivered.

Zaleshoff was still humming. It was a march of some sort. It went on and on, a steady, plodding rhythm. I found myself involuntarily beating time with my foot.

"Stop that!"

It was the wheel-tapper who had spoken. It was said angrily, in irritation; but in his eyes there was a watchful, worried look that puzzled me. I had a sudden feeling that there was something going on that I did not understand. The greaser was watching Zaleshoff closely. Outside an engine clanked slowly past. Then it happened.

Zaleshoff pulled the brandy bottle out of his pocket.

"Can we have a drink, comrades?" he said.

The greaser made a motion forward as if to stop him; but the older man nodded.

"He's up to something," exclaimed the greaser suddenly. He turned on his companion accusingly. "You dirty Red!"

The wheel-tapper raised his hammer menacingly. His mouth tightened. "Keep your mouth shut," he said slowly, "or I'll knock your brains out."

I was bewildered. I looked at Zaleshoff. As if nothing had happened, he was uncorking the bottle. He extended it to me. I shook my head and stared at him.

"You won't have another chance for a while," he said with a shrug. "They don't serve it in prison."

He put the bottle to his mouth and tilted it. There was not much left in the bottle and I could not help seeing that the liquid did not get as far as his mouth. He lowered the bottle and smacked his lips.

"That was good," he said.

He got slowly to his feet and extended the bottle to the greaser.

"Have some, comrade?" he said.

The man scowled and opened his mouth to refuse. Suddenly Zaleshoff stepped forward and the bottle moved quickly in his hand.

The next moment the greaser was staggering back, his hands clapped to his eyes and brandy streaming down his face. Almost simultaneously Zaleshoff's arm with the bottle in it flew up and smashed the electric-light bulb.

After the naked glare of the lamp, the half-light of dawn seemed pitch blackness. The greaser was shouting and swearing violently. There was a quick scuffling, a sudden stamping of feet and a sharp grunt. The greaser stopped shouting. There was a sudden silence. For a split second I stood there bewildered, then I came to my senses and jumped towards where I knew the door to be. It was madness. I knew it. The man with the hammer would brain us before we could get out. Then a hand gripped my shoulder. I spun round, drew back my fist and drove it into the shadow behind me. The next instant my wrist was caught and held.

"It's me, you fool!" hissed Zaleshoff. "Get out quick!"

He flung the door open and we tumbled out into the air.

"But . . ."

"Shut up!" he snarled. "Run!"

Even as he spoke, I saw the foreman's torch bobbing towards us at the end of the concrete path.

We raced across the lines. Then I caught my foot in a sleeper and went sprawling. Zaleshoff dragged me to my feet. There were shouts raised behind us.

"Quick, Marlow! Down by the engine shed!"

I saw the bulk of it outlined against the bluing sky. We clattered across the steel turntable in front of it and turned down a cinder track alongside a line of trucks. Zaleshoff dived under the coupling between two of them. I followed. On the other side we paused. As far as I could see we were going in the direction of the station proper. There were lights ahead and a large open space criss-crossed by rails. Zaleshoff turned round.

"It's no good this way," he muttered. "There's no cover. They'd see us before we got to the station."

The shouts were growing nearer. I heard a man calling for more lights.

"Come on," said Zaleshoff, "we've got just one chance. Follow me and do exactly as I do, and for the love of Pete do it quietly."

He started to walk quickly back along the line of trucks towards the engine shed and to the men approaching on the other side. I could hear their footsteps now and the voice of the foreman exhorting them to hurry. Zaleshoff walked on steadily for a bit and then stopped. For a minute we stood behind a truck. Then we heard our pursuers pass to the right of us.

"Come on!" said Zaleshoff.

We walked on down the line of trucks. Towards the end of it there were four cattle vans. Opposite the first of these he stopped.

"Up on the roof for us," he said.

He reached up, grasped the bottom staple and clambered up. I followed. A moment or two later we were lying spread-eagled on the roof. I glanced back and saw that torches were flashing at the end of the line. My heart gave a leap.

"They're searching the trucks," I whispered.

"I know. Keep absolutely flat and lie still."

I obeyed. My nose was jammed against a conical ventilator. There was no doubt about it being a cattle truck; but I scarcely noticed the smell. I was listening to the voices coming nearer and nearer. I could feel my heart beating against the curved hard surface of the roof. There seemed, I thought, to be about eight of them. I could distinguish the foreman's voice and that of another man obviously in authority. Both seemed anxious to propitiate that man. He was, I guessed, a policeman.

"Certainly we shall recapture them," I heard the foreman say; "certainly. Without a doubt. They could not have got away in this time. If they have doubled back, your own men will catch them. There is no way out. When it is a little lighter . . ."

The policeman emitted an exclamation of impatience.

"We cannot wait for the light." He paused. "If *I* see them I shall shoot immediately. I do not believe that these men are tramps. That they have no identity cards is very suspicious." Another pause. "See that your men search thoroughly. Not a centimetre of this train must be left unsearched. Do you hear?"

There was silence again. My heart pounded. Then, out of the corner of my eye, I saw Zaleshoff's hand moving slowly to his side. It stayed there for a moment, then it moved slowly upwards again. By the growing light I saw that he had a revolver in his hand.

Instinctively I stretched out my hand and clutched his sleeve. He shook me off and wormed his way slowly towards the edge of the roof.

They were only two trucks away now and on both sides of the line. I could hear them panting over their exertions as they climbed up the sides of the trucks and stripped back the tarpaulins. Then something struck the side of the truck on which we were lying. A moment later the sliding doors below us were rolled back. There was a pause. They were evidently flashing a torch round the interior. One of the men muttered *"niente."* Then a boot grated on the bottom staple and a man began to climb up to the roof.

I listened to the man's feet as he clambered up. One, two, three, four . . . another step and the top of his head would be visible. We were caught. I waited for his shout. I wondered desperately whether it would not be better to stand up there and then and surrender. The policeman might not shoot. As I swallowed down the saliva that kept filling my mouth I saw that Zaleshoff had moved so that he was near the edge of the roof at the point where the man would appear. The next moment the top of the man's head came into view. He took another step and the white shape of his face appeared. At that moment Zaleshoff's left arm shot out and he grasped the man's collar. I saw his right hand jab the revolver against the side of the man's head.

It was done in a fraction of a second. With his hands grasping the staples on the side of the van he could not attempt to defend himself. I heard him give a stifled sob of terror. Then, too softly for me to hear, Zaleshoff whispered something to him. The next moment the man was climbing slowly on to the roof. I could see his face more clearly now. His mouth was half open and his eyes were moving quickly from side to side seeking some way of escape. He bent forward to steady himself by putting his hands on the roof. Zaleshoff lifted his right arm. I saw him twirl the revolver round by the trigger guard and grasp the barrel. Then he brought the butt down with all his strength on the back of the man's head.

The man gasped once and slumped forward half on the roof and half off it.

"Pull him up," whispered Zaleshoff.

I grasped the man's outstretched arms and pulled. I saw Zaleshoff trying to draw the feet sideways on to the roof. It was difficult to exert any force while we were lying on our faces, but somehow we managed it. There was a movement from below and the policeman called up to know if there was anything to be seen on the roofs of the other cattle trucks.

Zaleshoff squirmed across the roof to the far side.

"*Niente*," he called back. He slurred the word so that it was little more than a grunt.

There was a curse from below. I heard the doors of the next truck being rolled back. The unconscious man's head had begun to bleed profusely, and the blood was trickling slowly down the curved roof and soaking into the shoulder of my overcoat. I tried to move, but Zaleshoff stopped me with a warning gesture. I heard the search go on to the third and then the fourth van. Then I saw Zaleshoff beckon. I edged across to him. He brought his lips close to my ear.

"We'll go down one at a time now," he whispered. "You go first. When you get to the ground turn right, away from them, and walk, *walk*, mind you, slowly and quietly along by the trucks. Keep close in to them. They'll miss this poor sucker any minute now, and we've got to get clear. I'll catch you up."

With infinite care and feeling as conspicuous as an aeroplane caught in searchlights, I swung my legs over the edge of the roof, rolled over on my face and felt with my toes for the staples. A moment or two later I reached the ground. I gave one glance at the torches still flashing about twenty-five yards away. I wanted badly to run; but I controlled myself carefully. Zaleshoff had said walk. I turned and walked. I heard a slight sound behind me and Zaleshoff had caught me up. We reached the cover of the engine shed in safety.

It was possible by this time to distinguish something of our surroundings. Far away to the right of us was the weighbridge office. Facing the engine shed about a hundred yards away was a long low building that looked like a warehouse. I remembered what I had overheard.

"I heard the foreman say that that way was guarded," I said quickly, for he was peering in that direction.

"So did I. We're not going that way. We've got to get across those lines on to the station side, and I guess there's only one way to do it. Come on. We'll see what we can find in here."

I felt suddenly irritable. My nerves were raw. He was treating me, I thought, like a child. And I was feeling sorry for the man he had clubbed.

"What do you expect to find? Are you planning to pinch an engine and ride out on that?"

"Don't be damned silly. Come on."

We walked to the end of the cinder path and turned into the engine shed. It was a large building constructed on a slight curve so that the lines on which the engines ran under cover converged on the turntable. The glass roof was practically obscured by soot deposits and it was very dark inside. There were five or six engines in it.

Zaleshoff led the way round behind them. Then I heard him give a grunt of satisfaction. We stopped. I could see him fumbling with something in the darkness near the wall. Suddenly he straightened his back and thrust something greasy and soft into my hands.

"What is it?"

"What I was looking for. A driver's coat. Get your overcoat off and put it on. There's a cap here, too."

I put the coat on. As my eyes got used to the darkness I could see that he was doing the same. On his head was a beret. He handed me a cap with a shiny peak. The coat smelt strongly of coal, grease and sweat.

"Have you kept your scarf?"

"Yes."

"Good. Give me your overcoat and hat."

I did so and he stuffed them behind a steel locker.

"I don't," I said, "see the point of all this. Do you imagine that we're going to get past the police on the strength of a couple of coats?"

"No. What we are going to do is to walk across the lines into the station and . . ."

"And hide in the lavatories, I suppose," I supplemented ironically.

"Maybe. Let's go."

A minute later we broke cover and began to walk across the tracks towards the end of the line of trucks that separated us from the main lines.

It was a nerve-racking business. Out of the corner of my eye I could see that Zaleshoff's victim had been found. They had lowered him from the roof of the van and he was sitting on the ground, his hands clasping his head. A group of them, including the foreman, was standing round talking excitedly. The policeman with his revolver at the ready was stalking rapidly in the direction of the warehouse. A railway official was trailing anxiously in his wake. We passed the line of trucks safely and started to cross the main lines diagonally towards the station. It may have been my nerves or it may have been that the driver's coat was a good deal thinner than my overcoat, but by the time we had reached the station I was shivering violently.

The station platforms were practically deserted; but there were two bored-looking militiamen leaning against the wall by each exit. There was also a man with a trolley buffet talking to a porter on one of the eastbound platforms. Zaleshoff changed direction suddenly and began to walk towards it.

"What's the idea?" I muttered.

"That buffet means that there's a night train due in. If it's got third-class coaches, we'll jump it."

"What about tickets?"

"We've got uniforms on. We can go third-class free."

We reached the platform.

I think that those ten minutes we had to wait for the train were the worst part of it.

The sky was grey and a thin drizzle had begun to fall; but it was now light. The goods yard seemed very near. The station was very quiet, and small sounds, the scraping of a foot, a cough, echoed from the curved roof. To my overwrought imagination, the porter, the buffet attendant and the militiamen seemed all to be staring at us suspiciously.

"For God's sake," muttered Zaleshoff, "don't look so darned sinister. You look as though you'd just made arrangements to blow up the station. Don't look at them, look at me; and look as if you liked it. Come on, we'll try a slow walk towards the buffet. We can't stand here all the time. It looks too exclusive. Have you got your cigarettes?"

"Yes."

"Break one in half in your pocket, stick one end in your mouth and light up. If those two start talking to us, keep your mouth shut and leave it to me. They'll spot your accent."

My fingers were shaking so much that it took me over a minute to light the cigarette. By that time, Zaleshoff was sauntering, hands in pockets, towards the buffet. Suppressing a desire to run after him, I followed slowly. I caught him up as he was nearing the buffet. The porter and the buffet attendant had stopped talking and were watching our approach. I felt sick with apprehension. Then the porter nodded to Zaleshoff.

"Trouble over at the goods yard, they tell me," he said.

He was a youngish man with quick blue eyes.

Zaleshoff shrugged. His voice when he spoke was thick, as though he had a cold, and he slurred his words. It would have been difficult to detect any accent.

"They found a couple of tramps hiding in a truck," he said. "One of them hit one of our chaps with a bottle and they got away. They must be hiding in another truck now. But they won't get out of the yard."

The porter leaned forward confidentially. "We've had a message here to look out for them. It is said that they may be the two foreigners that escaped from Milan."

Zaleshoff whistled softly.

The porter smacked his lips. "Ten thousand lire! That's something, isn't it?"

"Not so bad. But"—he looked puzzled—"I thought there was only one of them."

The porter whipped a newspaper out of his pocket. "No, two. The police think that he has another man with him, this foreigner. They were seen in a *caffè* near Treviglio the night before last. The *padrone* recognised one of them from the photograph in the paper. Look, here it is. No photograph of the second man, but a description. You know, I think that these are not Englishmen, but French, or perhaps English spies working for the French. The French will stab us in the back if they can. Yesterday I carried the baggage of a Frenchman, three heavy suitcases, and found him a good corner seat with his back to the engine as he wished. He gave me five lire. Five lire only!" He gazed at us in bitter triumph.

"Ah, the French!" said Zaleshoff. He glanced at the paper idly and laughed. "Well, it won't be you or me that'll collect that ten thousand. It'll be a policeman. You mark my words."

"Policeman!" chimed in the buffet attendant suddenly. He lowered his voice. "A man was telling me in the *caffè* last night that it was not the police whom these men escaped from in Milan, but—well—you know who I mean." He looked from one to the other of us meaningly.

Zaleshoff shrugged again. "Perhaps." He turned and dug me jovially in the ribs. "Hey, what about ten thousand lire, Beppe?" He turned again to the other two. "He's sulking. His woman is at home in Udine, and he's thinking that there will be a couple of his mates underneath the bed when he gets back."

The three of them roared with laughter. I scowled. Zaleshoff dug me in the ribs again.

"Where did you say you came from?" said the porter suddenly.

"Udine, and that's where we're going back to."

"Then how did you get this way?"

He was looking puzzled. My heart missed a beat. Zaleshoff must have blundered in some way.

"Brought a train of refrigerator vans up from Padova. Special job." He said it easily enough; but I saw a wary look in his eyes.

The porter nodded, but I could see that he was thinking this over. I saw the blue eyes flicker once from me to Zaleshoff. It was with an inward sigh of relief that I saw that the train had been signalled. Zaleshoff nodded towards the signal.

"Where's this one going?" he said.

It was the buffet attendant who replied.

"Belgrade and Sofia *direttissimo*, with a slip coach for Athens. It's got third all right as far as Trieste."

"Venezia'll do for us."

The porter opened his mouth to speak and then shut it again. I saw him shrug slightly as if dismissing a thought from his mind. Then he strolled away up the platform and began to manoeuvre a trolley into position ready to transfer the packages with which it was loaded to the luggage van on the train. But I noticed that from time to time he glanced at us. Another porter appeared with a postal official and a mountainous load of mail bags. The buffet attendant began to test the automatic coffee urn on his trolley. The smell of hot coffee was exquisite torture. The attendant looked at our empty hands.

"Aren't you eating to-day?"

"We have eaten," said Zaleshoff promptly; "an hour ago."

"Coffee?"

Zaleshoff grinned. "At a lira a cup! What do you take us for?"

The attendant laughed and began to push the trolley towards the end of the platform. We were left alone.

"That porter . . ." I began under my breath.

"I know," he murmured; "but we'll be out of it in a minute. Heavens, I could have done with a cup of coffee." He glanced up at the clock. "Two minutes after six. It'll probably be late." He looked casually along the platform at the porter. "It would be our luck," he muttered vindictively, "to strike a guy with eyes in his head. The only consolation is that he's feeling afraid of making a fool of himself."

"I don't know that our luck's been so bad."

"If it hadn't been for a piece of lousy luck we shouldn't have been found in that truck. I couldn't fasten the tarpaulin from the inside, and the wind blew it back. When we stopped in the yard they spotted it and had to climb up to pull it back. We shouldn't have been spotted otherwise."

I glanced sideways at him. "I wasn't thinking about that and you know it. Why didn't that wheel-tapper stop us? And it was he who stopped the other man shouting, too, wasn't it?"

"Why should he? I wish this darn train 'd hurry."

"It'll look better if we talk," I said spitefully. "What sort of game were you playing in that office, Zaleshoff?"

"Game?"

"Yes—game."

For a moment our eyes met. "This isn't the time . . ." he began, then shrugged. "Back in nineteen-twenty," he went on slowly, "a lot of the Italian workers used to tattoo a small hammer and sickle on the forearm. It was just to show that they didn't care a hoot who knew they were Communists. Sort of badge of honour, see. When that guy was holding me, I saw that he had a round scar on his arm. I guessed then that he might have had one of those tattoo marks at some time, but that he'd found it safer since to cut away the flesh with the mark on. I thought I'd find out if I was right. I called him comrade. That scared him, because the other guy was too young to remember anything except *fascismo* and he might talk. But I knew I'd got him. Once a Communist always a Communist. I started humming the *"Bandiero Rossa"* —that's the old Italian workers' song. Then, when I was pretending to take that drink, he winked at me. I knew he was O.K. In the darkness he gave that young chap a clip under the jaw that knocked him cold. I had to do the same for him then, so that he'd have something to show when they questioned him. The poor sap!"

I thought for a moment. "You know," I said then, "I wouldn't call him a poor sap, and I don't think you would either if you didn't feel that you ought to behave like the traditional right-thinking American citizen."

But he did not answer. The train was coming in.

Through the windows of the sleeping-cars I could see the white sheets on the upper berths. The sight made me start yawning again. I felt suddenly very tired.

There was a concerted rush for the buffet from the three third-class coaches at the front of the train. We got into a second-class coach and walked along the corridors to the front.

The three third-class coaches were very full and very hot. There were soldiers on the train, and their equipment was piled up in the corridors. Through the steamy windows of the compartments I could see weary, harassed women trying to pacify howling children. The air smelt of garlic, oranges and sleep.

"We'll stick in the corridor," murmured Zaleshoff.

Five minutes later the train drew out. We were leaning on the rail gazing out of the window. The blue-eyed porter was standing on the platform looking up. Our eyes met his, and his head turned slowly as the coach slid past him. Zaleshoff waved.

But the porter did not wave back. I saw him raise one hand slowly as if he were about to do so. Then the hand stopped. He snapped his fingers and turned on his heel.

"Damn!" said Zaleshoff softly. "He's made up his mind."

Chapter XVI

TWO GENTLEMEN OF VERONA

WHAT ARE we going to do now?"

It was the second time I had said it; I seemed always to be saying it; but he looked as if he had not heard me the first time. He was gazing out of the window vacantly, watching the side of a cutting slip by as the train gathered speed. Again he did not answer.

"I suppose that they'll be waiting for us at Verona."

He nodded.

"Then there's nothing we can do?"

"Sure, there's plenty we can do; but not yet."

"I don't see . . ."

"Shut up; I'm thinking."

I shut up and lit a cigarette. I had a pain in my stomach and could not decide whether it was nerves or hunger. Then I noticed that he was examining my face.

"You're pretty filthy," he said.

"You don't look any too clean yourself." For some reason, I felt suddenly very wide-awake and very quarrelsome. "I've always heard," I added venomously, "that the Russians are a very dirty race. But then, of course, you're an American, aren't you?"

I saw the muscles of his face tighten beneath the grime. "I should not have believed, Marlow, that the schoolboy could persist to such an absurd extent in the adult. I wonder if you are typically English. Maybe you are. One can see, then, why the Continental mind fails to understand the English. I have often suspected it. The Englishman is no more than an intellectual Peter Pan, a large red-necked Peter Pan with a grubby little mind and grubby false wings. Sublimely ridiculous."

I made some angrily cumbersome retort. We bickered on. We snapped and snarled at one another steadily for a good five minutes. It was childish, absurd; and it was Zaleshoff who put a stop to it. We had lapsed into a sulky silence. Suddenly, he turned to me and grinned sheepishly.

"Well, thank goodness we've got that out of our systems."

For a moment I frowned sullenly at him, then I was forced to grin too.

"O.K.?" he said.

I nodded. "O.K."

"Good. Then let's get down to brass tacks."

"Do you really think that porter'll do anything?"

"I'm afraid so. He was suspicious, all right. I must have made a bloomer somewhere. It was the mention of Udine that got him. They probably don't send goods trains up direct from Udine. Anyway, we can't afford to take a risk. Somehow we've got to get out of these clothes and make ourselves look different between here and Verona. We haven't got much time to do it in."

"But how . . . ?"

"Listen."

For a minute he talked quickly. At the end of it I pursed my lips.

"Well, I suppose we shall have to try it. But I must say that I don't feel very happy about it, Zaleshoff."

"I didn't think you would. I don't. I shan't feel happy until we're across the frontier."

"If we ever do get across the frontier. If they catch us now, they'll . . ."

"Forget it."

"Yes, I know, but . . ." I broke off helplessly. I was past caring what happened to me. All I wanted was food and more sleep. "I suppose that we just wait now for the ticket inspector."

"Yes, we just wait."

We waited. It takes just under an hour by train from Brescia to Verona, and half that time had gone by the time the ticket inspector came round. As the minutes went by Zaleshoff became increasingly anxious.

"Perhaps he doesn't inspect the tickets on this run," I suggested.

"If he doesn't," he retorted grimly, "we're sunk anyway, because that means they'll be inspected at the Verona barrier."

When at last we saw the inspector appear at the end of the corridor, Zaleshoff gave a sigh of relief. "Keep your face turned away from him as far as possible," he murmured.

I gazed steadfastly out of the window. But the precaution was unnecessary. The man passed us with no more than a casual nod. We waited until he was a few compartments away. Then Zaleshoff nudged me.

"O.K. Let's go."

We strolled slowly to the end of the corridor out of sight, then we increased our pace and walked rapidly through the second-class coaches. When we reached the leading first-class coach we slowed down again as we walked through it. At the end we stopped.

"There's a hat and an overcoat in the third compartment from the end," Zaleshoff reported under his breath; "but there's a woman passenger in there. The man's probably in the restaurant car having coffee. We'll try the next one."

We walked on again. Half-way down the next corridor I heard Zaleshoff stop behind me.

"Stand where you are," he muttered; "and don't look round."

Ten seconds later, he prodded me in the back.

"Let's go back."

We returned to the end of the corridor and stopped outside the lavatory. I opened the door. As I did so I felt Zaleshoff push a soft bundle under my arm. A moment later I was inside the lavatory and had locked the door.

I said "phew!" very loudly to restore my self-possession

and looked round. Then I jumped violently. A man was looking at me, and he was one of the ugliest-looking customers I had ever seen. Then, I saw that I was looking at myself in the mirror. I could understand now the blue-eyed porter's uncertainty. I have a dark beard and there was the growth of two nights on my face. I was filthy—Zaleshoff had been right there. The dust of the previous day, the grease from the shells, transferred by my fingers together with the soot from the roof of the cattle truck, the sweat—all had contributed. Beneath it all, my face was haggard. My eyes were red and bleary with fatigue. The dye from the muffler, soaked out by the sweat, had made a dark ring round my neck. The greasy driver's cap completed the effect. No, it was not surprising that I had not been identified with the picture in the newspaper.

But I had work to do. I stripped off the driver's coat and hat, rolled them up in a ball and threw them out of the window. Then I took off my jacket, waistcoat and shirt, retrieved the safety razor and shaving cream from the jacket pocket and set to work on my face.

Following Zaleshoff's instructions, I left a thin line of moustache and side-whiskers that descended down my jaw to the level of my nostrils. When I had washed I combed my hair straight back.

I was surprised by the result. As Zaleshoff had predicted, the long side-whiskers altered the proportions of my face. My mouth and chin looked somehow smaller. My forehead had become high and narrow. The hair brushed back accentuated those tendencies. The slight moustache made the nose more prominent.

I put my shirt, waistcoat and jacket on again and turned to the bundle Zaleshoff had stolen. It consisted of a good soft hat and a raincoat. Both were grey. I put them on and looked at myself again. Except for my dirty white collar and crumpled tie I looked "respectable." Cheered by this and by the wash, I unlocked the door and stepped into the corridor.

Zaleshoff was lolling against the window outside. He looked round and I saw his shrewd eyes travel quickly from my head to my feet.

"Not bad," he commented; "but you've been a helluva time. We'll be in in another ten minutes. Give me the razor and comb and get back inside there until we begin to slow down."

I gave him the razor and comb.

"What about your clothes?"

He tapped his stomach and I noticed that there was an oddly shaped bulge to the blue tunic.

"While you're waiting," he said, "you'd better do something about your boots. Polish them as best you can. They're the only part of you that doesn't look right. And your hat's a bit big. Put some paper in the band."

"What about suitcases?"

"Leave that to me. I'll tap three times on the door when I want you to come out. You'd better wait for that."

He vanished along the corridor in the direction of the second class. I retired once more to the lavatory and attacked my boots. I had let the turn-ups of my trousers down in the engine shed, but now that I had to turn them back again the uppers looked bad. They were of crude and unpolished leather and were much scratched. I rubbed at them furiously with the muffler, but without much result. The top part of me was that of a respectable Italian business man; the bottom that of a labourer. I gave it up after a bit, and having let out my braces so that my trousers covered as much of the boots as possible, I lit a cigarette and composed myself to wait.

After a seemingly interminable eight minutes, I felt the train slowing. I pitched my cigarette away and prepared for Zaleshoff's knock. I was in a fever of anxiety. The thought that was gnawing at my mind was that Zaleshoff had been caught taking the suitcases or that the owner of the hat and coat which he had stolen had seen him wearing them and given the alarm. The train had nearly come to a standstill, and I could hear the station bell tolling and people moving along the corridors to get out, when there were three quick taps on the steel panels of the door.

I wrenched it open and nearly fell over a suitcase standing just outside. Zaleshoff was standing by the exit door; but for the moment I did not recognise him.

He had on a dark green overcoat and a green Alpine hat; but it was his face that had altered. He was clean shaven, but the shape of it was different. It was rounder. His upper lip projected slightly over the lower in an odd way.

He was handing down a suitcase to a porter below. Then, for a moment, he half turned and his eyes met mine. Then they dropped meaningly towards the suitcase at my feet. The next moment he was gone. I picked up the suitcase and went to the door.

Another porter was standing on the platform looking up at me expectantly. The suitcase was heavy, and I grasped the rail to swing it out for him to take. The next moment I nearly dropped it on his head. Standing on either side of the porter and looking up at the train were two blackshirt militiamen.

I could have hesitated only a fraction of a second; but in that moment my brain worked overtime. I saw that their hands were resting on their Mauser pistols and knew that it was no use turning back. They would shoot me in the back, and even if they missed there were probably more of them on the other side of the train. Had Zaleshoff got through, or had they caught him too? I felt the sweat start out from the pores of the skin.

The porter grasped the suitcase and I swung myself down to the platform. Then the unbelievable happened. I looked at the faces of the militiamen. They were not looking at me but past me up into the train. For a moment I stopped, hardly able to believe my eyes. Then:

"Where to, Signore?" said the porter.

I was gaping. I pulled myself together. "To the cloak-room," I muttered.

My legs trembling, I followed him along the platform. There were two militiamen posted at every exit from the coaches. As the last of the alighting passengers left the third-class coaches at the front, I saw two of them, accompanied by an officer, board the train. Heads were being thrust out of the windows. The other passengers had realised that something out of the ordinary was happening.

Ahead of me I saw Zaleshoff, preceded by his porter, disappear through the door leading to the street. There were three more militiamen standing by it. I walked on. I was acutely conscious of my boots. They seemed to be making as much noise as a regiment on the march. They made a clumping, hollow sound as they touched the asphalt. I noticed for the first time that one of them squeaked. To take my mind off them I tried to decide what I should do if the owner of the suitcase, which the porter was carrying, were to identify it from a window of the train. It was a large, expensive-looking thing and easy to recognise. Should I run or attempt to brazen it out? But no! If I did that they would notice my accent. They might want to see my passport, they . . .

But I was approaching the exit. There were only a few yards to go now. I could see the faces of the militiamen turned towards me. I was sure that one was looking at my boots. Their faces came towards me and, in my panic, I could not make up my mind whether I was approaching them or whether they were coming towards me to seize me. My feet felt ungainly and awkward, as if I were wearing snowshoes. Instinctively I altered my direction slightly to bring the porter ahead of me between myself and them. He passed them. I felt the calves of my legs go taut as I walked. The militiamen stared at me. I was almost level with them. I could see the details of their uniforms, the texture of the black cloth, the shape of the black leather revolver holster, the shiny brass stud that secured it. I waited for a black arm to go up blocking my path. I prepared to play the farce out to the end. To be indignant. Instinctively, my face screwed up into an indignant scowl. A moment later I was past them.

For a moment I could scarcely believe my good fortune. I walked on, expecting at any moment to feel hands grasping my arms, pulling me back. But no hands came. Then I was standing in a dream by the cloakroom counter and the porter was standing there waiting for a tip. I plunged my hand into my pocket and pulled out the first coin my fingers touched. I saw the porter stare at it as I dropped it into his hand and realised, too late, that I had made a mistake. I had given him ten lire. He would remember me. I waved away his thanks irritably and turned to go. The cloakroom attendant called me back. I had forgotten my counterfoil. I took it and, sweating profusely, clumped towards the station yard.

Zaleshoff was waiting for me a little way away. I told him what I had done. He shrugged.

"It can't be helped. Have you got your cloakroom check? Well, tear it up and throw it away. I picked suitcases with name and address tags on them. The owners'll get them back eventually. Now let's go and have some breakfast. The shops won't be open for an hour or so yet."

By the time we had established ourselves in a *caffè* some distance from the station, reaction had set in. I was trembling from head to foot. The last thing I wanted was food. Zaleshoff grinned sympathetically.

"You'll feel better when you've had some coffee. It wasn't so bad as all that. Don't forget that they were looking for a couple of guys in drivers' uniforms."

"Maybe. But I've got the jitters."

"Well, we've got plenty of time. We can take it easy for a bit. As soon as the shops are open, we'll get some shoes, two new hats, two shirts and a couple of small suitcases. I'll get you a pair of glasses, too. They're not much good as a disguise, but they'll give you confidence. We can change in a lavatory somewhere and put this stuff we're wearing now into the suitcases. Then we'll buy tickets, like ordinary respectable folks, for Vicenza. We ought to get to Udine this afternoon."

"If we don't get caught here." I noticed that his face was looking normal again. "What did you do to your face?"

"Tore my handkerchief into strips and made me some little wads like the things dentists put in your mouth. They were poked inside my cheeks. They nearly made me throw up as I walked down the platform. I've shaved my eyebrows a bit, too." He got up. "I'll be back in a minute, I'm going to get a paper."

By the time he returned I had drunk some coffee and was feeling cooler, both mentally and physically. He was looking solemn.

"What's the matter?"

He gave me the paper. As the blue-eyed porter had said, Zaleshoff's description had been added to mine. We were still believed to be in the vicinity of Treviglio. But the paper had been printed some hours before.

"I don't see," I said, "that this makes it any worse."

"No, it doesn't make it any worse. But it's what they haven't printed that I'm worrying about."

"Such as what?"

But he did not answer. "There's something inside that may interest you," he said: "page three, column two, near the top."

I found it. It was a short paragraph under the caption:

"THE POLICE SUSPECT SUICIDE"

It went on:

MILAN,
Friday.

A woman was found late to-night behind a house in the Corso di Porta Nuova. She was seriously injured, and is believed to have fallen from a fourth-storey window. She died on the way to the hospital. A servant, Ricciardo Fiabini, identified the dead woman as signora Vagas, wife of Maggiore Generale J. L. Vagas of Belgrade, who is well-known in Milan musical circles. The General is at present abroad.

I looked up. "Why did she do it?"

He shrugged. "She was crazy; and when Vagas got away . . . but you can't begin to explain how the mind of a dame like that works." He stopped and looked at me quizzically. "What are you thinking about? Want to send a wreath?"

I shook my head.

"No," I said slowly; "I was wondering if Ricciardo would attend the funeral."

As soon as the shops were open, we made our purchases. Soon after nine we boarded a slow "omnibus" train to Vicenza. We arrived there at about half-past ten. From Vicenza we doubled on our tracks by bus to Tavernelle, where we caught a train to Treviso. We repeated the doubling-back process at Castelfranco and later at Casarsa. We reached Udine at half-past nine that evening.

It was a worrying day. Most of the stations were heavily guarded and we travelled in constant fear of being asked to show our papers. From time to time we dozed fitfully. The early drizzle cleared away during the morning and it became sunny and very warm. As we drew out of a station our heads would nod forward and for a minute or two we would sleep, only to wake up with a nerve-racking jerk if the train slowed for a signal or crossed points. My eyes ached and smarted with fatigue. This misery was aggravated by the pair of thick pebble glasses which Zaleshoff had bought for me at a street market stall, and which rendered me practically blind when I was forced to look through instead of over them. To add to my discomfort, I developed a bilious attack. Zaleshoff ate a solitary luncheon out of a paper bag. The only redeeming feature of the journey was that for most of the time we travelled with compartments to ourselves.

At Udine we left our cases in the cloakroom.

"Do you feel like something to eat yet?" said Zaleshoff as we walked warily out of the station.

"I might tackle an omelette."

"Then we'll find somewhere good. We may as well take our time about it, too. We've got time to kill."

I groaned. "Isn't there some small shady hotel where we could spend the night without being asked for our passports. I know we've had a nap or two to-day, but it's a bed I want. My back feels as if it's got a hole in it."

"So does mine. But you'll find that the shadier the hotel the more fuss they'll make about passports. Still, if you know of a place we'll go there. Otherwise . . ." He shrugged. "We've spent a lot of money to-day one way and another. We've got to wait for the banks to open in the morning or we shall run short."

"Supposing the police . . ."

"They won't. I've got an account in another name with the Rome branch of the Industrial Bank. I told Tamara to write a letter in that name to the Rome office telling them to arrange drawing facilities at their branch here."

"That sounds to me as if she'd have to forge a signature."

"Your hearing's perfect. That's just what she has done."

We found a restaurant and stayed there until it closed at

midnight. The next two hours we spent in a *caffè* drinking coffee. Then we went for a walk. Towards three we returned to the station, found that there was a Vienna-Rome train due at a quarter to six and spent the rest of the dark hours at a nearby wine-shop on the pretext of waiting for it. We played a card game called *scopa* with the proprietor and two of the railway workers, for whose benefit the place was kept open all night. At five o'clock we ordered spaghetti, ate it and left soon after, ostensibly to catch the Rome train. Actually we went for another walk. Twice we had to scuttle down side-streets to avoid encountering patrolling policemen, but a little before seven we found an open *caffè*.

By this time the sight and smell of coffee had become unbearable, and we disposed of the coffee we had to order by pouring it over the roots of the privets which stood in green wooden tubs along the pavement in front of the tables. I was feeling sick and wretched. Zaleshoff looked ghastly. We had sat there for an hour, and I was wondering how on earth we were going to spend the time until the banks opened, when I saw his face light up. He snapped his fingers.

"Got it!"

I grunted. "What?"

"A Turkish bath."

My spirits rose. "But will there be one?"

"More likely than an ordinary bath and in a town this size. . . ." He broke off and summoned the waiter.

There *was* a Turkish bath. It opened at half-past seven and we spent the next four hours in it. We had left instructions with the attendant that we were to be called at half-past eleven. We slept soundly. Both of us, I think, could have slept the clock round and we were still tired when we were awakened; but we felt immeasurably better, and a cold shower apiece temporarily stifled the desire for more sleep.

It was decided that it would be wiser for Zaleshoff to go to the bank alone, and I went for a walk in the public gardens. He rejoined me there soon after twelve and displayed his bulging notecase with a grin. Over our lunch he expounded his plan of campaign.

"The first thing," he said, "is another change of clothes. I don't think for a minute that we've been traced this far, but it won't do any harm. Besides, where we're going, these clothes would look a bit curious."

"Where are we going, then?"

"Up into the mountains."

He brought the map out again. I looked at it while he traced a line north-east towards the Yugo-Slav frontier with the handle of a fork.

"That's all very well," I objected; "but why clamber about mountains when we can go due east towards Laibach?"

"I'll tell you. The Gorizia-Laibach road may be more direct, but we'd have to cross the frontier between Godovici and Planina. The frontier along that line is pretty well dead straight, and there's a road running along it on the Italian side. That means that it's an easy stretch to guard. If we go northeast, the frontier between Fusine and Kranjska on the Yugo-Slav side is no farther away from Udine, and the country round there is better from our point of view. A mountain frontier is fine from a military standpoint, but it's darn difficult to patrol effectively. We'll go as a couple of hikers. Can you speak German?"

"Not a word."

"Pity. German hikers are more usual. Still, we shall have to do the best we can with our Italian. As to the clothes, we shall need plus-fours, skiing boots and jerseys, and sticks—oh, and rucksacks."

"Rucksacks!"

"All right, all right! we can bulk them with paper. Talking of paper. They've got my name in this morning's issues. And what do you think? Saponi has been arrested. That makes you laugh, doesn't it? I suppose that because they found his name on my office door they thought he had something to do with me. They'll let him go again, but"—he chuckled—"it serves the dirty double-crosser right." He was as gleeful as a small boy with a new catapult.

I regarded him suspiciously. "I thought you said that that hard-luck story of yours was untrue."

"Not the bit about Saponi. He sold me a pup all right. I knew he thought he was making a sucker out of me when he sold me that agency, but I let him go on with it. It suited me to do so."

"In your rôle of respectable American citizen?" I said sarcastically, and thought I saw the beginnings of a blush spreading from his neck. Without answering, he referred to a slip of paper in his pocket.

"I called in at the station. There's a train at three-five to Villach in Germany. It stops at Tarvisio, which is about twelve kilometres from the Yugo-Slav frontier. We should be at Tarvisio at about five. It's a slowish train. Then we can start hiking. We'll cross the frontier after dark." He beamed at me. "We've done the worst now. I said I'd get you out, didn't I? The rest'll be easy."

"Good."

I thought his jubilation a little previous, and for once I was right; but I did not voice the thought. It would have made no difference if I *had* done so. I remembered suddenly that I had done nothing about getting in touch with Claire. I mentioned the fact.

"You can telephone from Belgrade to-morrow. It'll be quicker than a letter and you can have the call on me."

That was unanswerable.

An hour later we emerged from the municipal lavatories in our new clothes. Zaleshoff had added peaked caps to the outfit. We looked, I thought, extremely silly and very conspicuous, and I said as much. He waved the idea aside.

"It's just that you're English and self-conscious," he stated; "when we get up in the mountains it'll be all right."

For the first part of the journey we shared a compartment with an old couple accompanied by their son-in-law. They took no notice of us. The woman and the son-in-law, an unpleasant young man with a huge wart on his chin, spent most of the time brow-beating the old man. He chewed unhappily at his toothless gums as he listened first to one and then the other. They were speaking a dialect and I could understand little of what they were saying; but I felt sorry for the old man. They got out at Pontebba. A man who looked like a farmer got in and slung a bundle on the rack.

We had been following a river valley, but now we began to climb more steeply. Through gaps in the lower hills I could see great pine-clad slopes rising steeply into drifting mists that seemed to move like long filmy grey curtains hanging from a lofty ceiling. I saw Zaleshoff frowning at them. The farmer had gone into the corridor and was leaning on the rail smoking. Zaleshoff got up and followed him. I remained where I was. The scene fascinated me. The clouds were constantly shifting, forming new shapes; their movements were like those of a conjurer's hands moving mysteriously to invoke magic. There was a dramatic quality to them drifting sulphurously like that among the hills. They made me think of illustrations to *Paradise Lost*. There was no sun and the sky was leaden. I noticed suddenly that it was getting very cold. The train went into a tunnel.

Outside in the corridor, Zaleshoff was talking to the farmer. By the yellow electric light I could see his lips moving, but the noise of the train drowned the words. Then I saw him nod to the other man. He came back into the compartment, slid the door to behind him and sat down facing me with his hands on his knees. He was looking worried. Suddenly we ran out of the tunnel.

"What's the matter?"

The corners of his mouth drooped. "Bad news."

"What is it?"

"That man comes from Fusine. It's been snowing for the past two days up there."

"In May!"

"Summer's always two months late in the mountains. It's bad, Marlow. He says it's a yard deep above the three thousand feet mark. He tells me they've had snow ploughs out on the roads, but that some of the villages higher up are still cut off. It's been freezing hard at night and all the snow isn't down yet. There's been no sun either to thaw what is down." He looked at the leaden sky. "That lot'll probably come down to-night. It's the devil's own luck."

"Three thousand feet's a long way up."

"When you start from sea level, yes. But round about Fusine it's over four thousand. Even if we stuck to the main road across the frontier we'd still be above the snow line. But we can't even do that. We've got to keep away from the road and that means going higher still. If the weather was good the walk would give us a nice appetite for breakfast to-morrow, but with a heavy fall of snow on the mountains and more on the way, we'll be in a mess."

"A little snow won't hurt us, surely."

He snorted. "A little snow! We're not in England now. Have you ever been in the mountains when it's snowing?"

"No."

"Well, then, don't talk out of the back of your neck. It wouldn't be a picnic if we could follow the road. Off the road it'll be blue murder. And another thing. You see those clouds? Well, if it doesn't snow to-night we're going to be trying to find our way through them."

"Well, what do you propose?"

He frowned. "I don't know. I'm darned if I know. If there was a train back to Udine to-night I'd say we ought to take it. But the only train going back comes from across the frontier and they might be examining passports on the train It might be O.K., but we can't risk it. If we hide out in the open we shall get pneumonia. Even if we stay below the snow line it'll be cold and wet with those clouds about."

"Isn't there a Turkish bath at Tarvisio?"

"Is that meant to be funny?" he snarled.

"Can't we do as we did last night?"

"Tarvisio is not much more than an overgrown village. Everything'll be shut by ten. They go to bed early in these parts."

"Well, if we can't go back and we can't stay at Tarvisio, we shall have to go on. Is that it?"

He grunted. "There are times, Marlow, when that sort of logic is just damn silly." He shrugged. "We'll have to spend some money at Tarvisio."

"What on?"

"Food and clothes. Wool caps to keep our ears warm, gloves, ski-ing gaiters to keep our ankles dry, an extra jersey apiece, woollen scarves, a bottle of rum and a better map than this one. I tried to pump that guy about routes. Naturally, I couldn't say any more than that we wanted some nice walks, but I did get out of him that there's an old disused road that runs over the frontier a few kilometres south of the motor road. Apparently it's overgrown by trees now and little more than a path. He mentioned it to warn me. It seems that last summer four hikers wandered out along it, got on to the wrong side of the frontier by mistake and were fired at by the Yugo-Slav frontier guards. That's the path we'll make for."

"I've always wanted to be fired at by a Yugo-Slav frontier guard."

"Don't be a sap! It'll be dark. Besides, it's the Italians we've got to worry about and they . . ." He broke off. The door slid open and the farmer returned to his seat. For the rest of the journey I watched the clouds in silence.

Shortly after six o'clock we left Tarvisio along a secondary road running south of Fusine.

Almost immediately we found ourselves climbing. The road was cut in a series of diagonals across the face of a range of grey stone hills. Below us the ash trees and pines grew against the hill-side like the quills on a porcupine. Through the dense mist that drifted down into the valley below I caught occasional glimpses of snow on the sides of the cloud-capped heights ahead. There was no wind, but it was bitterly cold. The air had an astringent quality about it that made the skin of my face tingle. There was an almost heady smell of pine resin. But for the cold I should have felt sleepy earlier than I did. It was not until nearly eight o'clock that we came upon the first traces of snow.

Shortly before we drew level with Fusine the road curled away to the left and we struck off up the hill-side to the right of us.

According to Zaleshoff's map and compass we were heading for the path mentioned by the farmer. We should, he had calculated, reach it before dark. For a time we climbed steadily through a dense pine forest, through which the mists drifted and curled like long eerie fingers searching absently for something lost. It was very still. Occasionally the loud, harsh croaking of mountain crows would break the silence.

But that was all. The sound accentuated the silence. When we spoke it was in whispers. Then among the trees ahead of us we saw a patch of white.

The patches became more frequent. At first they were thin and looked, as our boots crunched across them, like granulated sugar. Then they grew thicker and merged one with another so that soon we could see nothing but white through the trees ahead. The air became colder.

Then, quite suddenly, we found ourselves fighting our way round a deep drift of snow that had accumulated in a small gully. Beyond the gully, however, it was nearly as deep. As I scrambled on I kept thinking that it would get easier when we were clear of that freakish drift; and yet somehow it never did get easier. It became more difficult. Now drift seemed to merge into drift. The snow was half-way up our thighs. It was a dry, cloying powder that dragged at the feet. Now the forest was full of sound, a rustling, secret sound as the dense roof of pine needles far above us shifted uneasily under the weight of snow, allowing it to hiss softly through the lower branches in chalky cascades. The mist had become thicker.

By a quarter to nine we got to the top of what appeared to be a long ridge. We were both of us breathless and Zaleshoff called a halt. Then, when he had got his breath back:

"We ought to be above Fusine and slightly beyond it—about here." He jabbed the map. I did not bother to see where. "If we keep going level for a bit now we should strike the path where it tops the ridge. That is, if we can see it at all. If this damned mist would lift . . ."

We went on. In spite of the exertion of climbing, in spite of the two jerseys, I began to feel terribly cold. I could feel the snow, melted by the heat of my body, soaking through the thick woollen socks above the gaiters. The top of the ridge was rocky and we toiled through drifts of snow that came up to our waists. By this time, too, night was falling. The mist seemed to be closing in on us. I began to feel panicky.

As the light went the mist cleared. It seemed to dissolve into the shadows. At one moment it was all round us; thirty seconds later it had gone and we saw the lights of isolated cottages on the hillside far away down the valley. There were no stars. The night hung like a black fog overhead. A few minutes later it began to snow hard.

The top of the ridge was partly screened by trees, but the shelter they gave was negligible. The snow did not fall in flakes, but in great frozen chunks. There was a frightening savagery about it. There was no wind and it fell vertically:

but when we moved forward it beat against our faces with stinging force. Our arms shielding our faces, we blundered on a few steps at a time, pausing in between for breath.

We must have gone on for twenty minutes like that before we felt the ridge begin to dip slightly. Zaleshoff grasped my arm.

"We're getting near the path now," he panted; "keep your eyes open for it."

But that was easier said than done. I had long ago thrown away my spectacles. Now I wished that I had kept them. The strain of trying to peer through screwed-up eyes into the darkness beyond the streaming white mass in front of us was almost unbearable. The ridge dipped and rose again and still we had not found the path. My legs were beginning to feel leaden. We went on for another ten minutes. Then I stopped. Zaleshoff was a few paces ahead of me. I called out to him and he turned back.

"What is it?"

I waited to get my breath. "Zaleshoff," I said at last, "we're lost."

For a moment he did not move. Then I saw him nod. For a minute we stood there in silence, the snow hissing through the trees and beating down on us. I remember that it had piled up on my shoulders so that if I bent my head sideways I could touch it with my cheek. I had begun to shiver.

"Let's have a drink," he said, "it's in my rucksack."

I cleared the snow off the top of the rucksack and got out the rum. We took a stiff peg each. I could feel it, warm and sickly, trickling down to my stomach.

"What do we do about it?" I said as I replaced the bottle.

"We can't be so far away from the path. If we get down the side of the ridge here, maybe we can find some place among the rocks where we can shelter until it gets light."

"You mean spend the night out in this?"

"We've got the rum."

"All right. Anything's better than standing here."

We started to scramble down the side of the hill. It was steeper than the side by which we had come up and we slithered down most of the way. At last we came to rest on a shelf of rock.

"This isn't getting us anywhere," muttered Zaleshoff; "we shall end up on the floor of the valley. We'll try going forward."

We edged our way along the shelf. Soon it sloped sharply upwards and we were climbing back towards the top of the ridge.

The snow was coming down as heavily as ever. We were both soaking wet and numb with cold. We had stopped to get our breath back and take stock of our position when we saw the light ahead of and above us.

The side of the ridge was scooped out in a series of hollows like huge teeth marks. We were at the edge of one of these hollows. The shelf turned away sharply to the left and the light could only be coming from somewhere farther along the top of the ridge as it curved southward.

The light seemed to flicker.

"What is it?" I said.

"It might be someone with a lantern. But it's a bit too steady for that. We can't be more than a kilometre from Fusine. It may be a house. Come on, we'll see."

"What's the use?"

"If there's a house it means we must be near the path that guy was talking about. It starts from Fusine. Let's go."

We started to climb again. The way was steep and dangerous. With each difficult step I could feel my strength going. The cold and the altitude were slowly overcoming me. My heart was pounding furiously. But I floundered on up after Zaleshoff. I was afraid of being left behind.

The light had disappeared. A feeling of lassitude began to steal over me. Now it did not matter if I was left behind. My head was swimming. I heard myself calling out to him to stop. Then suddenly I felt my feet sink through the snow on to a level surface. The light reappeared and it was nearer. I could see the shape of a window.

Zaleshoff's hand was on my shoulder. I heard him telling me to stay where I was. Then I saw him disappear towards a blackness beyond the snow. I stood still. Behind the thudding of the blood in my head I could hear the quiet, incessant rustle of the snow.

Suddenly there was a shout from the direction in which he had gone. The next moment I heard him yelling out something in a language I did not understand. Involuntarily I stumbled forward up the slope. Then, out of the white darkness ahead loomed two figures. Hands gripped my arms. I heard Zaleshoff shouting again; and this time he was using English.

"It's O.K., Marlow. Take it easy. Don't resist. We're over."

Resist! I was too exhausted even to laugh at the idea.

Chapter XVII

"NO CAUSE FOR ALARM"

THE REMAINDER of that night we spent by the brazier in the concrete Yugo-Slav advance frontier post into which we had succeeded in blundering. As soon as dawn broke we were removed to a guard post a kilometre away.

The Yugo-Slav officials were suspicious but polite. There was an air of informality about the proceedings that I had not expected. The men who had arrested us stood about spitting and smoking while we were questioned. It was not until later that I learned that it was only the fact that we were not Italians that interested them. Italian refugees were still, apparently, fairly common.

Zaleshoff produced his passport and was released within the hour. I was allowed to telephone the Vice-Consul at Zagreb. It took a long time to get the call through, and they gave us coffee while we waited in front of the guardroom stove; but by eleven o'clock matters had been satisfactorily arranged and, on the understanding that we reported to the police immediately on our arrival there, we were permitted to proceed to Zagreb. That night, for the first time in five days, I slept in a bed.

The following morning, clad in a brand new Yugo-Slav suit and armed with an identity paper from the Consul, I travelled with Zaleshoff to Belgrade. The luxury of being able to face a ticket collector without flinching was delicious. I was extraordinarily excited and pleased with myself. I had telephoned to Claire, explained that I had had to leave Italy hurriedly (I did not say just how hurriedly) to escape a charge of bribery over a Spartacus contract, and promised to be home within the week. She had refrained manfully from asking for details. I had told Zaleshoff of the fact with some pride.

He had grinned. "If I were you, Marlow, I'd get busy as soon as I got to London. If you don't look sharp and marry her, some other guy will."

"That's precisely what I'd been thinking."

I had also telephoned Wolverhampton. Mr. Fitch had not been so accommodating in the matter of details. News of the warrant for my arrest had reached Spartacus via the

British authorities. Bombarded with questions, I had said that I had been staying with friends waiting for the thing to blow over, that I was now safe and sound, and that I would get to Wolverhampton as soon as possible. At that point the operator had intervened with the news that I had been talking for six minutes. I had suggested quickly that Umberto be empowered to carry on temporarily in Milan and hung up. I should, I reflected, have two months' salary to come from Spartacus.

But one thing that Fitch had said troubled me. He had raised the question of the Italian Government starting extradition proceedings. I mentioned it to Zaleshoff.

He laughed. "Extradition? Not a chance. Even if they knew you were here they wouldn't do anything about it. For one thing they'd know that it was too late to prevent your reaching Vagas. For another, they'd have to answer too many questions themselves to make it worth their while. What about that passport photograph they put in the paper? Supposing the British authorities wanted to know how they got it. No, I guess the only one they'll take it out of is Bellinetti. I wouldn't be in that bird's shoes for a good deal."

He had evidently been in touch with Tamara, for she was waiting for us at the Belgrade station. They kissed each other's hands. It was rather touching. She smiled at me.

"You're looking well, Mr. Marlow."

"He's done a lot of walking," remarked Zaleshoff; "there's nothing like walking for getting you fit." He grasped her arm. "Where's Vagas? Have you found him yet?"

"Yes. His house is shut up, but I put Fedor on to watch it. He went there yesterday and came out forty minutes later with a suitcase. Fedor followed him to the Hotel Amerika. He's got a suite there on the second floor. Number two hundred and ten."

"Good." I saw his eyes flicker towards me.

"Fedor?" I said. "That sounds like a good old American name." But he ignored the remark.

"Where are we staying?"

"I've taken rooms at the Acacia for us and one for Mr. Marlow at the Amerika—on the second floor."

"Let's go to the Acacia first."

At the Hotel Acacia we talked for half an hour. Or, rather, Zaleshoff talked and I nodded. Tamara had left us to ourselves, but presently she appeared with a large and expensive-looking suitcase containing a pair of pyjamas, a tooth brush and toilet necessities, and a number of second-hand books to add weight to it. Towards six o'clock I put the case into a taxi and was driven to the Hotel Amerika.

As I was registering I glanced at the key rack and saw that the key of number two hundred and ten was hanging there. Vagas was out. I went up to my room, deposited my hat, unpacked the sponge bag and the pyjamas and then descended to the lounge. There I selected a table from which I could see across the foyer to the main entrance, ordered a drink and sat down to wait.

He would, I thought, be returning to the hotel to change his clothes for the evening, and I was right. I had just finished my second drink when I saw him come through the revolving doors, collect his key and walk towards the lift. I put my drink down quickly and dashed for the stairs. I just had time to reach the lift entrance on the second floor and press the button as if to summon the lift, when the doors opened.

Vagas stepped out and we met face to face.

His eyebrows went up; but as evident as his surprise was his suspicion. I affected amazement and delight. Before he could say a word I seized his hand and wrung it heartily.

"General Vagas! the very man I've been looking for!"

"Mr. Marlow! this is most unexpected."

"Very unexpected," I said warmly. "I've been wondering all the afternoon where I could find you. I looked up your address in the directory, but your place was shut up. I'd given it up as hopeless. And all the time, we were on the same floor in the same hotel!"

He smiled faintly. "Well, now that you *have* found me, Mr. Marlow, perhaps you will join me in a drink."

"I should be delighted. This is remarkable," I babbled enthusiastically as we walked along the corridor. "When I found your place empty, I naturally thought that you must be away."

His lips still smiling, he listened. I could almost feel his suspicion of me. Inside the room, he went to a cupboard and got out some glasses and two bottles.

"When did you arrive, Mr. Marlow? Brandy and Evian?"

"Thank you. This afternoon after lunch."

"From Italy."

But Zaleshoff had coached me carefully. "No, from Vienna." I laughed. "That little business transaction of ours did not end very happily, did it, General? You know, I was in Naples at the time, and if my assistant had not telephoned me when I was in Rome and warned me, I really believe they would have arrested me when I got back. Naturally, my Consul would have put *that* right quick enough, but I thought that I had better play for safety. I managed to get a boat for Villefranche. I tried to telephone you in Milan, but your manservant told me that you had left." I delivered a long tirade against the interference of the Italian police in private business matters.

He listened politely. "I understand that the Commendatore was arrested. Most unfortunate. It was reported in the papers. By the way, have you seen the Italian papers lately, Mr. Marlow?"

"No. Why?"

"I thought you might have seen the reports of the case. Most interesting."

I wondered if he knew that the Italian papers had been quite silent on the subject of the Commendatore. I found out soon that he *did* know it.

He handed me a glass and bent down to fill his own.

"Mr. Marlow," he said over his shoulder, "I am most curious to know just why you came to Belgrade instead of returning to England and why you were so anxious to see me."

I registered astonishment. "You don't mean to say that you've forgotten about those questions you asked me in your letter? I took quite a lot of trouble over them, and then I did not have time to write to you before I left for Naples. After that, as I told you, I found that you'd left Milan. I . . ."

His hand with the bottle of Evian in it had been moving towards his glass. Suddenly it stopped. He straightened his back.

"One moment, Mr. Marlow. Am I to understand that you had actually secured that information before you left Italy?"

"You are, General." I grinned. "With a five thousand lire bonus at the end of it, can you blame me for taking a little holiday trip to Belgrade. I don't suppose that Spartacus will be very pleased with me over this bribery business. It's not my fault, of course. But the Italians may rat on that contract. I shall probably be glad of fifty pounds."

For a moment or two he looked at me in silence. Then: "You have the information with you, Mr. Marlow?"

I smiled and tapped my forehead. "In here, General." I had, I hoped, the air of a cunning, stupid man who knows that he has the whip-hand and is determined to use it.

He contemplated me thoughtfully. His eyes were very dangerous, and I could feel my assumed confidence oozing away, leaving only a wooden empty smile behind it. Then he put his hand in his breast pocket and drew out a wallet. Slowly he counted out five *mille* notes and tossed them on to the table in front of me.

"Well, Mr. Marlow?"

I repeated the second part of Zaleshoff's lesson and had the satisfaction of seeing his eyes gleam with interest. He went to a bureau, drew out a piece of paper and told me to repeat what I had said. I did so. He jotted down a note or two. At last he stood up again.

"I am glad to state, Mr. Marlow, that this information has the appearance of accuracy and may be of use to us. I think I should remind you, however, that this transaction must be our last. I should be quite unable to persuade my superiors that there is any reason for continuing to pay your salary now that you are no longer *persona grata* in Italy. You understand that?"

"Oh yes, General." I hesitated and looked at him rather furtively. "With regard to the matter we discussed in the car that night, I should like some assurance that the information concerning my employers' business will not be used in any way . . . er . . . prejudicial."

A glint of amusement appeared for an instant in his eyes; but he assured me gravely enough that I need have no fears.

"Can I persuade you to have dinner with me, Mr. Marlow?" he added.

"I should like to, General, but I am leaving for London in the morning and I have some letters to write. I feel sure you will excuse me."

It was feeble enough as an excuse, but he nodded. Clearly, he had not expected me to accept.

"A pity. However"—he held out his hand—"*bon voyage*, Mr. Marlow, and thank you. My wife will be sorry that she missed you."

I almost jumped. Was it possible that the man did not know of his wife's death? Then I realised that the statement was a trap. I had said that I had not seen the Italian papers. I ought not to know that his wife was dead, that she had killed herself. He was grasping my hand, and I was afraid for a moment that he might have felt the involuntary contraction of my muscles. That was, of course, why he had taken my hand before he had mentioned his wife.

I managed to keep my voice level. "Please convey my respects to Madame Vagas."

Then a curious thing happened. Before this, I had not seen him in the daylight. His *maquillage* was not as heavy as that which he wore at night. Now, as his cheeks creased momentarily into the first genuine smile I had seen on his face, I saw that beneath the paint his face was pock-marked.

The smile was gone; but when he spoke his voice held laughter, the laughter of a man who is enjoying a good joke.

"I shall do my best to convey your respects to my wife,

Mr. Marlow," he said deliberately; "I shall make a point of doing so next time I see her. *A rivederci*."

I fumbled with the door-knob. I was feeling slightly sick. "Good night, General."

As the door shut behind me I heard him laugh.

I got my hat from my room and went downstairs on my way to report to Zaleshoff. I was not sure that I had not been made a fool of. Then, as I stopped by the desk to leave my key, I heard something which made me change my mind. The telephone stood adjacent to the clerk's desk and I heard the operator repeat the word "Berlin" twice and then *"danke."* Someone in the hotel was putting a call through to Berlin.

I turned to the clerk.

"I wonder if that Berlin call would be for me," I said in Italian.

"What name, Signore?"

"Marlow."

He turned to the operator and said something to her in German. I did not understand her actual reply, but two things I did understand. One was her impatient shake of the head, the other was the name "Herr Vagas." That was enough.

"No, Signore," said the clerk; "it is not for you."

The following morning Zaleshoff and Tamara saw me off on the Paris train.

We were standing on the platform with about two minutes to go when I remembered something that I had forgotten to ask him.

"Zaleshoff, what did you mean the other morning when you said that you were more worried by what that paper didn't print than what it did?"

It was Tamara who answered. "He was afraid that they might have detained me. He's always afraid for me."

"I see." I hesitated. Then: "Look here, I've got a finicking sort of mind. Do you mind telling me exactly what you did with those queer files of yours. You surely didn't leave them for the police to find and I really can't see how you could burn such a mass of paper without attracting attention."

They looked uncomfortable.

"Well," said Zaleshoff airily, "those were Saponi's old files."

"But what about those cards that . . ." I stopped. I was beginning to understand. "I suppose," I went on slowly, "that it wouldn't be that the two cards I saw, Ferning's and Vagas', were the only two cards there were?"

For once Zaleshoff had nothing to say. I nodded grimly. "I see."

Just then the whistle blew and I climbed into the train. They were both standing on the platform, looking up at me. The girl was smiling, but Zaleshoff's jaw was stuck out defiantly. I wanted suddenly to laugh at him. The train began to move.

I leaned down.

"Don't forget to send me a postcard from Moscow."

They had begun to walk along by the side of the train. Suddenly he grinned. "I will," he called back; "that is, if I ever get around to the place."

And then, as the train gathered speed, he began to run. Almost immediately he cannoned into a porter's trolley; but he scrambled to his feet again and ran on. When I last saw him he was standing on the end of the platform waving a bright red handkerchief after me. No, you could not help liking Zaleshoff.

I spent two days with Claire before I went up to Wolverhampton.

When I had arrived, there had been a letter waiting for me. It was from Hallett. In it were the five pounds which he had borrowed from me just before I had left for Italy and, more important, the offer of a job under him with his new employers. Having telephoned my grateful acceptance, I travelled north armed.

I saw Fitch first. He greeted me with gloomy enthusiasm. "The bottom's out of the export market," he said; "and, of course, just as we'd got hold of a really good man to handle the Milan end, this had to happen. It beats me, Marlow. We've been using that special appropriation ever since we started over there. Ferning never had any trouble. Some new broom, I expect. We were pretty worried about you. Did you have any trouble getting out?"

"Well, it was a bit awkward because they had my passport. But I made for the Yugo-Slav side and sneaked out across the frontier."

"And you heard nothing about it in Yugo-Slavia, I gather. Well, all's well that ends well, I suppose. But where we stand now, I don't know. I don't see how the ice-creamers could wriggle out of their contracts with us even if they wanted to. Pelcher's going over in a few days to straighten things out. Everyone here is doing well except the export department," he went on sombrely; "we've started supplying the shadow factories. Pelcher's very pleased."

"What does he think about this Milan business?"

"He says that it's the fortune of war. I don't quite know what he means, but he's stuck that label on to it, so there we are. You'll find him very cheerful. Apart from the shadow factories, he's had a spirit level let into the head of his new driver, and reckons that it's going to bring his handicap down to eighteen. He thinks it'll be worth nearly a stroke a hole to him; but, as I told him, even if St. Andrew's would permit it, it's not the club head but the ball that he ought to keep his eyes on. He'll never make a golfer."

Soon the message came that Mr. Pelcher was disengaged and would see me.

His reception of me was overwhelming. He pressed me into a chair, ordered tea, and gave me a cigar. Then he sat back, tugging at his collar and beaming while I repeated once more the prepared version of my experiences.

"Well, Mr. Marlow," he said breezily when I had finished, "I must congratulate you on extricating yourself from a very difficult position with skill and discretion. Frankly, we were a little worried until we heard from you; but, as I said to Fitch, I had considerable faith in your tact. There was never, I felt, any *real* cause for alarm."

"It is very kind of you to say so."

"And now," he went on, "we must think of the future. It is out of the question for you to return to Italy."

"Utterly, I am afraid."

"Ah well—the fortune of war, you know." He tugged at his collar. "Let me see now. Fitch badly needs an assistant and I dare say . . ."

"One moment, Mr. Pelcher," I interrupted. "I think I should tell you now that I have been offered and have accepted the post of production engineer to one of the Cator & Bliss branch factories. Perhaps I should have told you before. I am afraid that I assumed . . ."

"That we should let you down?" He looked hurt, but I could see the relief in his eyes.

"Not exactly that, Sir; but I have come to the conclusion that I am far more suited to a works job."

"Once an engineer always an engineer, eh? Well, I can sympathise with that." For a moment I thought I saw a shadow cross his face; but that was, no doubt, my imagination. He stood up. "Well, my boy, we shall be sorry to lose you so soon, but, of course, we can't stand in your way. And besides," he added jovially, "we've just started supplying S2 machines to Cator & Bliss. You won't be losing touch with us altogether, eh?"

"It's very good of you to put it like that."

"Nonsense, my dear chap! You'll fix the financial details

with Fitch, of course. You might spend some of your remaining time with us making him familiar with the Milan details so that he can give me a report. Meanwhile"—he held out his hand—"let me wish you the very best of luck." We shook hands warmly. I thanked him again. We walked towards the door.

"By the way," he said suddenly, "I'd like to have your technical opinion on my new driver. Fitch is sceptical; but then you know what these scratch golfers are. You don't play, so I think you'll see the beauty of the idea."

I had dinner with Fitch. It was dark when I left Wolverhampton. I shared a compartment with a well-dressed, beefy man who sat under an enormous suitcase perched rather precariously on the rack. Tied to the handle was a travel agency label. For a while he read a Birmingham paper. I looked out of the window. Then, in the distance, I saw the glow of blast furnaces.

The paper rustled. "Nice to see them working like that again, isn't it?" he remarked.

"Yes, very."

"Are you a Birmingham man?"

"No."

"We're not doing so badly up here. Can't turn the stuff out fast enough."

"That must be very heartening."

"Yes. I'm off on a tour, through Italy. First class all the way after London, and all tips included in the ticket. No need to worry about the lingo either."

"It sounds good."

"I was there for a day or two last Easter. It's a fine place for a holiday is Italy. Now that Mussolini's on the job, the trains run nearly as good as ours. You ought to try it."

I settled back in my corner. I was feeling tired.

"I'm afraid," I said, "that Italy would be a little too hot for me."

He nodded understandingly. "Yes, there are some people who can't stand the heat. My late wife was like that. Either you can stand it or you can't. It's just the way you're made, I always say."

THE THIRD FACTOR

THERE FOLLOWS a short extract from an article which appeared in a French periodical during the summer of the year in which the events described by Mr. Nicholas Marlow occurred. The title of the article was *The Shifting Sands of Europe*.

" . . . any assessment . . . of the situation must be based on the knowledge gained during the past few weeks.

"Several factors have operated to produce the present easement of tension. The first and most potent has been the hardening of American financial opinion in relation to possible aggressor states. The clear expression by responsible persons of the opinion that, from the point of view of capital, a falsified national balance sheet is no better for being national instead of private, was timely. The second has been the decision with which the Anglo-French *bloc* has functioned now that misunderstandings have been disposed of. A third influence has been the unexpected coolness which has developed lately between two partners of the Axis. The cause is understood to be of a military nature and to concern the Brenner Pass. The details are obscure, but it appears that the mutual assurances given in Rome not so long ago have not proved as durable as had been expected by the parties concerned.

"This much is clear. Extended co-operation on the part of the three great European democracies, France, Great Britain and our ally, Soviet Russia, backed by the moral support of the United States, would be an irresistible force for peace. But . . ."